CRY TERROR!

She tried to put an entire message in her glance: *I'm in trouble. Please help me.*

But if the attendant understood, he didn't let on. . . .

Doyle put pressure on Kate's elbow. He started steering her out of the office.

She stopped suddenly, turned back to the attendant at the register.

"Sir?"

He looked up. "Yes, ma'am?"

"I—"

Then she felt the gun. . . .

RUN
TO
MIDNIGHT

CHRIS SHEA McCARRICK

DIAMOND BOOKS, NEW YORK

This book is a Diamond original edition, and has never been previously published.

RUN TO MIDNIGHT

A Diamond Book / published by arrangement with the author

PRINTING HISTORY
Diamond edition / December 1992

ISBN: 1-55773-825-4

Diamond Books are published by The Berkley Publishing Group,
200 Madison Avenue, New York, New York 10016.
The name "DIAMOND" and its logo are trademarks belonging to Charter Communications, Inc.

PRINTED IN THE UNITED STATES OF AMERICA

10 9 8 7 6 5 4 3 2 1

This novel is for my sister Julie
with love and appreciation.

Acknowledgments

Several people helped me with this novel, notably Jan Holton of P&N Flying Service; Tim Banse; and Carol Gorman, who did a wonderful edit of the first draft.

Kevin D. Randle, a fine writer and a fine friend, spent many hours going through the second and third drafts, righting technical errors and making many valuable suggestions about the story itself.

Finally, this novel is a variation on a theme that Rex Miller and I talked about for many months.

Thanks to all of you.

1

HE had slapped her again last night, viciously, and afterward he had, as usual, taken her hand with great and tender care and asked her to forgive him.

"It's just that I don't understand," he said. "It's just that if you do it I'll—I won't have you anymore. Not the way I have you now."

She smiled her ruthless smile. "It's your fantasy, anyway."

"What is?"

"That you 'have' me. Nobody has ever 'had' me and nobody ever will."

"I'm just afraid. I can't help it."

"It's going to happen, no matter how much you fight it." She touched him then, as only she could touch him. "Please, darling, please trust me."

That had been in the spring when they'd gone for long lilac walks along the soft blue river, when they took dinner at a sidewalk café they favored, where the wine was excellent and the handsome waiter played sentimental love songs on the accordion. The perfume of the May night had been exotic and exhilarating.

He'd tried to be happy about what she was going to do, tried to rationalize that it would be best for everybody concerned, but late at night, in his lonely little bed in his lonely little sleeping room, he knew that what she was about to do was wrong and that she would eventually leave him behind.

But there was nothing he could do.

Nothing.

In the autumn, when it was done with and final and she was exulting in it, he tried to take his life with a pistol, but at the last moment fear overcame him, and his trembling finger jerked the gun from his temple and fired the bullet into the wall.

Forever after, he would hear the sound of that gunshot.

It was the sound of his humiliation, and of how useless he had become to her.

2

THE blizzard that hit Chicago that morning was more an invasion than a storm. Just after slate-gray dawn, snow, ice and furious wind came screaming across Lake Michigan and began benumbing the city. Snow buried cars, ice made streets treacherous and wind made even walking a dangerous task. All this took place before 8:30 A.M.

It was a morning to stay snuggy warm in a blue cashmere sweater and designer jeans and nubby red argyle socks, and to sit in an elegant Lake Shore Drive apartment looking out over the foggy gray waters of Lake Michigan. In order to keep from feeling self-indulgent and lazy, a forty-five-minute aerobic workout was mandatory. There was a Stairmaster and a treadmill in a large, empty room that had been converted into a gym of sorts.

Thirty-one-year-old Kate Evans once more counted her blessings. If she'd been a teacher, a clerk or a "radio personality" like one of her friends, she would have been forced to bundle up and try to impose herself on the howling day.

But when you write songs for a living—and hit songs at that, as she had to keep reminding herself—you had the option of staying inside whenever you chose, and doing your work on a Steinway concert piano.

Kate was a slight girl, red of hair, worn now in a fashionable bob, with clear intelligent gray eyes and a quick white smile that made her fetching indeed. Of late, her morning mirror had been a little too honest, showing wrinkles in the corners of the eyes and flecks of gray in her silky red hair. But most days, she didn't mind so much. Given what had happened to Sally, Kate simply felt grateful for her life and health.

She forced herself to think of last night's phone call. No point in thinking of Sally now . . .

Kate was not yet jaded by being around celebrities and rock stars. Getting a personal phone call from the woman known simply as Riki, currently the most popular young singer in America, still made Kate feel as if she were living in the sort of dopey fantasy high school girls frequently had.

Riki had called Kate last night to say she hoped Kate's new song would make both of them a lot of money. "You know me, Kate," Riki had laughed. "People think I'm this really sensitive, poetic type. But deep down I'm just a greedy bitch who loves platinum records." Which had been followed by Riki's familiar, throaty laugh.

Sometimes Kate had to keep reminding herself that all this was real . . . But such thoughts inevitably led back to Sally . . .

After her forty-five-minute workout, Kate took a quick shower. She put on sweater and jeans and argyle socks again and left the steaming bathroom. She liked showers only a few degrees cooler than saunas.

She went into what she called her workroom, a large white room with a huge window overlooking Lake Michigan. The morning's river traffic—tugs and barges, mostly—looked grubby and isolate in the angry snow.

Near the window sat a beautiful concert Steinway and when she saw it, her thoughts turned back to Sally.

Five years ago, Kate had come to Chicago with her husband, Greg Mullin, an amiable and handsome farm kid she'd met at a small liberal arts college in Cedar Rapids. Superficially, Kate and Greg were a great deal alike. They didn't go in for all the clamor that their classmates seemed to favor. A good day for them was hopping aboard Greg's motorcycle and shooting off into the countryside. Unlike most of her dates, Greg hadn't even pushed her about having sex. If he found her freakish for being a virgin at age twenty, he hadn't let on. When the time came, it was the right and proper time, and the night had been tender and fulfilling.

They were married eight months after graduation. Greg's parents had some money, so Greg was able to attend law school in Iowa City. And it was then he began to change, six or seven months into their marriage. He was no longer satisfied with countryside trips or nights of renting Laurel and Hardy movies or simply walking around the leafy university campus on soft spring nights.

Greg was in the top five percentile of his class and he began to regard himself as somebody quite special. He bought a small red sports car and started dragging her to noisy university parties at which he was one of the reigning gods. It was at one such party that she'd walked in on Greg kissing an imposing blonde who only laughed when Greg, scarlet-faced, introduced his wife. "He's been a very bad boy tonight, Mrs. Mullin," the blonde undergraduate had said, making Kate feel not only betrayed but ancient as well. The blonde was probably nineteen. Kate was twenty-three.

Their marriage survived. After law school, Greg graduating second in his class, they moved to Chicago. In Iowa City, during Greg's law school years, Kate had worked as an elementary teacher and had loved the work. Though she knew that children could be cruel, she learned that they could also be much more insightful and astute and giving than most adults. They were just what they were . . . with no pretenses . . . and Kate liked and admired that.

But teaching jobs were hard to come by in Cook County the year she arrived. After three months of looking, the only work she could find was as a kind of glorified gofer in a recording studio that created jingles for a long list of national clients. Sally Beaumont ran the studio. A onetime Broadway singer, Sally was determined to show both New York and Los Angeles that Chicago could create commercial music just as good, just as creative, as the music on both coasts. Though twenty years her senior, Sally made Kate her closest friend and confidante. And when she found out that Kate used to write songs and play them for her family on long, wintry farm nights, Sally started pushing her to start writing again. At first, Kate produced very little—sketchy, hackneyed product songs that were bad imitations of what she heard on TV and radio.

But eventually Kate wrote a song good enough to present to one of Sally's clients. Or so Sally insisted, anyway. And her intuition was proved correct. The client, a sportswear manufacturer, loved Kate's composition, and even took her refrain and made it into his advertising campaign theme for the year.

More successes came quickly. Kate started writing full-time and making a good deal of money with residuals, income earned every time a product song was played on radio or TV.

None of this success did much for her marriage. Greg was threatened by her success, especially when local TV stations and magazines began doing pieces about her. He was already a senior partner in an old-line law firm. Greg seemed to be saying if there was any prominence to be had by this family, that prominence had better by God belong to him. She suggested that they see a counselor. He refused. She suggested that he start coming with her to the studio, to get to know Sally and the staff better. He refused. She confided all this over and over to Sally. She was confused and hurt and afraid. Soon enough, Greg took a mistress. One night, with great relish, he announced that he was leaving Kate. He also announced, with equal relish, that his lover was pregnant. They would have the family Kate and he had never shared.

Kate lived through a year of pain unlike any she'd ever known before. She saw a shrink occasionally, even tried hanging out in bars a few times, something she soon began to view as a chore. Nothing worked. She hadn't wanted a divorce. In ways, she still loved Greg. But there was anger and remorse and confusion. Despite this, her musical work was better than ever. Her product songs sold to such premiere clients as Dodge, Arrow shirts and Brut. She found herself in demand on both coasts as writer and producer, not only writing songs but also working with the band to achieve a certain "sound." Her work was constantly on network television.

That was how the rock star Riki had first heard of her. Riki was a beautiful but mysterious young singer that men developed hopeless crushes on and women envied for her sensitivity and femininity. Riki heard a product song Kate had done for an insurance company, a lovely and tender song about old age. Riki liked it so much she bought rights to it and then hired Kate to write new lyrics to it. Soon after the song was released, Kate had her first gold record for songwriting.

Then one spring day, Kate's world once again collapsed.

Kate and Sally were having lunch at one of the restaurants favored by the top ad agencies when Sally said, "You're finally going to meet my son."

"Why, Sally, that's great!" Kate had said. But then she noted how pale and tense Sally looked. Sally had been married three times, the second marriage producing a son on whom she doted with abiding pride. Son Michael was now a dentist in Seattle with two kids of his own.

"He's coming in tomorrow," Sally said.

Kate smiled. "Did I forget your birthday?"

Sally said, "No, kiddo. I've got to have a little surgery. They found a tiny lump on my breast."

Kate would never forget the cold shadow of death that touched every part of her being. She knew she had to be bright and chipper for Sally's sake but . . .

"I'll be fine, kiddo. You know me. I'm too mean to die."

And then Sally had reached across the table and taken Kate's hand and said, "I'm scared as hell, kiddo. I hate to admit it but it's the truth."

Then began eight desperate months. There was surgery and there was chemotherapy, Sally beaten and sad-eyed following each debilitating session. There was a trip to the Mayo Clinic for experimental drug therapy. There was a trip to California for vitamin treatments ("I know it's probably bullshit, kiddo, but what have I got to lose?"). And all the time, Sally was getting paler and weaker, as if a vampire were visiting her at midnight and draining the life from her. There was laughter so hard that Sally's frail body seemed consumed with it, and tears so bitter and hopeless that all Kate could do was just hold her and let her spend herself until sleep was the only recourse.

Very near the end, Sally's son set up a hospice in Sally's Lincoln Park town house. He was there twenty-four hours a day. Kate was with him most of the time.

Neither of them heard her die. Michael went in to check on her one drab rainy afternoon, rain like teardrops on the summer window, and she was gone.

As she had done following the loss of her marriage, Kate turned to work as an escape. She wrote an entire album for Riki. The album went double platinum. Kate was now working on the follow-up album and helping to plan Riki's summer tour for next year. Riki wanted special material written and had decided Kate was the woman to do it. That's why Riki had called last night, to see how the material was coming along.

This gorgeous Steinway concert piano was Sally's legacy—a gift when Kate's song had landed them their biggest product song account to date—and Kate could never play it without thinking of the very funny, very dear woman who had been her best friend for two and a half years.

Restless, Kate got up from the piano and went into the living room.

A small fireplace was set into the brick wall. The bricks had been painted to complement the off-white carpeting and the oak-framed sofa with off-white pillows. Kate had decorated the room with a country-house air, with lots of rattan furniture and plenty of thriving green plants. All the moldings were white with wine-red wall covering to lend the room boldness. One entire wall was a sprawling bookcase, with titles running from her childhood favorite *Black Beauty* to later favorites such as *The Catcher in the Rye* and *Childhood's End*.

The fire took five minutes to come crackling to real life. She was just closing the glass doors when she heard the buzzer in the living room.

Somebody was downstairs, wanting to come up. But at 10:15 on a Monday morning?

Walking to the front door, she reasoned that the caller must be a delivery person of some sort. Her friends were all musicians and songwriters, both breeds known for sleeping all day and working all night.

"Yes?" Kate spoke into the small white-painted speaker set into the molding around the front door.

"Kate. It's me, David Greene."

She knew instantly that something was wrong. The publicist always sounded bright and confident no matter what the time or circumstances.

But not this morning. His slow, drugged voice hinted at something terribly wrong. He sounded as if he were about ready to collapse.

"What's wrong, David?"

"I need to come up. Please."

"Of course."

She buzzed him up.

While she waited for him to get on the elevator and ride up to the sixth floor, she speculated on what could possibly make David sound this way.

She knew, with a melancholy pang, that her nice, settled morning of working at the piano and sipping hot cider had most likely been canceled by forces beyond her control.

The weatherman had promised the season's first blizzard. She always liked to stay inside, watching the big, lovely flakes splatter on the window glass and become beautiful water crystals. Tomorrow, Chicago turned beautiful by the mantle of white, she would walk up to Grant Park and build a snowman. She'd done this for the past four years, on the second snow day of each season.

David's knock was so weak Kate almost didn't hear it.

She opened the door and he fell straight down into her arms, his blue eyes rolling backward, blood bubbling red and ugly in the corner of his mouth. Beneath his open topcoat, she could see a bloody wound on the right side of his stomach. He winced every time he took a step, as if his ribs had been broken.

By the time she got her hands underneath his arms and helped him over to the couch, David Greene was very near slipping into unconsciousness.

Even so, he continued to mutter things but nothing she could understand.

She got him laid flat on the couch, a throw cushion beneath his head for a pillow.

She was just parting his coat for a closer look at the wound when she realized she was wasting her time.

She was neither a doctor nor a nurse. She had no idea how to treat what was clearly a gunshot wound.

Dark blood pasted his shirt to his chest. When she leaned closer, she saw a neat little hole in the fabric, not much bigger around than the head of an eraser on a number two pencil. The blood was spreading over much of his white oxford, button-down shirt, like spilled cranberry juice on the white tiles of a kitchen floor.

Sweat beads stood out dramatically on his forehead. Sweat turned his collar grimy. His entire body trembled. His teeth literally chattered.

"I'll get you an ambulance," she said, even though she was sure he couldn't hear her. And after she called an ambulance, she'd call the man she'd been dating, Homicide Detective Robert McGivern.

She turned and rushed over to the telephone. She was just picking up the receiver when, from behind her, he said, "Don't call anybody, Kate. I'm in serious trouble."

She turned back to look at him. He was crazy not to let her call an ambulance.

She was going to make her argument, force him to let her get some medical help, when she saw his trembling hand reach deep into the pocket of his overcoat and pull something out.

Before she could quite believe what she was seeing, David Greene, the handsome successful publicity agent known for his business acumen and his highly placed show business friends, was holding a gun on her.

"I don't want you to call anybody. Just come over here."

Even in his weakened condition, it was clear he meant what he said.

Afraid suddenly, knowing that she had just become involved in something terrible, she replaced the receiver and walked reluctantly back to the couch.

"I hope to God he didn't follow me here," Greene said.

All Kate could do was listen.

3

DETECTIVE Robert McGivern had at some time or other seen every kind of killer in the interrogation room. Some were angry, some were boastful, some were jubilant, some were sad.

The room was fifteen feet long and ten feet wide. A table with cigarette scars accommodated six folding chairs. On top of the table was a black, box-like Sony tape recorder. The floor was tiled. About every third tile was badly worn or missing. The ceiling was also tiled. Cigarette smoke had turned the tan color gritty brown in places. The door leading in and out was metal. There were several deep indentations from fists, some put there by cops, some by suspects. At least one had been put there by a public defender sickened by the man he was forced to defend.

McGivern sat staring at the man sitting on the other side of the table.

George Bayer was a thirty-six-year-old accountant. He was tall, gaunt, balding. He wore rimless glasses that gave him a somewhat helpless, nearsighted look. The arresting officer had been forced to subdue him and in so doing had broken Bayer's nose. His yellow dress shirt was a mess.

McGivern had had nothing to do with the case. He had been sitting at his desk in the homicide bureau when they'd brought Bayer through. He'd looked up and his gaze had met the suspect's. McGivern had promptly forgotten all about the man. That was two hours ago.

Ten minutes ago, Clymer, the homicide detective who had made the arrest, came back from the interrogation room and walked over to McGivern's desk.

Clymer said, "He wants to see you."

McGivern glanced up. "Who wants to see me?"

"The guy who shot his wife this morning. Bayer."

"The guy you brought through here a while ago?"

"Right."

"It's your case. Why's he want to see me?"

"He says it's your eyes."

"Right."

"True facts, McGivern. He says you've got kind eyes and he'll only talk to you. I mean, I don't think he's gay or anything. He's just kind of crazy. You know, after killing his wife and all."

So now here McGivern sat in the interrogation room. "Mr. Bayer?"

Bayer had been making a study of his folded hands. He looked up. "Why don't you call me George?"

"All right, George. Detective Clymer said you wanted to see me."

"I want to tell you what I did."

"Detective Clymer also tells me that you don't want a lawyer present."

"Not right now I don't. Maybe later." He nodded to the Sony. "Is that machine running?"

"Yes, it is, George."

"In grade school we had this priest. Seventh grade. Father Tomlin. He had eyes like yours."

"I see."

He kept looking straight at McGivern. But for a time he didn't say anything. "You know how I found out?"

"How you found out what?"

"About her other guy."

"Your wife's other guy?"

"Right."

"No, I guess I don't."

"A pubic hair."

"Oh."

"Last May I wake up, this really sunny morning, and I get out of bed all happy and pumped up because it's spring, and then I put on my glasses and happen to look down at the sheet and there it is. A red pubic hair. So I tore the top sheet off—she was in taking a shower—and I started really looking the bed over carefully. I found a lot of little red hairs. And Doris is a natural blonde and so—" He shook his head. Stared at McGivern. "You really do."

"I really do what?"

"Have eyes like Father Tomlin's."

And then, just as McGivern expected him to, George Bayer put his head down on the table and started sobbing.

Five minutes later, after McGivern had read him the Miranda again and given him careful warning about waiting for a lawyer, Bayer made a complete confession.

Half an hour later, a uniformed officer stood at the front of the homicide bureau and said, "Hey, McGivern."

Deep into paperwork, his battered desk covered with forms of at least six different bureaucratic hues, McGivern glanced up. The detective bureau consisted of eight desks, each with its own phone and adjacent gray metal typing table on wheels. The other detectives were off on various assignments. The phones ringing in the gray, empty room had a melancholy echo.

Garvey, the uniformed man, held up a small white sack. "There's one Danish left. Everybody downstairs is on a diet.

You want it?" For emphasis, Garvey patted his basketball of a stomach.

"No, thanks."

"You sure? You don't have any reason to watch your weight."

McGivern smiled. "I will if I start eating stuff like that."

"All right, then," Garvey said, and started away, his footsteps loud in the big room.

He had just about walked out of the homicide bureau when he snapped his fingers and said, "Hey, that's why that name sounded so familiar."

McGivern paid no attention. He was already lost again in his paperwork.

Garvey came back to where he'd been standing. "Where does your lady friend live?"

This time McGivern looked up. "The Remington. Why?"

"That's why it sounded familiar."

"What sounded familiar?"

"This squawk we got downstairs a few minutes ago. Somebody who lives in the building reported seeing a man who looked like he'd been shot."

McGivern wasn't sure why, but he had this sudden animal panic. He needed to talk to Kate, make sure everything was all right.

"Thanks for telling me, Garvey."

"You bet." Garvey held up the small white sack again. "You sure you don't want this?"

"Positive."

Garvey shrugged and disappeared down the hall.

The Remington was an unlikely place for a wounded man to be wandering around. McGivern wanted to know what was going on over there.

He grabbed the phone and dialed Kate's number.

4

KATE could see the death in him, the faint glaze of eye, the tight draw of lips, the sinking fall of chest. Even now he was a dead man, though he did not yet know it.

"Key," David Greene said, looking up at her with his dull scared gaze. "Key."

The blood was worse now. He lay on the couch, too drained to even hold the handgun up any longer. It lay on his abdomen, rising raggedly with each breath.

"Key," he said again.

She knelt next to him. Over the past months, David Greene had become one of her best friends. She was angry, just as she'd been angry with Sally. People you loved had no right to desert you. No right at all.

And it wasn't only Kate that David was about to desert.

David Greene was the husband of a beautiful former model, and the father of two children, the younger of whom, Alana, had been born two years ago with Down's syndrome. Those who knew David well saw that Alana's fate destroyed him. He loved her too much to feel anything but devastation at her condition.

Most children with Down's syndrome are usually turned over to a public or private institution where they are raised by nurses and their aides. David Greene had decided to keep Alana at home and help raise her in the family. This was a costly decision in two ways. One was the emotional expense. Such children, no matter how much you might love them, were sometimes difficult to deal with and teach. Two, raising such children yourself required a lot of money, only a fraction of which would be needed if David had given Alana up to a special school.

David was gifted at his calling of public relations—he had handled some of the biggest rock stars of the past decade—but he was a terrible businessman. He kept two fully staffed offices, one in Los Angeles, one in Chicago. The latter had not ever paid for itself, yet he kept it open because he wanted to be close to his family, who lived in a nearby suburb. Alana was the expense that began to sink David Greene Associates. He began taking on more work than he could handle, and not doing the quality of work expected of him. He began letting go key employees, which not only hurt him with the work load but also ensured that industry gossip would soon take its toll. The word was that David Greene would soon be forced into Chapter Eleven. And when this word was sent forth with all the malice the gossips could summon . . . David Greene started losing clients. What kind of rock star wanted to have a loser for a public relations man? The jungle beasties with their hundred-dollar haircuts and their San Juan tans began feeding on him.

David was Riki's public relations man. One night, after Riki and her manager, Brad Doyle, and the record label CEO, Frank Sayler, had left the Gold Coast restaurant where they'd all had dinner, Kate found herself walking out the door with David. He was too drunk to drive. She said she'd drive his car back to his office for him, and from there they could both take taxis home. He was one of those little sad cuddly animals she adopted from time to time. She looked at it as good practice for motherhood.

On the way to his office, David had told her all of it. The too-big mortgage on the too-big suburban house; the offices in L.A. and Chicago; the flight by three big clients within the space of forty-one working days; and then Alana.

He started crying. He just simply crashed and burned. They were three blocks from his office when she took a sudden turn eastward. He didn't seem to notice. She drove to her apartment building and had the night doorman help load David into the elevator.

While he was stretched out on the couch, snoring, she went into the bedroom and closed the door and called his wife. She explained who she was and what had happened and said that she was afraid he might be getting suicidal and that she didn't trust him to a cab.

David's wife arrived thirty-eight minutes later. By that time, David was sitting up drinking steaming black coffee. He looked vaguely ashamed of himself, which was probably a good sign. At least he had a modicum of self-respect left.

After that night, the three of them became good friends. Kate was invited to their house many nights for dinner. She met Alana. And fell in love with Alana. She understood exactly why David was willing to go through financial hell to keep her.

David's business continued to decline. Only Riki, of all his major clients, remained loyal to him. Nobody in the business could understand that, or explain it. Riki was *big* big business. Why would she want to be associated with a loser like David Greene?

Then one day, over lunch, David ordered a particularly good wine and toasted Kate. He'd stopped in at a small Chicago recording studio to watch Riki lay down some tape of two songs Kate had just written for her. Then he'd asked Kate to join him for lunch.

"You look happy," Kate said.

"I am. Very happy," David said.

"You picked up a new client?"

"Better than that. An old client paid me a lot of money he'd owed me for a long time."

"That's wonderful!" Kate said.

"I'm back in business again. No doubt about it."

But as they'd finished their lunch, Kate sensed that David seemed anxious about something.

After handing the waiter his American Express card, David said, "You're going to L.A. next week, right?"

"Right. Riki wants to show me her new studio."

"Wondered if you could do me a favor."

"Of course."

"I want to take out a safe-deposit box and I wondered if you'd cosign for it with me. You and I would be the only two authorized to open it."

She suddenly stared at him and said, "You didn't tell me the truth, did you?"

David tried a boyish grin. "Hey, what're you trying to do, spoil the mood?"

"There wasn't any 'old client' who paid you a lot of money, was there?"

The grin vanished. Worry gave his eyes a desperate brightness. "I need somebody I can trust."

"And that's me?"

"That's you, Kate." He paused. "I'm putting a very important document in the safe-deposit box. I just want to know that if something should happen to me, you'd—well, you wouldn't let it fall into the wrong hands."

"What kind of document?"

The nervous grin was back. "If something happens to me, you'll be able to read it for yourself."

The waiter returned. David signed for the lunch. Kate stood up. David sat in his chair, watching her. "I wouldn't ask you if it wasn't important, Kate. Very important."

A week later the two of them were in Los Angeles. David

found a Beverly Hills savings and loan he liked and they went in and cosigned for a safe-deposit box. Polaroids were taken of them, the photos placed in a book for future identification.

All this stayed in Kate's mind for a month or so. Why was David being so secretive? What kind of document had he put in the box?

Then she forgot about it.

Till this morning . . .

"Key," David Greene said again.

"The safe-deposit box key?"

He nodded. "I'm sorry, Kate. Sorry I got you involved."

She leaned forward and put a soft damp nubby washcloth to his forehead, cheeks and mouth.

"I'm burning up, Kate."

"Just lie still, David."

And then he was gone from her. As Sally had been gone from her.

She knelt next to him, staring at eyes that no longer saw, at lips that no longer spoke.

The door buzzer sounded.

Before getting up, she took the washcloth from his forehead and kissed him on each of his eyes. His flesh was cold and tasted salty.

She went to the door. She was trying hard not to cry.

"It's me. Brad Doyle. I need to see you."

"But David—"

"That's why I need to see you."

Not until she'd buzzed him up did she recall what David had said to her earlier. "I hope to God he didn't follow me here."

Could he possibly have meant Brad Doyle . . . ?

The knock, three minutes later, was short and angry.

She opened the door on a man whom many people mistook for a certain hunky blond movie star. Until they looked at the deep blue eyes, that is. True, there was a similarity in the square, regal set of kingly head and imposing classical jut of nose and jaw. But the eyes . . . In the movie star, you saw quiet sensuality and a hint of male sensitivity. But in Brad Doyle . . . there was just a curious emptiness until something angered him. Then the blue gaze turned so harsh that you no longer noticed how handsome the face was. All you saw was the rage accumulating in the pitiless blue depths of the eyes.

He was dressed fashionably as always, blue cashmere topcoat, double-breasted gray Armani suit, red-striped shirt complete with gold collar pin, gray silk necktie. A lank piece of blond hair fell with perfect theatrical grace across his wide forehead. He was six foot two of hard male grace.

He didn't wait for an invitation. He came right through the door.

And saw David Greene on the couch.

"He's dead," Kate said. "I was just going to call an ambulance and then the police."

"Let me look at him first," Doyle said, crossing to the couch.

"But Brad, I—"

He paid no attention. He obviously didn't trust her diagnosis.

After reaching the couch, he checked neck and wrist for a pulse. He found none. He took Greene's gun.

"Bastard," he said.

And then did something Kate could not have imagined anyone doing. Ever. He raised a chunky slab of well-muscled hand and brought it down hard across David Greene's face.

The report of the slap echoed like a rifle shot in the large, silent apartment.

"Brad!" she screamed.

Unaware of what she was doing, she lunged forward several feet. His back was to her. She hoped to push him off balance in case he tried to slap David again.

But he was too quick for her. By the time she reached him, he had turned around and pushed a large silver handgun right in her face.

"You're the one, aren't you?" He didn't let her answer. "You're the one with the key to the safe-deposit box. I knew he'd lead me to the right person."

He raised the gun. He put the barrel directly against her forehead. She smelled metal, and oil.

"You're going with me," he said.

"To where?"

"To L.A. You're going to open that safe-deposit box for me."

"But—"

He slapped her then, a chopping, angled blow strong enough to lift her heels a quarter inch off the floor, strong enough to blind her momentarily.

"I don't want any bullshit, Kate. Do you understand me?"

She felt so confused and afraid that all she could do was meekly nod her head. Warm blood had started trickling from her nose to her lips.

Her sight was coming back. She saw him reach into his coat pocket and pull out a square white unused handkerchief.

He raised the handkerchief to her face. With surprising gentleness, he wiped the blood from her nose and then put the handkerchief in her hand.

"If you do this the right way, Kate, you won't get hurt." He beckoned with the gun. "Now I want you to walk over to that closet and get some warm boots and a warm jacket because it's very cold outside, and then I want you to go down on the elevator with me and out to the limo. All right?"

He sounded like a father briefing a young daughter on what she was to do for the next twenty minutes.

"All right, Kate?" he said.

She nodded again and put the handkerchief to her nose, the blood starting to flow for the second time.

He took one of her slight shoulders in his wide vise of hand and marched her to the front closet. He opened the door, looked inside and decided to do the choosing for her. He took out a buff blue ski jacket with a yellow stripe on each arm. Then he bent down and picked up a pair of fleece-lined hiking boots.

"Remember," he said, "I don't want any bullshit of any kind."

He watched Kate get dressed, then he accompanied her out the door and over to the elevator.

5

TWO years before, Captain Ralph Helman's son Don had dropped out of high school and started hanging out with a group of boys who spent most of their days around the worst section of Rush Street, which, by night, was famous for its jazz clubs. But in gray light of day, a few parts of Rush Street were mostly panhandlers, hookers and sad shambling junkies. Don's decline had begun when his eleventh-grade girlfriend dumped him for another boy. Don was disconsolate, not seeming to care what happened to him. One night Don's friends stuck up a convenience store. One of the trio shot and killed the clerk. When the boys were arrested, they insisted that Don had been with them, obviously (but mistakenly) believing that if a cop's kid was involved, the justice system would go easier on them. Don was arrested and charged with robbery and accessory to murder.

Though only fifty-two, Captain Helman had already suffered two heart attacks. He tried to prove his son's innocence, but the stress brought on by the extra load only made him sick. McGivern worked on the case in his off-duty hours. It took him three months of nights and weekends, but he finally found an eyewitness who had seen the three masked boys enter the convenience store. There had been no fourth boy waiting outside, as the other boys insisted. Don was freed. Grateful for his freedom, he decided to return to high school, get his grades up and go on to college. Soon enough, he even met a new girl. Captain Helman never forgot what McGivern had done for him.

Helman sat in his office now. He wore the dark uniform of Chicago police officers. With his bulky body and his salt-and-pepper hair, he looked to be exactly what he was, a tough man who'd come up through the ranks and achieved his present status through hard work, a modest amount of luck and endless hours at night school. He possessed an M.A. in criminology.

"Morning, Robert," Helman said, walking over to the Mr. Coffee atop the metal bookcase sitting along his west wall. "Care for a cup?"

"No, thanks."

Helman poured himself a cup.

From behind him, McGivern said, "I need a few hours off this morning."

McGivern's tone troubled Helman. He turned around and looked at his friend. Around the precinct, McGivern was known for being unflappable. The only time he'd been known to go a little bit berserk was one day when he'd jumped into a swimming pool to rescue a three-year-old girl, but he'd been too late. His inability to save her had made him crazy for several weeks afterward. He began drinking heavily and sleeping in when he should have been at work. Helman had worried about him. McGivern's wife had left him two years earlier for the surgeon she worked for, a situation not unlike the one Don Helman had gone through. Helman started going over to McGivern's apartment at night, slowly nurturing him back to life, convincing McGivern finally that he was not responsible for the little girl's death. Could Helman do any less for the man who had done so much for his son?

"What's up, Robert?"

"I'm not sure. I've been calling Kate's apartment for the past twenty minutes and I don't get any answer."

"Is that unusual?"

McGivern grinned. "It is for Kate. She's neurotic about her phone machine, afraid she'll miss a call. She buys a new one every six months just to make sure she's got a good one." The grin faded. "Somebody reported seeing a wounded man in her apartment building this morning."

"You think Kate's involved somehow?"

"I don't know. It's just damned funny about her answering machine not being on."

Helman fondly surveyed his office. Though small, it was clean and orderly and filled with ten framed photographs of his wife and three sons at different stages in their lives. Various precinct wags referred to this as the Helman Museum. He didn't mind. Pictures of his family nurtured and consoled him. The grim business of being a cop—not to mention all the political headaches of being a captain—was much easier to bear when you were surrounded by photographs of the people you loved most.

"Sounds like you'd better get over there," Helman said.

"I was afraid you wouldn't want me to go. Nobody else is around the office to catch."

Helman smiled. "You sure don't do much for my ego, buddy-boy. You seem to forget that I was a homicide detective once myself. And a pretty good one at that."

"A damned good one," McGivern said.

"Don't waste your time flattering an old goat like me," Helman said. "Go find out what's happened to your lady friend, Robert."

"Thanks," McGivern said.

A minute and a half later he was in his car and heading for the expressway.

6

RICHARD Conroy remembered the trouble he'd had asking Bunny Sullivan to the ninth-grade dance. Though he was generally regarded as the handsomest boy in class, Conroy had always been exceedingly shy around girls. He didn't believe they saw him as anything special. He phoned Bunny three times and walked her home twice, nice long autumn-afternoon walks with bright leaves falling from the trees and the wonderful smoky scent of October on the air, but he still never worked up courage enough to ask her. His tongue just wouldn't form the words "Will you go to the dance with me?" His palms got sweaty and his heart hammered and he felt so dizzy he wondered if he was going to pass out. And the words still wouldn't come. Ultimately, he went to the dance alone, and stood in the corner all night and watched as Bunny danced with Jerry O'Hara. He never forgot how beautiful she looked that night in her blue formal, or how desperately isolated he felt, as if he would never be a real part of the humanity he saw dancing in happy couples on the floor of the gym.

Now Richard Conroy was all grown up, thirty-one years of age and a full-time flight instructor for Ames Aviation School, and he still had the same problem.

For the past three weeks, he had been teaching Jenny Stivers how to fly. So far she had completed ten hours in the air, which meant that she had learned how to do everything from the preflight check to gauging the fuel to running all radio communications to taking the controls herself. In a week or two, she'd go solo for the first time, which meant running the patterns in the small single-engine Piper Cherokee. She would take off, make several turns, land and then take off again, doing this many times over the course of an hour.

"It's getting bad, isn't it?" Jenny said.

"Yes, it is," Conroy said. "I think we'd better turn back."

The weather this morning was bad and getting worse. A blizzard was starting in the Rockies and rapidly spreading eastward. They were just seeing the first front of it now. For a time, Conroy had taken them above the clouds to that bright, sunny province that he never tired of seeing, his own personal Shangri-La.

But he hadn't wanted to risk their lives by staying up there. Like most good pilots, Conroy knew that most aviation accidents were the result of pilot error, not structural defects or failures. Even when presented with a problem, good pilots could use their knowledge and skills to overcome it—if they stayed calm and thought rationally. Stress and panic were a pilot's two worst enemies.

So now Conroy made a sober, reasoned judgment to land the plane and get them out of this weather before icing or visibility became a problem.

Landing would take approximately six minutes. Which meant he had six minutes to ask Jenny Stivers about next Saturday night.

Jenny was twenty-nine, owner of her own advertising consulting business, and an attractive if not beautiful dark-haired young woman with large brown eyes that managed to convey both wry humor and hard intelligence. She had been married once but that had ended a few years ago. Several times she'd mentioned the loneliness of singles life. She'd taken flying lessons, she'd told him, because without a man in her life, she had plenty of extra time on her hands.

Conroy had tried not to interpret her remarks as an invitation to ask her out. He considered himself a pretty dull guy and what would a woman like Jenny—who had, after all, run the governor's last two political campaigns—see in a guy like him?

Now he was down to it. Saturday night, aviation people from in and around Chicago were having their annual holiday party. Conroy needed a date.

He glanced over at her. She was in place, hands taut on the wheel, watching the private airport below them appear as they banked leftward. Ames Aviation was located sixty miles outside of Chicago. She took obvious pride in her flying skills, a pride he admired.

She must have sensed his eyes on her. She looked over at him with her huge brown eyes and smiled. "You still going to that party Saturday night?"

Last week, he'd managed to get all the way to the point of mentioning that there was going to be a party. This week he'd planned to ask her to go with him.

He felt his face burn. He was back in seventh grade. "Uh, yeah."

"You get a date yet?"

"Not yet."

"A big, handsome guy like you shouldn't have any trouble. Especially somebody who flies charter flights for big rock stars like Riki."

He'd told her about the three times he'd flown the rock singer Riki to important concerts. "Well—"

He felt the words on his tongue. *Why don't you go with me Saturday night, Jenny?*

He willed himself to speak them.

He opened his mouth.

He started to form a word.

And just then they hit some turbulence that was bad enough to pick up the Piper and slam it back down hard again.

"Wow," Jenny said, skillfully easing the plane through the turbulence.

The opportunity for asking her had passed, Conroy thought.

Another week, another lesson, and he still hadn't asked her out.

She was going to get away from him because of his stammering shyness. Stand-up comics had a phrase for it—"flop sweat"—fear of failure come true.

He would spend his whole life trapped inside this handsome mask, looking out enviously at the couples who strolled by.

"You want to handle the landing?"

"Great!" she said.

"You remember everything?"

She laughed her wonderful laugh. "I guess we're about to find out."

She was all concentration suddenly, hands tight on the yoke as the plane began its descent through the gray, snowy morning.

She executed the landing perfectly, touching down perfectly, wheeling the Piper into place over near a long row of other craft that sat to the right of the vast metal hangar.

"Did I do good?" she said as she took her hands from the yoke.

"You did great." He smiled, fighting an overwhelming desire to lean over and kiss her right on her cute little mouth.

"Well, if I did so great, then why don't we celebrate?"

"Celebrate?" he said, swallowing hard, feeling like a klutzy fifteen-year-old.

"Sure. My first perfect landing. Isn't that kind of a special event?"

"Well, yes, I guess it is."

Then she did what he'd been wanting to, the Piper cockpit so small she didn't have any trouble reaching him.

She leaned over and kissed him quickly but tenderly on the mouth. He felt exhilarated, scared, disbelieving and enraptured all at once.

She sat back in her seat and said, "So what time're you going to pick me up?"

"Pick you up?"

"For Saturday night."

"For Saturday night?"

"Gee," she laughed, "my dream date. A real live parrot."

She put her small white hand on his. "Wouldn't you like to take me to your dance Saturday night?"

"Yes." He swallowed again and then managed to say, "Very much."

"Good. Because I'd like to go with you very much. So why don't we say you'll pick me up at seven-thirty. All right?"

He nodded, unable to speak.

She opened her door and started to climb down from the plane the way he'd showed her.

She glanced back at him abruptly and said, "Are you just going to sit there grinning, Conroy, or are you going to go about your day?"

"Am I really grinning?"

"Yes, Conroy." She laughed again. "You're really grinning."

He knew then, with a wonderful self-confidence he'd never felt before, that Jenny Stivers wasn't going to get away from him the way Bunny Sullivan had in ninth grade.

7

DOYLE'S face didn't offer a clue to his thoughts. He stood on the other side of the elevator car calmly looking at Kate.

"You shot David earlier, didn't you?"

He smiled his handsome blond smile. "Things happen."

"I don't want to go to Los Angeles."

"Believe it or not, neither do I. But we're going, anyway."

As she watched him, Kate found herself wishing that Doyle would act nervous. His easygoing manner made her feel that he was in complete control of everything. She had seen him slip his gun into the pocket of his camel-hair coat. His hands were nowhere near it now. Obviously he believed he could get his gun in plenty of time no matter what Kate might do.

"What if I told you I didn't have the key to the safe-deposit box."

The smile again. The quick, easy and utterly artificial smile. He reached inside his coat, into his shirt pocket, and brought forth, with the overwrought flair of a second-rate magician, a small gold key.

"This belonged to David. It's all we need. When we get there, I give you this key and you go in and get the papers from the box." He put the key away. "So even if you don't have yours, I have mine."

"L.A.'s a long way away."

He leaned back and stared at her awhile. The smile was gone. He seemed to be looking at her, really looking at her, for the first time.

"You know, Kate, I've always liked you. I mean that. The hell of it is, you've never liked me."

"I don't like the way you treat Riki sometimes."

Personal managers were notorious for the possessive way they treated their clients. But even by those standards, Brad Doyle was legendary. Kate had seen him shout at Riki when he didn't like what she was wearing for an evening out. Or grab her when he saw her paying too much attention to another man. Kate had once even seen him slap Riki, much like he'd slapped David, and only because Riki had had too much to drink. She was a sweet drunk the few times she imbibed, but for some reason her drinking had enraged Brad and he'd cut her down for it.

"I do what I think is best for her. If I didn't care about her so much, I'd let her go."

"She's a grown woman, Brad. You shouldn't treat her like a prisoner."

Ice settled in the blue gaze now. He was a beast sensing a sudden adversary. All his playfulness was gone. "I'd say that's between Riki and me, wouldn't you?"

Kate, sensing his anger, shrank back from him. The car was small, the walls painted blue, the floor tiled in a darker blue. If he wanted to, he could be all over her in moments.

The rest of the trip was made in silence.

Three feet from the elevator, Kate saw Mrs. Roberts lugging in a bulky sack of groceries from a nearby health food store. No doubt the overweight widow was trying out a new diet. She was one of those people who could easily lose fifteen pounds and gain twenty back just as easily. She wore a wine-colored cape that came to her knees and a somewhat ratty fox stole, its sad animal eyes forever glassy in death. Her white hair, tinted electric blue, was the texture of cotton candy.

She was preceded by a tiny mincing creature known as "Dodie," some kind of "golden mutant Pekinese," as one of the apartment house's bitchier tenants had once remarked. Kate felt sorry for the little dog. It seemed to be in a constant state of agitation.

Hefting her grocery sack with one hand, tugging on Dodie's leash with the other, Mrs. Roberts said, "Would you mind hitting the elevator button for me, dear?"

Mrs. Roberts loved playing the dowager, giving the impression that she was one of those flutey women who worried about nothing more than the condition of her mink stole and her supply of Fanny Farmer chocolates. But Kate knew better. Mrs. Roberts personally managed the investments of her late husband and did quite well by her modest fortune.

"Thank you, dear, I appreciate it," Mrs. Roberts said after Kate had pushed the button.

Kate stepped in front of Mrs. Roberts just as she was stepping onto the elevator. Kate started to turn away from Doyle so she could mouth "Help me" to Mrs. Roberts.

Doyle saw what she was going to do. He grabbed her elbow so hard Kate had to swallow a cry.

Mrs. Roberts looked first at Kate and then at Doyle. "Is everything all right, dear?"

Doyle increased the pressure on Kate's arm.

"Everything's fine," Kate said, the pain nearly intolerable.

Dodie sashayed over to Doyle. She tilted her ugly little face up to him and began yipping in tinny, pathetic tones.

"Be quiet," Mrs. Roberts said, leaning down to scold the dog. "Or you won't get any pizza tonight." Mrs. Roberts returned her gaze to Kate. "Dodie loves pizza. Pepperoni, especially." Then, "You're sure everything's all right?"

"I'm sure."

"Well, then, I guess I'll go upstairs and listen to the news. This is supposed to be the worst blizzard we've had since 1967."

"Goodbye, Mrs. Roberts," Kate said over her shoulder as Doyle pushed her toward the glass front doors.

Maybe they weren't going to Los Angeles, after all, Kate thought hopefully. Maybe if somebody found the body upstairs and the police started looking for Doyle . . . maybe Doyle wouldn't dare go to O'Hare and try to board a plane.

All Kate could hope was that some unforeseen piece of good luck would stop them from going to L.A.

8

RICHARD Conroy sipped at steaming black coffee as he watched the computer screen fill with information about the winter storm roaring across the plains states from the Rockies.

He always double-checked every bit of important information. First he consulted his own computers and then he called the weather service for backup. The computers were valuable as quick reference for common weather patterns, but something as potentially dangerous as a winter storm necessitated calling the weather service.

The take on the storm was this: Snow and freezing rain were causing severe icing conditions. Many flights had already been grounded.

When the computer screen went dark, Conroy carried his cup of coffee over to a desk and sat down. He thumbed through his Rolodex. In the next ten minutes, he made three phone calls. In weather like this, he wasn't going to be giving any flying lessons. He told his three students that he was canceling and would carry over their lessons to next week.

Finished with his calls, he sat back and picked up a flying magazine. He had been meaning to finish an article on some new studies on "accident-prone" pilots. Always a dutiful pilot, he wanted to make sure he wasn't sliding into any bad habits of his own.

He looked up fifteen minutes later to see Tom Warner

standing on the other side of the desk. White-haired, chunky, possessed of a face that suggested Santa Claus, Warner owned 100 percent of this flying service. Twenty years ago the service had been little more than a small runway and a handful of Piper Cubs. Today sleek new small aircraft of every kind could be found in its hangars and on its runways.

Warner had smudges of grease on his apple cheeks. His coveralls and hands were coated with grease. Even though he was now a successful—and, some hinted, wealthy— businessman, he had never forgotten his origins. At twelve years of age, he'd fallen in love with the world of small aircraft. At the time, his only entrée into this sacred realm was assisting the mechanics at the small airfield near the farm town where he grew up. He had started as a mechanic and he would die as a mechanic. Even though he now belonged to prestigious country clubs, even though his wife had been known to buy Bob Mackie originals on their annual trips to L.A., Warner was still the same unaffected, easygoing guy he'd always been.

He was smiling.

"What's so funny?" Conroy said.

"You."

"Me?"

"Yeah. You've got your head stuck inside that magazine and you're grinning like a schoolboy."

"Oh." Conroy felt his own cheeks heat up. They were probably as red as Warner's usually were.

"You going to let me in on the joke?"

"Joke?" Conroy said.

Warner nodded to the magazine. "Yeah, what you're reading that's so funny."

"Uh, nothing. Not in the magazine, I mean. I—" He hesitated. He had grown up in one of those fundamentalist Christian homes where any talk of romance or sex was strictly forbidden. That's why he was always so tongue-tied when he went to ask a woman out. He felt he was doing something vaguely sinful. That's why, as now, he couldn't just come right out and tell Warner what was making him so happy. He couldn't just come right out and tell him about Jenny Stivers.

Warner's blue eyes shone with paternal kindness. He leaned over so nobody else in the office could hear him and said, "She was grinning just as much as you were."

The office was a big open area with a counter for customers in front and four desks, telephones, a Xerox copier, government-issue filing cabinets that somebody had bought from the National Guard many years ago and four full-time employees, each of whom was busy on the phones right now. Because of the weather, the service was going to virtually close down today. Many people had to be notified.

Warner looked around, making sure nobody was eavesdropping, and said, "She told me."

"She did?"

Warner winked at him. "Said you had a date Saturday night. Good for you. I was wonderin' when you were going to ask her out."

"You were?"

"Sure." He glanced around, then lowered his voice even more. "Couple weeks ago I saw you walking off the field together. I thought to myself, now there's the kind of nice young woman Conroy should be taking out."

Conroy's cheeks burned again. "Uh, she's real nice."

"And she's nuts about you."

"She is?"

"Sure. Can't you tell?" Warner studied Conroy a long moment and then said, "No, I guess you couldn't tell. You don't know the signs to look for." He grinned again. He had a nice grandfatherly grin. "But take my word for it. I know about these things, Richard. I used to cut quite a swath myself. She's crazy about you."

With that, Warner wiped his greasy hands on a clean oil rag that had been sticking out of his side pocket, nodded goodbye and started off in the general vicinity of the hangar.

Ordinarily, a day like this would be a long and tedious one for an active flight instructor like Conroy. The most excitement he could expect would be washing a few planes in the hangar, fueling up empty tanks and taking calls from nervous owners who wanted to make sure that the planes they kept at Warner's were safe from the wiles of the storm.

But today was going to be different.

Because something had happened to him, something that felt silly and wonderful, something that was almost narcotic in its effect.

The girl he'd been waiting for all his life had just said yes to their very first date.

While the other Warner employees stood at the windows and looked out at the somber, threatening skies, Conroy was so happy it might well have been a sunny day with soft blue butterflies in the air.

She was crazy about him, Warner had said, and Warner knew about such things.

Crazy about him.

9

KATE'S last hope was the giant Haitian doorman named Ted Manderly. Ted was a fixture at the Remington, wry of eye, courteous but not toadying of manner. He wore a red greatcoat with sparkling gold buttons and a festive matching Douglas MacArthur hat and gloves so white they seemed to glow. He worked the day shift, and if you lingered with him at all, he'd whip out color photos of his grandkids and tell his plans for each one—doctor, teacher, lawyer.

Ted stood with his back to them, between the glass front doors and the interior doors where it was warm. Out front, Kate saw a giant black stretch limo. The smoky windows made it impossible to see inside. Snow made everything seem distant, opaque.

Doyle still had painful grip of her arm. As they approached the six-five doorman, Doyle's fingers bit even more deeply into her elbow.

Kate prepared herself. She was going to have to give a small theatrical performance here. She could only pray that it worked.

As soon as they reached the interior doors, Ted heard them coming and turned around. "Morning, Kate."

"Morning, Ted."

"I sure hope you have better luck getting around out there than some of the cars I've seen already."

She smiled up at Ted's dark, friendly face. The eyes were

knowing. Only sometimes did they reveal the sadness she occasionally heard in his deep, clear voice.

"Oh, nuts," she said.

Both Ted and Doyle looked at her.

"What's wrong?" Doyle said.

"I forgot my purse."

Doyle saw instantly what she was up to.

"Why don't you wait here with Ted and I'll run back up and get it?" she said.

"I'll go with you."

As Doyle spoke, his fingers clamped down so hard on her arm that she gave a little gasp of pain.

Ted saw her expression. And then saw how tightly Doyle was holding her.

"Is everything all right, Kate?" Ted said. He was looking straight at Doyle.

"No, it isn't, Ted. I need help."

"That's what I thought."

He took a step toward Doyle and then stopped.

Doyle had taken his gun from his topcoat pocket. He pointed it directly at Ted's chest.

"No reason for you to get hurt," he said. "I'm going to walk out to that limo with Kate here and then you won't have to worry about anything anymore."

Ted started forward. Kate said, "It's all right, Ted. There's nothing you can do."

"C'mon, Kate," Doyle said, "let's go."

She tried to jerk away from him. This time he yanked her to him and shoved the gun against her neck. "Remember what I said about not giving me any bullshit? I'm trying to be nice about this, Kate."

Kate looked desperately at Ted but knew there was nothing he could do.

Doyle said, now that she was no longer fighting his grasp, "Just keep on being a good girl and everything will be fine."

She sighed and let him take her out the front doors.

She was not prepared for the lashing wind or the numbing cold. Even walking the few feet to the limousine, her cheeks felt chafed and her fingers frozen. She had a pair of leather gloves in her coat pockets. She was probably going to need them.

Doyle opened the limo door. She ducked down and climbed inside. The backseat was as wide as a small couch, plush and soft in leather. There was a bar, a telephone, a twelve-inch TV.

The limo driver had the interior panel of glass rolled down. His gloved right hand rested on the back of the front seat. There was a gun in the gloved hand, obviously intended to keep Riki in check.

Riki, in a red ski jacket, stonewashed jeans and a pair of knee-high leather boots, sat next to the other back door. Her short dark hair, which one critic had called an "erotic version of Joan of Arc's," was mussed slightly and her eyes were red from crying. "I'm sorry about all this, Kate. Brad just showed up at my door and forced me into the limo at gunpoint. I don't know what's going on."

Doyle got in and closed the door.

"You remember where I said to go if flights got canceled at O'Hare?" Doyle said to the driver.

"Right."

"That's where I want to go. Fast."

"We may have some company."

"What?"

"There's a squad car coming down the block. That doorman is waving to him."

"You sure it's a cop car?"

"One thing I know is from cop cars. Trust me."

"Get the hell out of here!"

"That's what I was thinking."

The intercom clicked off. The massive limousine pulled away from the curb, its gathering speed amazing given its bulk.

10

MCGIVERN was one long block from Kate's apartment house when he saw her march across the sidewalk and get into the waiting limo.

Both by her stiff, reluctant body language and by the way the man kept hold of her arm, McGivern knew that something was wrong.

Then he saw Ted standing out at the curb, waving him down with his big, white-gloved hands flailing through the snowy air. Ted had obviously recognized the unmarked police vehicle McGivern sometimes drove.

McGivern pulled into the curb, opening the door for Ted even before the car stopped.

Ted, breathless, sweating despite the cold, shoved his head into the car and said, "A man with a gun just took Kate in that limo!"

"Thanks, Ted," McGivern said.

Ted slammed the door shut.

McGivern floored the police vehicle, meanwhile grabbing the portable siren and affixing it to his dashboard.

The limo driver showed no sign of being intimidated. By now, a full block ahead of McGivern, the limo was rolling, maybe seventy miles per hour.

McGivern drove even faster.

Two blocks away on the narrow one-way street, the limo

reached an intersection. The traffic light was red. The limo barreled right on through it.

McGivern took out his Police Special and laid it on the seat next to him. It comforted him to have his weapon ready even if he knew that in reality it probably wasn't going to be much help. He grabbed the walkie-talkie and let other cars in the vicinity know what was going on.

By now, the limo had led McGivern over to Lake Shore Drive, the limo driver apparently feeling that he could lose McGivern on a straightaway. But for the first time, McGivern had started to gain on him.

He tried not to notice the blur in his windows. He was traveling at a dangerously high rate of speed, especially given the road conditions.

People stopped on the sidewalk, shocked, to watch the pursuit going on in the middle of one of Chicago's most fashionable areas.

Drivers honked and cursed as the two cars weaved in and out of lanes, swooping up on slower vehicles and then shooting on around them when the other lane came clear.

All McGivern could think of was Kate. In the past eight months, she had become more important to him than anybody else on the planet. He had no idea what was going on here. He simply knew that she was in danger and wanted to save her.

To his right, McGivern could see the vast, choppy lake. Snow and ice were already crusting the water. The few boats that could be seen looked frail and lonely.

The limousine abruptly turned left, taking the corner so wide and so fast McGivern wondered for a breathless moment if it would roll over on its side and skid down the block.

McGivern went around the corner, too, gripping the wheel till his knuckles were white.

The throughway was now a maze of narrow, twisting streets.

An old lady in the middle of an intersection saw the limousine bearing down on her. She dropped her sack of groceries in the street and turned around and ran back to the curb for safety.

The siren continued to scream out.

Two blocks west, a college student on a small motorbike made a bad move when McGivern swooped up behind him.

The student, terrified, made a near-fatal mistake. He turned directly into McGivern's path.

McGivern grabbed the wheel and jerked leftward with all his power.

Thank God no parking was allowed on this side of the street today.

McGivern went up over the curb and then brought the car back under control, guiding it for a time with two wheels over the curb and two wheels on the street.

The limousine took another sharp left.

McGivern saw now that the driver was headed for the Eisenhower Expressway.

McGivern came roaring back to the street with all four wheels in place.

He went squealing around the corner and powering down the street the limo had taken.

He was angry now. The distance between his vehicle and the limo kept lessening.

He would soon be right on top of it and would be able to safely shoot out its rear tires. He needed to be close to cut down the risk to citizens.

Closer, closer, his foot flat to the floor, the rear of the limo growing larger and larger in his windshield . . .

In a minute or two, Kate would be in his arms. Safe. He was sure of it.

He picked up the Police Special with his right hand, then transferred it to his left. He was ready now.

The Budweiser truck came out of a blind alley on McGivern's left. A rank of fir trees had hidden the truck until it was well out into the street.

The driver was just now looking to his right and seeing McGivern coming at him. Recognizing what he'd done, the driver stopped the huge truck and tried to back up so McGivern could get through. But by the time sufficient space had been cleared, the limo was long gone.

McGivern had had to brake down hard to keep from plowing into the cumbersome truck.

Sweat slicked McGivern's face. A sick feeling gripped his stomach. He had been in car wrecks before. His entire body had anticipated the terrible sound of the collision, metal and glass and human flesh and bone smashing into one another.

But somehow, he had managed to slow his car before anybody got hurt.

Three feet short of the Bud truck, McGivern came to a fishtailing stop.

He fell forward, almost as if he'd been wounded, setting his head on the edge of the steering wheel, letting his trembling body work through the shock of nearly hitting the truck.

But his mind was filled with Kate.

Who had taken her? And why?

Somebody was pounding on his rolled-up window.

The guy kept on pounding until McGivern slowly raised his head and looked over at him.

The beer truck driver was scared and shouting, over and over again, "Are you all right?"

Poor bastard was probably afraid he was in some sort of legal trouble.

Behind the driver, ringed like a Greek chorus, stood a semicircle of neighborhood people, staring at him. Staring.

Only then did McGivern realize why the driver was shouting so loudly.

The siren was still going.

McGivern was sitting here in the middle of the street, a massive beer truck blocking him, and he had left the siren on.

And Kate was gone.

Gone.

Gone . . .

11

THERE had been a goddamn three-car smashup on the goddamn Santa Monica Freeway this morning and so Frank Sayler was a goddamn hour late reaching his private reserved parking space in Century City.

Of all the goddamn mornings.

On the walk through the parking lot on his way to the sun-dappled glass and steel building that a Japanese investment group had bought last year, his stomach started giving him serious trouble.

On the elevator up, he gnawed on three Maalox tablets. They tasted like baby shit.

On the walk down the cushy seventh-floor hall to his offices—carpeting so deep you could twist your ankle in it—his eyes scanned the saucy bottoms of three secretaries walking to the elevators . . . but he felt nothing. Not even one of those teensy inadvertent midlife-crisis erections he'd been having so frequently lately.

He was just too goddamned worried to think in any serious way about sex.

Scimitar Records claimed three entire floors of this twenty-story building. As president of Scimitar, Frank Sayler had most of this particular floor to himself. When you had to pander to the tastes and predilections of rock stars, you had to have office space to satisfy every urge: there was a Jacuzzi, there was a Stairmaster and assorted other gym equipment, there was a state-of-the-art Japanese high-definition 45-inch TV screen, there was even a big double bed replete with silk sheets and bright red packets of Trojans in one of the headboard drawers. You never knew when a rock star—fried on drugs and used to being catered to—wanted to have an orgy.

"Good morning, Mr. Sayler."

"Morning, Mr. Sayler."

"Lovely morning, isn't it, Mr. Sayler?"

Even now, even given the miserable morning building before him, Sayler had to pause and marvel at his success. He'd come a long way for a nerdy Cleveland kid whose old man had punched a factory time clock and worked nights as a janitor to keep his family fed.

But that of course was why Sayler was so upset this morning. He wanted to make sure that he was blessed with continued success.

"Good morning, good morning, good morning," he said to each respective secretary. There were three desks beneath the huge tan wall of framed platinum and gold records. Thirty-six massive hits, a track record unequaled until two years ago when it had all started coming to an end for Frank Sayler.

How could you be forty-three years old and be ready for retirement?

Well, that was certainly possible in the record industry. Like most members of his generation, Sayler defined "quality" in certain ways. He had grown up listening to such stars as Stevie Wonder and the Jefferson Airplane and Janis Joplin. They were quality. He had carried this particular sensibility into the record business with him. At twenty-one he worked in the publicity department at Columbia, not so happy that he'd been assigned to bland middle-of-the-road acts but pleased to be a part of the "business."

Soon enough he met a man in the artist and repertoire end of the company and became his assistant. Here, he was assigned the task of finding new acts for the label. When you grew up as Sayler had, this particular job was almost impossible to imagine. Sayler had walked around pinching himself and muttering, *Yes, this is really happening to me.*

Mostly what he did was go into clubs and check out bands. See if they had a marketable "sound," see if there was an especially cute girl or boy that the label could exploit. It was a powerful gig. You sat in a dark club, the owners "comping" you drinks because they knew you were with the label and thought it was pretty nifty that you were in their dingy little club at all. And you had your own groupies. Thank God this was the seventies, before AIDS, because Frank Sayler, who had not lost his virginity until he was nearly twenty years old, slept with more women than a lot of studly movie stars ever had.

Unfortunately, there had been one problem. Frank Sayler fell in love with virtually any woman nice enough to go to bed with him. And invariably he got dumped. Groupies didn't want pledges of love and talk of a nice new home in the suburbs. They wanted quick explosive sex and dope and proximity to the rock stars they'd sleep with as soon as Sayler's back was turned.

For all his newfound money, for all his newfound power, Frank Sayler was still this sort of geeky-looking guy who just didn't know how to handle women. With one, he'd gotten so desperate that he'd followed her around for days, jumping out of his car and pleading with her to take him back (he'd had the gall to ask her to marry him). With another, he'd caught her balling one of his rock stars in his own bed. And instead of being ashamed of themselves, they'd been angry. "You've got a lot of nerve walking in on us like this," the rock star had said. "But this is my apartment,"

Sayler had whined. "Yeah, but you wouldn't have this apartment if you weren't exploiting poor downtrodden working-class kids like me," the rock star had shouted back. Like most rock star millionaires, the kid was a devout Communist.

Sayler might not have been able to handle women but he sure knew how to pick talent.

In 1976 Frank brought three acts to the label. Three of them went gold. In 1977 Frank brought three more acts to the label. Once again, all three acts went gold. By now, Frank had given up club girls. He was working in New York and dating models exclusively. If he was going to get his heart broken, better it be done by a girl who looked like Cybill Shepherd than a somewhat scruffy girl who might say, of an evening, "Did you ever take drugs anally, Frank? It's a real turn-on."

His image began appearing in tabloids and gossip rags. *Time* did a piece on the three most powerful producers in rock-and-roll and Frank Sayler was one of them. In 1979, just as disco was waning, Scimitar Records, a small but very hot label, offered Frank two million dollars a year to become CEO. He would not only find and develop his own acts, he would also have the final say in how the acts were marketed. The offer was too much to refuse. Frank moved to Hollywood, married a decent, sturdy woman who'd grown up rich in Beverly Hills but had the same values as a small-town Midwestern woman, fathered two children in quick order and then proceeded to place three albums in the Top Ten in one week's time, something no producer had ever been able to do before, not even George Martin with the early Beatles albums.

By now it was said that Sayler and Sayler alone had a sense of "yuppie" rock (or "corporate" rock as some chose to call it), that soaring, melodic kind of rock that acts such as

Journey and Nazareth built careers on. Frank made it even more soaring and he made sure that the band members were also the sort of boy-men that brought screams to the lips of teenage girls. His four most important acts shipped platinum. When *Time* did a follow-up piece on rock producers, only one man was mentioned now: Frank Sayler.

Near the end of the eighties, however, the record business began to change. Superstars remained much sought by record companies, but "niche" recording also became a factor. Ignored forms of music such as jazz, country, rhythm and blues and New Age began to produce major new stars of their own, stars that did not "cross over" to the pop charts but still generated steady and sometimes massive earnings for their labels. The Japanese businessmen who owned Scimitar began asking Frank why their label wasn't adding "niche" stars.

The truth was, or so he sometimes believed late at night when not even an extra Halcion could induce sleep; the truth was, for a nerdy kid from Cleveland who still thought that Sly and the Family Stone was about the coolest act he'd ever seen, Sayler found himself unable to operate in the Japanese fashion. It was music Sayler loved, not business. The Tokyo board of directors had sent over three men to work with Sayler on making Scimitar even more profitable. But Sayler worked on instinct. He found the Japanese concept of *nemawashi*, consensus building, and *ringi*, shared decision-making, an inhibiting way to do business.

Two and a half years ago, Sayler had seen his biggest acts begin to founder.

First it was concerts, drawing half-full or even quarter-full houses. Then it was TV gigs. Acts that Jay Leno had pleaded for a year ago were now regularly being turned down. Finally, it was record sales themselves. No audience base was more fickle than teenagers. Ask New Kids or Tiffany or the Partridge Family.

Sayler had entertained notions of getting out. But how could he retire at forty-three? Especially when he was so much in debt.

And then one day this terribly shy, very wistful Midwestern beauty walked into his office. An agent Sayler knew had sent her over and Sayler, more as a courtesy than anything else, had said he'd talk with her.

Her name was Riki and within twenty minutes, Sayler was smitten with her. He had always carried in his heart, almost like a memento, a mental picture of Elizabeth Taylor when she was fifteen years old—the raven hair, the violet eyes, the rich mouth that was both proper and erotic at the same time. And that's who Riki reminded him of: young Elizabeth Taylor. Her music was a bonus. She sang wan and painful songs of lost love and lonely nights in a style that was part jazz and part folk, a unique and fetching blend that would require careful marketing to entrap a crossover audience. In one gorgeous person, Sayler had both his first niche performer and his next superstar.

The only thing that spoiled the afternoon was the coldly handsome man who sat next to her, a man named Brad Doyle, who was her personal manager. Sayler had frequently seen relationships like this—an angry, possessive manager almost psychotically in love with the beautiful young girl he had discovered. On the one hand, these managers never wanted any other men around. On the other, they knew that the only way they would gain wealth and power was to feed their women to the carnal male appetite.

Sayler sensed this sort of dynamic in the relationship between Riki and Brad Doyle . . .

Over the next three weeks, lawyers like sleek black crows spying a fresh bloody road kill began descending on the offices of Scimitar, conducting meetings that involved both Sayler and, as Riki's representative, Brad Doyle.

Sayler's idea was to pitch Riki (real name Nancy Caine) as everyman's dream of a captivating, virginal innocent. Unfortunately, Frank learned quickly there was a problem with that. At seventeen, Riki had had a child out of wedlock, a girl who now lived with Riki's grandmother. Sayler and Doyle agreed that the child should be kept a secret, the kid not doing much for the "captivating, virginal innocent" image Frank had in mind for Riki.

One year later, Riki's first album appeared. Sayler had greased all the skids—including big payments to Mob "hit men," men who used bribes, threats and blackmail to ensure that certain records got a lot of airplay on certain major radio stations around the country—and Riki was launched. *Lonely Nights* became the fastest-selling debut album of the decade. Riki became a major instant star. At present, she accounted for nearly half of Scimitar's gross income.

Frank Sayler was once again on top. Unfortunately, there was not a number two star at Scimitar. Riki was their one and only. And if anything ever happened to her or her reputation . . .

All he had left was Riki. Thank God she was still so big she could compensate for all the other losses these past two years.

"Mr. Doyle called," his secretary said. "Four times already this morning."

"Did he leave a number?"

Marcia handed him four different pink phone notations, each bearing the same number.

As he took the notes, he felt his stomach constrict and stomach acid send searing heat up into his chest. Brad Doyle was not a man given to panic. When he called four times in one morning, something was wrong . . .

• • •

Before he called Brad Doyle, Sayler sat back in his nice leather executive chair in his nice fashionable executive office and closed his eyes.

He was doing the deep-breathing exercises his doctor had recommended.

He needed to be nice and calm when he talked to Doyle.

Whatever the problem was, he had to greet it rationally and confidently. He had to forget he was actually this sweaty little daydreaming music nerd from Cleveland and pretend he was . . . he was the man *Time* magazine claimed he was.

He dialed the number.

And after two rings the receiver was snapped up and Brad Doyle shouted, "Frank? Is that you?"

"Sure it's me, Brad. Why are you shouting?"

"I'm in a limo, Frank, and a cop is chasing us! I'll call you back later!"

Doyle slammed the car phone down.

Calm. Sane. Rational. A man in perfect control. That's who Frank had to be now.

Sure it sounded like some bad movie script that Brad Doyle was in a limo being chased by cops. Sure it was very threatening that Riki herself was probably involved in all this. Sure it was upsetting that Frank's one and only star was probably headed straight down the toilet . . .

But calmly, sanely, rationally. That was how he had to approach all this.

Then he jumped up from his nice leather executive chair and proceeded to destroy the shit out of his nice fashionable executive office, hurling everything on the desk to the floor, grabbing a huge bookcase and pulling it down, taking the Mr. Coffee and smashing it against the wall, coffee splattering all over the expensive flocked wallpaper . . .

Marcia, terrified, opened the door and carefully stuck her head in and said, "Are you all right, Frank?"

And Frank, standing like a conqueror on a huge pile of fallen hardcover books, said, "I'm fine. Just getting a little exercise is all."

The secretary, who was inclined to call a mental hospital, smiled nervously and said, "Well, everybody can use a little exercise."

Then she quietly closed the door and vanished.

An hour later, with no explanation or apology to his secretaries, Sayler left his office and went down the hall to an empty office. He'd wanted to say something to his secretaries, of course, make some kind of amends for his juvenile behavior, but what could he say? "Exercise" was probably as good an explanation as any.

Three minutes later, Sayler sat tense and miserable behind a desk. The door was closed. The radio was on. Maybe there was a news story . . .

At first, the stories were just the usual. Inflation rising. Trouble in the Middle East. A crazed employee shooting up the factory he worked in. A black gay alcoholic senator announcing tearfully that he was also a drug addict and an embezzler.

Then . . .

"From Chicago, a breaking story involving the apparent murder this morning of record publicist David Greene, a man most closely associated with recording star Riki . . ."

Sayler sat there in shock and disbelief.

David Greene . . . murdered.

My God . . . he had to get ahold of Doyle, and fast. What the hell was going on, anyway?

Frank Sayler reached into a pocket of his new pin-striped suit, bought at Bijan on Rodeo Drive, and dug out three more Maalox tablets.

12

THE limousine was now twenty minutes away from the alley where the beer truck had suddenly appeared.

Kate sank back in the deep, cushiony seat. A terrible image of Robert McGivern filled her mind: his car smashing into the beer truck, an explosion of glass and metal and gasoline, and Robert dying in the midst of it.

She put her face into her hands.

Every few moments, she was startled by the unreality of all this. David Greene dead. Brad Doyle holding a gun on her. Nothing in her life had prepared her for a situation like this. Every moment seemed both chillingly real—and not quite real at all.

There was no way to tell what Riki was thinking. She only stared out the window at the freeway they had just entered. She was capable of withdrawing in a way that was almost frightening to watch. At long formal dinners, Kate had seen Riki have what seemed like an out-of-body experience to the point where she wasn't in the room at all.

Face still in her hands, Kate became aware of the odd sound, the odd smell: thrum of tire, monotone of motor, Doyle's musky after-shave.

She looked once again at Riki.

The rock star had her head tilted back. Her eyes were closed. Tiny headphones no bigger than hearing aids shone in her ears.

Kate felt the massive automobile veer rightward. As it came down the off-ramp, the rear end began to slide. If a limousine slid this way, the ice storm that had been predicted all week must really be landing hard.

The driver's voice came over the speaker. "I've got to get some gas."

"Great," Doyle said. "Of all times."

"I told you about it earlier. You said—"

"I know what I said. So do it."

On the other side of the window, Kate saw the neighborhood the driver had entered, one of the venerable old working-class neighborhoods of Chicago. The small homes had been built well and they'd been kept well, with obstinate immigrant pride. Even eighty, one hundred years later the homes looked clean and tidy, the yards slavishly kept. Warm gray smoke curled from the chimneys. Kate wanted to be inside one of the houses now, snug and warm and safe.

The limousine turned into a service station and passed over a hose that started dinging.

A young blond man in a 1956 crew cut and a clean pair of coveralls came out to the pumps.

On the other side of the glass separating front from back, the driver rolled down his window and told the young man to fill it up and check the oil. The driver pulled the hood latch. The hood looked as big as a rowboat as it lifted up into the air.

"I have to go to the bathroom," Kate said.

Doyle turned to her and smiled. "I was waiting for that."

"Waiting for what?"

"Some pathetic little attempt to escape."

"I really need to go to the bathroom."

"Right."

Kate tried reason. "After all that's happened in the last hour, you don't think I need to go?"

He stared at her, then glanced over at Riki. Her head was still back, eyes closed, earphones in place.

"You know what happens if you try anything, Kate?" Doyle said.

"I know."

Doyle rolled down his window, looked out on the station. On the corner of the plate-glass window was a sign with an arrow pointing to the right: *Rest Rooms*. Below, it said: *Ask attendant for key.*

"C'mon," Doyle said.

Doyle got out first. He stood by the door, as if holding it open for Kate.

As her feet touched the concrete, she was surprised to find that her legs were shaky. Fear and stress had taken a much greater toll than she'd realized.

Doyle took her arm. They probably looked like any other young couple. Except for the limo, she thought sardonically.

Inside the station, they stood at the cash register while a redheaded attendant finished making out a credit slip. The station smelled of oil from the two-bay garage to the left. Two men in the bay laughed about something, their voices echoing.

When the attendant finished with his previous customer, he nodded a hello to Doyle. "Help you, sir?"

"Rest room key, please. For my wife."

"Oh, sure."

Momentarily, Kate saw an expression on the young man's face that said: *If your wife wants the key, why doesn't she ask for it herself?*

But the attendant just shrugged, reached below the cash register and brought up the key. He handed it to Kate.

She tried to put an entire message in her glance: *I'm in trouble. Please help me.*

But if the attendant understood, he didn't let on. After

handing her the key, he moved over to the cash register, punched *No Sale* and started working in the cash drawer.

Doyle put pressure on Kate's elbow. He started steering her out of the office.

She stopped suddenly, turned back to the attendant at the register.

"Sir?"

He looked up. "Yes, ma'am?"

"I—"

Then she felt the gun.

Doyle had draped his coat over his weapon again.

"I just wondered if you knew the time."

He nodded to a big 7Up clock on the wall. It was right in front of her. Impossible to miss.

For the first time, the attendant looked as if he might suspect there was something wrong with this nice young couple.

"There's a clock, ma'am."

"Oh, yes. Thank you."

Doyle practically shoved her the rest of the way out the door.

Ice bit at her face; the temperature had dropped even more.

"I really need the bathroom," she said.

They stood on the corner of the station. The crew-cut attendant was scraping ice from the limo windshield. The driver, dressed in a black uniform replete with a small black cap, stood on the far edge of the station, smoking a cigarette in the lashing wind.

Doyle squeezed Kate's arm so tight, pain traveled up into her shoulder and neck.

"That was pretty goddamned cute."

"I still need to go to the bathroom. There's nothing I can do in there."

"Pretty goddamned cute," Doyle repeated.

She watched as he visibly tried to calm himself. His pride was obviously that he was always in control of every situation. But his rage was something to contend with. She'd once seen him savagely beat a busboy whose service had displeased him. The busboy, properly, sued Doyle. The matter was resolved with an expensive out-of-court settlement. The tabloids had feasted on the matter for months. Frank Sayler had been extremely unhappy that anybody associated with Riki would be involved in such an incident.

Doyle guided her around the corner and down the walk leading to the rest rooms.

She kept watching for a means of escape but she saw none. Angry as he was now, Doyle would kill her for practically any reason. In his rage, he would forget that she had something he needed.

The rest rooms were near the back of the concrete-block building. The women's was on the very end.

When they reached *Ladies*, he handed her the key. "You've got two minutes."

"It may take a little longer."

"Two minutes. No more."

She looked at him, shook her head.

Then she turned, and inserted the key.

She started in but he tapped her on the shoulder. "I keep the key."

She dutifully handed him the miniature rubber tire with a Yale key dangling from it.

Even with the door only halfway open, the overly sweet scent of "outhouse perfume" nearly gagged her. All she could think of was one of those too-cute little skunks that emitted saccharine scents.

She got inside, closed the door.

On the left was a sink and a toilet. On the right was a metal wastepaper basket that was as high as the sink. Above the basket was a window. There was no heat.

In the cracked and faded mirror, she saw her breath plume silver.

She really did need to go to the bathroom. She did that first and quickly, her bottom never quite touching the seat. "Hovering," her mother had called this method while instructing her daughters in the proper use of "city" toilets.

She finished quickly, washed her hands, then immediately climbed up on the sink and stepped across from it to the metal wastepaper basket. The window was wide enough for her to squeeze through. If she could just climb out before Doyle got suspicious . . .

The window did not open easily. She cut several knuckles while pushing the glass back. The square through which she would shimmy was no more than two feet wide and two feet tall.

Through the open window, she looked out at a patch of gray, turbulent sky and felt freezing ice crystals blow through the opening.

She vaulted upward, grabbing desperately on both sides of the window.

Now began the almost impossible task of wiggling and wriggling and twisting her way through the small, square opening. Shoulder muscles strained to the point of ripping; the palms of her hands started to tear on the metal window frame. And for a terrible moment she felt stuck, unable to move in any direction. She should have taken her jacket off. Panic fluttered in her chest.

Doyle, predictably, began pounding on the door, his fist on the metal sounding murderous.

She whimpered, exasperated that she couldn't propel herself any faster, enraged that she wasn't big enough and tough enough to confront Doyle in a fight.

Doyle kept up the pounding.

He even salted the air with a few expletives.

In moments, he would use the key and let himself in.

Three quarters of her body was out of the window now. She felt as if she were struggling to be born.

Below her she saw winter-hardened ground and three rusty barrels filled with greasy, empty oil cans.

She could drop down there and start running before Doyle figured out what had happened and—

She had only inches to go when she became aware of the sudden silence. The noise from the station was lost in the wind.

The wind was the only sound, an icy wind laying a crystal coating on roadways and naked black tree limbs.

She was looking left when he came around right, Doyle did, and stood below her and pointed his gun directly at her face.

Curiously, he seemed more amused than angry. "You always were cute, Kate. You're even cute now."

The smile vanished.

"Now get your ass down from there."

A minute later, free of the window, she dropped in a tumble to the ground.

He jerked her to her feet and shoved her toward the walk.

Kate was again a prisoner.

13

WHEN he reached Kate's apartment, McGivern found an entire police department team at work. There were people from the police lab, the police photo unit and the precinct commander's. There were also people from the medical examiner's, the district attorney's and the Mobile Crime Lab. It was the work of the latter group that put the stink of chemicals on the air. A half dozen solvents and solutions were used in recovering latent prints and blood samples that would then be taken to the lab for DNA testing.

Overseeing this small circus was Captain Ralph Helman.

He stood in the center of the living room half shouting into a walkie-talkie. On his way inside, McGivern had seen three mobile trucks from the TV stations. Reporters wanted upstairs where the juicy TV shots were to be found—a corpse, lots of blood and, even better, celebrity. The dead man had been Riki's publicist, after all. Even a city as big as Chicago only infrequently got a story this good.

"You may come up, Jonas, when I say you can come up. There's nothing more to talk about."

With that, Helman broke communication and handed the walkie-talkie to a uniformed officer standing next to him.

"How're you doing?" Helman said, careful to lose his angry tone. Via police radio, McGivern had informed him of what had happened, how close he'd come to getting the limo until a beer truck got in his way. The limo's license number was now being broadcast to all cars.

"Pretty good."

Helman smiled bleakly. "Better than *he* is, anyway, huh?" He nodded to where David Greene still lay sprawled on the couch. A sheet covered him. In places, blood had soaked through the white cotton.

"I met him a few times," McGivern said. "He seemed like a decent guy. Always talking about his wife and kids."

"Well, somebody sure didn't think he was a nice guy. He got it close up, three times."

McGivern shook his head. "Anything at all on the limo?"

"Not yet. Sorry." He pointed to the window. Ice had started to harden along the window frame. "The weather isn't helping. Most of the cars that might ordinarily be looking for the limo will be checking out fender-benders instead."

Chicago was typical of most midwestern cities on the first few snow days of the season. Drivers gave in to panic. Otherwise perfectly safe, sensible drivers did foolish things such as slamming on the brakes and causing three-way pileups.

"I kept thinking of how she looked when I pulled up to the apartment house. Just the way he was holding his coat, I knew he had a gun to her back." McGivern's voice was fraught with melancholy.

"You ever see him before?"

"No."

"We'll get him."

"Hopefully."

Helman nodded toward the couch and said, "Come over here a minute, Robert."

They walked over to an end table. On their way, the familiarity of the place overwhelmed McGivern. In that chair, Kate had sat in his lap as they shared a huge bowl of popcorn and watched a Warner Brothers cartoon festival. On that dining table, only an edge of which was visible around the corner, she'd served him a delicious meal of braised beef tips and sautéed vegetables. And in the bedroom . . . he thought of their first night together, how it had not exactly been spectacular sexually—both of them nervous and somewhat shy—-but how it had been loving and tender and nurturing for both of them.

Helman took a yellow number two pencil from his uniform coat and pointed to a wrinkled plastic bag bearing a bright yellow evidence tag. Inside it was a small tan envelope with a set of numbers stamped in black at the top and a line of bold black type at the bottom that said *Safe-deposit Box*.

Helman then pointed to another wrinkled plastic bag. Inside it was a United Airlines envelope.

Helman said, "The safe-deposit box key envelope was stuffed inside the United envelope, which probably means that the key envelope is from Los Angeles because that's where the ticket is to. In Greene's pocket."

"Anything in the key envelope?"

"There's printing on the back about being careful with your key, informing them immediately if you lose it and so forth."

"But was there a key in there?"

"No. And that makes me curious. Maybe Greene was killed for that key. Maybe that's why it's missing."

"Can you check with various L.A. banks and see if they have numbering systems similar to this one?"

"We're already doing that," Helman said. "You say Kate and Greene were friends?"

"Right."

"Close friends?"

"I guess so. Why?"

"What if he came up here to hide the key? Say he knew that the killer was after him. Would he trust Kate with the key?"

Much as he didn't want to, McGivern thought about that. If Kate had the key and the killer suspected she did . . .

"It's possible, I suppose," McGivern said. "If Greene didn't know he was being followed and he came up here and—but don't you have to have two keys for most safe-deposit boxes?"

Helman was about to respond when a familiar man stepped up.

"Excuse me, Captain, could I speak with you a minute?"

Dr. Fineman was from the M.E.'s office, a small, white-haired man who was a favorite with the police force because he always spoke in plain English, never jargon, and because he seemed to have real respect for cops. Some of the M.E. folks treated cops as if they were gorillas.

While Helman and Fineman stepped to the center of the living room and spoke in whispers, McGivern thought over what Helman had said.

Greene came up to the apartment to give Kate his key, thinking it would be safe with her. Not knowing that he had been followed, he had no hint that he'd gotten Kate into trouble. Then the killer was at the door and—or had Greene given a key to Kate before today?

Finished talking, Helman came back to where he'd left McGivern standing. "How you doing, Robert?"

"Hanging in there, I guess," McGivern said.

"Things'll turn our way, Robert. You wait and see."

McGivern sure hoped Helman would soon be proved correct.

14

DOYLE'S limo driver had had many names in his twenty-nine years on planet Earth. He had been Ed Rollings when he was running bad checks in New Orleans. He had been Sandy O'Toole when he was supplying hookers to a group of seemingly insatiable Denver businessmen. He had been Dave Swarthout when he was on the edges of the big-time drug trade as a broker of sorts, bringing buyer and seller together and bowing out before things got physically dangerous. So many names but so little luck, money that came quick and went quick, bad women and bad investments (a sporting goods store in Teaneck, New Jersey, that got urban-renewaled right out of frigging business six months after he opened it up) and any number of lazy-ass relatives who didn't want to know how he made his money just as long as he kept them on the dole every month. So one day he just said screw all the pressure, screw all the stress, I'll just be a gofer and enjoy the singular pleasures of being a nobody who nonetheless has ready access to women, dope and the occasional windfall of cash. The record business was an ideal place for such a goal. Especially if your bosses sometimes needed you to rough a few people up. Nothing permanent, he was hardly a hit man, but he was an expert at making someone's groin or back or head hurt for many, many months to come.

His real name was Fritz DeVrees and right now Fritz

DeVrees was looking in the mirror on the driver's side of the limo.

Fritz DeVrees said, "Oh, shit."

He punched the button that let him be heard in the back, in that private realm behind the smoky glass, and said, "We've got a cop car following us, Brad."

Then it was Brad Doyle's turn to say, "Oh, shit."

The limo was traveling at 55 mph on a sloping part of the interstate that was becoming more icy and treacherous by the moment. Every quarter mile or so you saw a car that had skidded out of control and run into the guardrails along the highway. You even saw a few of these drivers walking along the edge of the roadway, presumably in search of a tow truck and a telephone.

Fritz DeVrees drove carefully.

Mammoth yellow sand trucks with whirling neon eyes sprinkled gritty sand over the two lanes of the interstate, making all the cars behind it travel fifty-five even if they didn't want to.

"Maybe they're not following us. Maybe they're just moving slow because of the sand truck."

"What if they try to pull us over?"

"Where's the next exit?"

Fritz DeVrees said, "Half a mile."

"Take it."

"Should I wait and see what the cops are going to do?"

"No. Take it, anyway."

"All right."

Fritz DeVrees clicked off, put both of his black-gloved hands tight on the steering wheel and proceeded to cross into the exit lane. Even with all its massive weight, the limousine was having a problem with traction and would have even more if it had to suddenly increase speed.

His blue eyes watched his mirror steadily.

The cop car moved into the exit lane.

For the second time in the space of a minute and a half, Fritz DeVrees said, "Oh, shit."

The cop car had just turned its cherry on. No siren as yet; just the whipping red light.

Fritz DeVrees knew what he had to do.

He applied his right foot heavily to the gas pedal. He gripped the steering wheel even tighter.

The big dark limousine jumped ahead to the exit and raced down the sloping off-ramp.

Now the siren came on, cutting through the privileged air of the limo's interior.

Fritz DeVrees saw a T-intersection straight ahead. Either way he went, turning the heavy automobile at this speed would be difficult.

He tamped the brakes lightly, needing to slow by ten miles per hour or so.

The limo started to skid. The ice here was a bitch.

Fritz DeVrees stayed in control, however. He used the skid to his advantage, turning the wheel to coincide with the skid.

He was around the corner.

A long avenue filled with slow-moving cars lay ahead.

The siren seemed to grow louder and more insistent by the moment.

He glanced in his mirror again. The cops had also negotiated the sharp turn with little difficulty. They were now racing down the broad avenue after him. They were no more than seven or eight car lengths behind.

With the siren slicing through Christmas carols being broadcast over outdoor speakers in this suburban shopping district, cars started to pull over to the curbs to let the two cars pass.

Pedestrians stopped, pointing to the chase that was obviously in progress.

DeVrees heard the abrupt and unmistakable sound of gunfire. *Bakka, bakka, bakka.*

Fritz DeVrees, increasing his speed, watched the action in his rearview mirror.

Brad Doyle was leaning out the back window, firing again and again at the squad car, trying to hit its tires.

While movie stuntmen made such feats look easy, hitting anything from a vehicle traveling upward of 90 mph was virtually impossible. And dangerous for anybody in the vicinity.

Then, even above the gunfire, even above the siren, Fritz DeVrees heard Riki and Kate start screaming.

He put the pedal to the floor.

He almost didn't see the little old lady who had pulled her nice new Buick Regal into the intersection and, out of sheer fright, stalled the damn thing.

In a single moment, the eyes of Fritz DeVrees took in the following information: the little old lady had just gotten herself a sweet little old-lady perm; the little old lady was wearing a silly little old-lady hat with a prim little veil; the little old lady looked just like a woman he'd once raped back in his Newark days. He'd been fifteen and she'd been eighty-one. He'd always been attracted to old ladies.

He swerved the cumbersome mass of metal around the nice Buick Regal.

Swerved, and for a stomach-churning, bowel-loosening moment felt the limo begin to slide out of control.

He saw her now, a freeze frame of terror staring at him, baffled, out of her car window as the limo skidded toward her.

He jerked the wheel hard to the left, the rear end still sliding.

God, was he going to make it?

He made it.

He couldn't believe it.

The limo slid around the proud new hood of the Buick Regal.

Fritz DeVrees had a clear run again. He put the accelerator to the floor and continued down the straight shot of avenue.

He watched in the exterior mirror as the cop car, too, managed to slide around the stalled Buick.

The cop car was on a clear run again.

It came faster, faster, like a swooping predatory bird about to scoop up its prey.

Boyle resumed firing.

Riki and Kate resumed screaming.

The siren continued to wail.

Fritz DeVrees watched the road ahead. He could see two or three intersections down the avenue. They all looked clear.

Checking his exterior mirror again, he saw proof that on this day luck was with them.

Doyle finally managed to hit one of the tires.

The cop car spun instantly out of control, turning around completely in the middle of the broad avenue, and then plowing into a parked car.

Fritz DeVrees settled in for some more stunt driving. He was smiling, exultant.

Then he saw a second police vehicle round the corner ahead of him and come racing down the street toward him.

But the police vehicle was traveling too fast for the icy road. He saw the driver's face register this as, beneath him, his car began to spin out of control.

The police car was now on Fritz DeVrees' side of the avenue.

He tried to pull out of its way before they collided but it was too late.

The cruiser came abreast of the limousine and then started to slide again, spinning directly into the rear end of the massive vehicle. Seconds later, the rear end of the cruiser slid into the rear end of the limousine again. This time, the rear fender of the cruiser was struck by the limo, tearing open the cruiser's gasoline line. Fuel began to slosh across the back of the careening vehicle.

The cruiser bounced off the limousine one more time and then went into a 180-degree spin, turning and turning and turning until it finally went up over the curb into an empty space between parked cars and slammed into a utility pole.

The two officers were slumped over in the front seat and so neither of them saw the long power line dangling from the smashed utility pole.

As the pole began to creak and fall to the ground, the power line brushed against the cruiser's open gas line.

The effect was immediate.

The explosion sent pieces of the cruiser flying in different directions. The concussion was such that the safety glass in several nearby cars shattered.

Rolling flames and waves of greasy smoke made approaching the cruiser impossible.

Kate watched all this from the back of the limousine. The big vehicle was stalled in the middle of the street, the collision with the police car killing the limousine's engine.

Something else was wrong, too.

The limo driver was neither moving nor speaking. During the last collision, his head had cracked the windshield.

The horn sounded unceasingly.

Doyle had his gun out. He looked at Kate and Riki and said, flat and harsh, "We're getting out of here. Now."

Kate knew better than to argue with him.

15

TED Manderly had never been comfortable around white people. He had come from Haiti to Galveston, Texas, and finally on to Chicago thirty-eight years ago but still had never learned how to relax around white folks. His son, whom he had put through college and who had now become a black Muslim, openly hated white people and called his father vile names for working for them. But after all these years, what could Ted Manderly do? In a few years, he would retire and he would do so thinking that his lot had not been bad and was, by Haitian standards, enviable. Three children, each raised healthy, each graduated from college. A wonderful, faithful wife who had always been his best friend as well as his lover and partner. A well-kept little frame house in a decent South Side neighborhood (most whites didn't believe there was such a thing as a decent South Side neighborhood but there was; there were several, in fact). A five-year-old gray Oldsmobile that he babied the way he'd babied his children. Subscriptions to *Time* and *Atlantic* and *Ebony*, magazines his wife had long ago taught him to read even though he'd never gone beyond second grade in Haiti. Six years ago he'd had a cancer scare with his prostate but the problem was not malignant and was treatable with medication. Three years ago his second oldest daughter had presented him with a grandchild. And this year an old friend would visit from Haiti and bring pictures of other old friends and places. Ted Manderly knew why his son hated whites and why he had become a black Muslim, but Ted had made his peace with them and a few he even liked—even if he didn't quite trust them.

Ted took off his splendiferous uniform hat and stood on the threshold of Kate Evans' apartment.

A uniformed officer, a black man, had come down to the lobby and said he'd watch the door for Ted, that Captain Helman would like Ted to come upstairs.

Ted's first reaction had been fear. He had learned early on that when a white policeman wants to see a black man, there will inevitably be trouble for the black man, even if he is innocent. Ted had seen innocent friends of his hassled and beaten many times. Things were better in Chicago now but they were not perfect.

Ted was startled by the number of people working in the apartment. With their brushes and whisk brooms and vacuums, they looked like a cleaning crew.

He was happy to see that fully a third of the crew had skin the color of his own. As he often told his son, progress was slow but it was steady.

Then, for the first time, Ted looked over at the couch and saw what the two ambulance attendants were doing.

David Greene, a man Ted had often greeted at the door downstairs, was being zipped into a black body bag.

Greene had the pallor and rigidity of the dead.

When Ted had first come to America he had been without friends and so he had adopted a small stray dog.

One day the dog was hit by a car. Ted, in tears, had rushed into the street and lifted the dog tenderly and solemnly from the concrete and carried him over to a tree where there was shade and the sweet spring smell of lilacs.

Ted sat down by the tree and put the tiny dog in his lap.

The dog had died in jerks and spasms, Ted only weeping as life left the little animal.

Then the dog had suddenly been still. Ted liked to think that this was because the dog's soul had left its body. Ted fervently prayed that dogs had souls and that, just as the nuns had taught Ted that God took human souls to His side, Ted hoped that God would also take the little dog to His side.

David Greene looked like that now as the attendants lifted him from the couch and set him into the body bag: soul-gone.

McGivern saw Ted Manderly standing in the doorway looking intimidated and immediately went over to him.

"Thanks for coming up, Ted."

"Sure."

"Would you look through some photographs of people Kate knows in the music business? Maybe we can find the man you saw."

Ted nodded. "Fine."

McGivern knew that it was a stereotype to think of older black men as dignified, but dignity was just what Ted Manderly exuded. Along with patience, intelligence and his own quiet charm.

"Why don't you come with me?"

Ted nodded again and followed McGivern through an obstacle course of people and equipment scattered all over the living room and extending into the bedroom.

The den was three book-lined walls and a large window overlooking the lake below. There was a built-in twenty-seven-inch TV and a comfortable leather sofa. In one corner of the sofa was a neat stack of cassette recordings, songs that Kate had composed on her piano and that were in various stages of development. Sometimes songs came to Kate in blinding flashes and were complete in minutes. Other songs fought her all the way and took months to finish. She had explained all this to him one soft summer night when McGivern had first been falling in love with her.

As he came into the den now, a terrible melancholy overtook him. He heard her voice and felt her flesh against his and scented her subdued perfume.

Kate.

He went to work quickly.

Kate was not vain and so she tended to throw all her publicity pictures into two cardboard boxes hidden behind the sofa. She didn't value the pictures much.

Because she frequently traveled to New York and Los Angeles, she often dined, along with Riki and other recording stars, at posh night spots. Which meant breaking bread with various celebrities.

"I haven't looked in this box yet," McGivern said.

The two men sat on the leather couch. McGivern dragged the box over between them.

He started examining the black-and-white glossies and the newspaper clippings one at a time, showing each to Ted Manderly as he did so.

Here was Kate with Elton John. Here was Kate with Mariah Carey. Here was Kate with Vice President Quayle, a man she said she actually liked despite all his problems with the press.

And so on.

No sign of the man McGivern suspected Ted had seen this morning.

"She sure keeps to herself," Ted said at one point.

"Oh?"

Ted smiled. "Sure, if most people had met all these folks, they'd be bragging about it."

McGivern thought, Kate . . .

Sometimes they took turns playfully suggesting that their relationship would someday lead to marriage. One night, while Kate was tossing some of these photos into the cardboard box, she said, "Well, at least our children will think that their mom was really somebody special in her day."

Remembering that now, McGivern felt tears burn his eyes.

He moved even faster through the remaining photographs.

Paul Simon. Meryl Streep. Stevie Wonder.

Ted said, "There."

He pointed a long ebony finger to a faded yellow newspaper clipping that showed Kate, Riki and a handsome blond man sitting in a corner booth in a trendy Los Angeles restaurant called Spago.

McGivern held up the photo. "That's him?"

"Yes. I don't know what his name is, I mean he's never been here on my shift, but that's the man. I'm sure of it."

McGivern turned the photo over. On the back it read "Brad Doyle and I, 1990." "His name is Brad Doyle."

The men shook hands, then stood up.

"She's one of the real nice ones," Ted said as they were leaving the den. "I sure hope everything turns out all right."

Seventy-eight seconds later, McGivern was on the telephone with headquarters.

He ordered a computer search for any information on Brad Doyle or any aliases of Brad Doyle, and he gave a description of the subject and said that he was a suspect in a murder this morning.

McGivern then went out to where Helman was talking with two men from the Crime Lab.

Finished talking, Helman came over to McGivern and said, "Why don't I buy you a cup of coffee? You look a little wound up."

"Guess I am."

"C'mon, we can grab one on the way back to the precinct."

16

"HI."

"Hi."

"You know who this is?"

"Uh, huh-uh."

"Take a guess."

"Madonna."

"Very funny." Pause. "You really don't know who this is?"

"Of course I do."

"God, you really had me going there for a minute."

"I'm glad to hear from you. It's a nice surprise."

"Thanks for saying that," Jenny Stivers said. "I was a little insecure about calling you."

"Hey, I'm the one who has the shyness problem," Richard Conroy said.

A nice girlish giggle. "So I noticed. I practically had to plead with you to ask me out."

"Sorry. Just the way I was raised, I guess."

"Oh?"

"One of those fundamentalist Baptist congregations where just about everything you do is sinful. Including asking out pretty women."

"I didn't think there were churches like that anymore."

"If you look hard, you can still find them."

"And your folks looked hard?"

"Very hard, I'm afraid. So I've still got this hang-up about asking women out, I guess."

"We'll have to work on that."

"I look forward to that."

"I hope you're not flying any more today. On the way back to the office I started worrying about you."

"There won't be any flying today. All the planes that are outside are iced up pretty well already. And even though the icing's supposed to let up, the blizzard keeps getting worse."

"The predictions are six-foot drifts in some places."

"Remind me to move to Florida sometime," Richard Conroy said.

"You sure this was all right? Calling you, I mean?"

"It was fine. Great."

"I'm afraid I'll have to cut it short now. There's a client in the reception area. He hates to be kept waiting."

"Important man, huh?"

She laughed. "That's what he tells me." Pause. "I'm really glad we have a date."

"So am I."

"Maybe next time you can overcome your Baptist up-bringing and ask *me* out."

"I'll work real hard on it."

She laughed again. "Promise?"

"I promise."

Five minutes later, hunched inside his leather bombardier jacket, Conroy made the rounds of the airplanes parked near the runway.

Some of the more careful owners always tied their private craft down to eyebolts. This prevented the planes from flipping over in storms. Others showed much less concern, figuring that a storm of that force was an unlikely event. Today, they would find out differently. In winds like these, you realized how fragile small aircraft really were.

Above the blowing snow, he could hear a twin-engine plane coming in for a landing. The pilot would have to be flying IFR, on instruments. There was still time for most crafts to land safely, albeit with a savvy pilot at the controls.

He spent the next five minutes checking the remaining planes. A few of them were already creaking in the blowing snow, showing signs of stress, hinting that they might soon be tipped over on their backs.

He walked past the hangar, where his own plane was safe inside, and then went into the office.

He went straight to the coffee machine, where the owner, Tom Warner, stood drinking a can of diet Pepsi.

When he saw Richard, Warner smiled. "Just the man I wanted to see."

"Oh-oh. That tone sounds familiar."

"It's the I-really-need-a-favor tone."

"That's what I thought."

Warner shook his head. "My mother-in-law took the train into the city this morning and my wife is afraid of driving on ice. So guess who has to go get her?"

"As I recall, your mother-in-law is a very nice woman."

"Yes, she is. So if you wouldn't mind being alone here for a few hours—"

Conroy nodded to the snow tumbling furiously across the window. "I doubt we'll have much business the rest of today."

"Murray just landed. He asked if we had any space left in the hangar. I told him we did. He'll put his machine in there and then be out of your hair." Murray was one of their best customers, a charter pilot who was a nice enough guy but a little irritating to be around for any length of time. He tended to inform you that everything you were doing as a pilot was wrong.

Warner walked to the window, looked out. "There's Murray now. Getting in his truck and pulling away."

He went over and put on his parka, tugged on a wool cap and started over to the front door.

"I'll be back here as soon as I can."

"No problem," Conroy said. "I'm not going anywhere."

"Appreciate it, kid. I really do."

With that, Warner went out into the storm and was, within seconds, lost in the whipping white wind.

17

BRYCE Conlon was all the things Frank Sayler was not. Patrician background. Harvard business degree. Intimate of movie stars and politicians and network newsreaders. And handsome. And tanned. And so well spoken he sounded like those snotty British actors who did voice-overs for Jaguar. Oh, yes, and silver-haired. He was as vain about his hair as young ladies sometimes were about their legs.

And one more thing: bigot.

Bryce Conlon loathed, and not necessarily in this order, black people, gay people, women (except those he was currently humping), poor people, sick people, liberals, anybody who drew a paycheck from the government, and Japanese people.

The irony was that the Japanese owners of Scimitar had themselves brought Conlon on board. He had the kind of fuck-you attitude that people in Hollywood envied and frequently tried to emulate. The idea was that Conlon would go out and wine and dine prospective new talent and Frank would turn them into stars.

The Japanese loved him.

When Frank came into the room on the very top floor, he didn't get much respect. His Japanese superior sat behind his aircraft carrier of a desk, small hands folded neatly in front of him, and said, "Yes, Frank, what is it?" The man's irritation with Frank was plain. If Frank didn't have Riki . . .

But when Bryce Conlon walked in, the man on the top floor was always deferential . . .

The thing was, Frank wasn't a Japanese-basher. He admired them. America had fallen behind exactly because of men like Bryce Conlon who, during the eighties, had joined with another group of country club WASP thieves and debt-leveraged two major American record companies into Chapter Eleven. Afterward, he went from Bryce Conlon, patrician recording industry entrepreneur, to Bryce Conlon, bitter recording industry employee. He of course blamed the Japanese for his problems, even though it was Japanese paychecks that underwrote his *New Yorker* life-style . . .

Frank was sometimes tempted to send the man upstairs an anonymous note saying, "Guess who constantly tells demeaning jokes about the Japanese? His initials are B.C."

Pure fourth-grade, of course, but Frank frequently resorted to such embarrassing little mental games because they gave him temporary pleasure, like a sugar fix.

All Frank needed this morning was to hear from Bryce Conlon . . .

"Bryce Conlon on one," Marcia said on the intercom.

"Thanks, Marcia."

Frank was still hiding out in the empty office down the hall from his own. It would take two of the building maintenance staff a few hours to straighten out that mess . . .

Bryce Conlon.

Frank stared at the phone. He wished he could levitate it. Or set it on fire, the way sweet little Drew Barrymore had set things on fire in that Stephen King movie.

But he had no choice.

He-had-to-pick-it-up.

"Hi, Bryce."

"Hi, Bryce, my ass."

"And that means exactly what, Bryce?"

"That means have you heard the fucking news this morning?"

"If you mean about David Greene, yes, I have heard the fucking news this morning."

On paper, anyway, Frank was Bryce Conlon's boss, though it never seemed to work out that way. In a sentence or two, Bryce always put Frank on the defensive.

"He just called me," Conlon said.

"Who just called you?"

"Upstairs. The head Nip." Which was how Bryce invariably referred to their mutual boss.

"Why didn't he call me?"

"Because he wanted to talk to me about you."

Frank patted his shirt. No damn Maalox tablets left. "About me?"

"He said that he wants to see you in two hours and that if you don't have a plan for handling all the public relations aspects of this, I'm to take over."

"Why are you telling me this, Bryce?"

"Because I don't want the job. It'll just make me look bad. A murder like that . . . who knows where it will lead? If Riki's involved in any way . . . When I take over this company, I want everything to be moving along very well. I don't want to start with our biggest artist involved in some kind of scandal."

"So much for altruism."

"Huh?"

"I thought maybe, as my good and loyal coworker, you were trying to warn me—you know, for my own sake. But as usual, you're just trying to save your own ass."

"You've got to come up with a good way to handle this. I'll meet you upstairs in two hours sharp. You know how he hates meetings that don't get started on time."

"I'm not a P.R. man, Bryce."

"You are now, pal," Conlon said. And hung up.

Frank sat there for a long time. Just sat there. As if somebody had given him a sedative.

He knew only one thing for sure. He had to talk to Brad Doyle as soon as possible.

He had to find out exactly what had happened and what was going to happen . . .

18

IN Chicago, the talk around the precinct was that most city offices would be closing at 3:00 P.M., three hours from now. The storm was getting very bad.

About the only people happy with the weather situation would be kids. Kids loved getting off early for snow days.

Sometimes, Robert McGivern wished he could be that young and innocent again. A snow day meant snowball fights and building snow forts and snowmen. It meant having your cousin over for the day and maybe even staying overnight. It meant hot soup after a freezing afternoon outdoors, and hot cocoa and cookies before bedtime, and praying a fervent prayer that the next day would be another snow day, too. And it meant, best of all, no teachers, no books, no boring math problems or interminable lectures on boring periods of history. (Acceptable periods of history included any with dinosaurs, gladiators or goose-stepping Nazis who were about to be crushed by the Americans. Most other periods of history, face it, were pretty dull.)

McGivern sat in his office, grateful for the sentimental memory of what snow days had meant to him as a youngster, grateful for the respite from his concern for Kate.

Where was she?

Had the killer already shot her, too?

He sat behind his desk making useless fists, thinking that if he had only been a few minutes earlier in arriving at Kate's apartment house he might have been able to stop her from being kidnapped . . .

At 12:03 P.M., central standard time, his phone rang.

He snatched it up.

It was Helman.

"One of our cars reported seeing the limousine a few minutes ago, Robert. It gave chase. Now we've lost radio contact and somebody has just called in that a police cruiser was involved in an accident with a limousine and exploded. Let's get the hell out there."

McGivern thanked the man and slammed the phone.

Less than ninety seconds later, they were racing down the rear stairs to get Helman's car.

19

BRAD Doyle opened the driver's door of the limousine and then waved Kate to him with the gun he had concealed beneath his coat.

"See if he's alive." As he spoke, he glanced around. A crowd had gathered on both sides of the street. The police vehicle was a funeral pyre of lashing flame and oily smoke. The screams of the two patrolmen had died long ago.

Kate leaned in and examined the driver. Gasoline and oil smells saturated the air.

She moved her eyes quickly to the top of his skull. A segment of slick, bloody brain was exposed.

She lifted his left hand, eased her finger beneath his glove, felt for a pulse on the damp skin.

She pulled her head from the limousine and said, "I think he's dead."

Doyle glanced quickly around the street. The crowd kept getting larger.

"Both of you—walk over to that convenience store on the corner. I'll be right behind you."

Somewhere nearby, sirens wailed, closer, closer.

"Move," he said to both of them.

Riki took Kate's arm. "We'd better get going, Kate. He's crazy enough to kill us both right here."

Kate nodded. Started walking.

The convenience store was half a block away. Doyle

forced them into a kind of half-run, which was not easy on sidewalks coated with ice.

The onlookers were curious about where the three of them were going, walking away from the accident. But obviously none of them wanted to ask a man like Brad any questions. Even from a distance, he exuded a sense of barely controlled rage.

The convenience store was on a corner. Out front was a concrete island of self-serve gas pumps and inside was the usual mix of snacks, grocery staples and pharmaceuticals.

Except for a teenage clerk, the store was empty. The customers were likely up the block watching the vehicles burn.

The shelves were full, the tile floor was scrubbed, the packaged cold cuts and the dairy products all smelled fresh. The store gave the impression of being well organized and prosperous.

Doyle marched the two women straight up to the counter.

The clerk had black hair, brown eyes, red zits and very white teeth. He wore a silly red-and-white-checkered polyester jacket and a silly red-and-white-checkered hat.

"Wow," he said. "Did you see that accident up the street?"

"Uh-huh," Doyle said impatiently.

"Sure wish I had somebody to cover for me. I'd like to go up there and see if it goes up a second time." The kid sounded positively festive.

Doyle said, "You have a car, kid?"

"Huh?"

"I asked if you had a car."

The kid took his first hard look at Doyle. He looked, suddenly, very young and very afraid. "Uh, yeah, I have a car."

"Where is it?"

"Out back."

"Good. You're taking us for a ride."

"God, mister, I can't do that. I'm the only one on duty here and—"

Doyle raised the gun. Held it just over Kate's shoulder, pointed directly at the kid's face.

The kid said, "I don't have the combination to the safe. Wally does. He's the manager. He's down the street getting his hair cut."

"I don't give a damn about the safe, kid. Or Wally. I want you to give us a ride someplace."

The kid glanced at the two women, clearly hoping to find compassion and some sort of guidance in their faces.

"God, mister," the kid said, "I didn't do anything to hurt you."

"Where are the keys?"

"In my pocket."

"Good. Let's go out the back door."

Suddenly a second explosion came. The concussion was enough to rattle the store windows. People yelled and shouted. Emergency vehicles wailed their way onto the block.

"The keys," Doyle said.

"Yessir."

"Let's go to the back door."

"I can't leave the register unlocked and—"

"Kid, think about your mother."

"Huh?"

"What she'd be like at your funeral."

"Oh."

"Think of how she'd be crying and carrying on."

The kid looked overwhelmed with sadness. Kate wanted to take him in her arms and hold him, protect him from Doyle. But she knew if she made a move, Doyle would hurt somebody. She could sense that he was now eager to hurt anybody who gave him half an excuse.

Doyle slapped the kid.

It was a hard, clean shot with his open left hand, but so forceful she saw the boy start to sink to the floor.

Instead, fear and anger making him a little crazy, the kid started crying.

He tried not to, there being women present and all, but he was so confused, so scared—God, he'd just been standing at the cash register doing his job when these three people came out of nowhere—he couldn't help himself.

Doyle raised his left hand to hit him again but Kate grabbed it and bit hard into the flesh of his thumb.

"God damn you!" Doyle said.

He backhanded Kate so hard she felt her neck snap back and a rush of hot pain shoot up beneath her ear.

As Doyle started to move toward Kate so he could strike her again, Riki screamed, "Leave her alone!"

Her anger seemed to calm Doyle. He lowered his hand and looked around at Riki, the kid and then back to Kate.

"We've got to get out of here," he said, "and kid, we're going out in your car and you're driving us. You understand?"

Doyle's anger had been replaced by a coldness that was even more sinister.

The kid said, "Yessir, I understand."

Doyle smiled at the kid. He had broken the spirit of another human being and was proud of himself.

20

THERE were grimaces and there were tears but there were also quick guilty smiles.

No matter how tragic it was that two police officers—a female cop with two children, a male cop with three—had been killed, there was something exciting about the scene. Obscenely exciting.

At least this was the impression McGivern got from some of the onlookers as he and Helman worked their way past the crowd, past a mobile TV van and past an ambulance to get close to the circle created by fire fighters as they hosed the burning cruiser off with splashing silver water.

Gasoline fumes choked the air, as did the fumes of oily fire.

McGivern reached the fire fighters. Twenty seconds earlier or later he would have missed what he saw. And been happy to miss it.

Ambulance attendants, one of them a chunky young man with a punk hairstyle, dragged a corpse from the waves of gray smoke near the end of the vehicle. McGivern looked away. Once before had he seen a human being this badly burned. He didn't want to see another one.

By now, more than two hundred people ringed the accident site. Traffic officers on either side of the crowd rerouted angry drivers. This street was a main thoroughfare. Taking icy side streets was a pain.

By the burning hulk of the police vehicle, everything was very warm. Only a few yards away, it was freezing winter.

Snow continued. The water from the fire hoses froze on the street. Emergency lights were a bouquet of different colors: yellow for the street crews, red for the fire people, blue for the police. An old woman had spotted the charred corpse of one of the police officers and was pointing it out to half a dozen people who looked both disgusted and spellbound. This sight would burn the eyes of their souls for weeks to come.

Given the big rumbling fire engines and the police chopper hovering overhead, just above the dark tumbling smoke, Helman had to shout so his man in charge could hear him.

McGivern walked over to the limousine, which was damaged badly but intact.

The ambulance attendants were just now getting to the body sprawled across the steering wheel. He looked as if he were posing for a true-detective magazine cover, stage blood trickling down his temple and into his ear.

McGivern tried hard not to think about Kate similarly sprawled across a steering wheel.

"Sir?"

McGivern raised his eyes and saw a woman in a wheelchair rolling herself over toward him. She had curly gray hair and a weathered face but she was strong enough and nimble enough to use the wheelchair with great dexterity. He could see the girl in her grandmotherly face. She must have once been a beauty.

She wore a black-and-red-checkered woolen shirt and a merry red stocking cap. A heavy black scarf was wrapped around her neck and tan leather mittens with Santa and his reindeer on them covered her hands.

"Sir?" she said again.

"Yes, ma'am?"

"Are you a policeman?"

"Yes."

"Good. Would you come with me, then?"

"To where, ma'am?"

"See that convenience store down there on the corner?"

Through rolling smoke that was just now parting, McGivern saw a small store designed to look like one of the mom-and-pop groceries of his youth.

"That one?"

"Yes."

"What's going on there?"

"Kenny Brennan's gone." For the first time, worry showed in her handsome, sixtyish face.

"Kenny Brennan?"

"He's the young fellow that works there every morning."

"I see."

"I live three houses away from the store and every morning I go over there for my groceries. I know I pay more than I would at a supermarket but I like the little stores better. You know, more like the old days."

"Yes, ma'am, but what about Kenny?"

She looked up at him with innocent eyes. "Why, he's gone, that's what about Kenny."

"You're sure he's not out back doing something?"

She shook her head. "I checked. His car's gone, too."

"Maybe there was an emergency."

"Kenny's a very responsible boy. He wouldn't leave like that. Not without leaving a note or something."

He glanced over at the limousine. Some of the water had splashed over it and frozen, like ice sculpture.

"I may not have my legs anymore, Officer, but I'm not the kind who panics easily. Believe me."

He did believe her.

He followed her through the smoke to the other side of the street and then down the block to the convenience store.

21

FORTY-THREE minutes after forcing Kenny Brennan out the back door of the convenience store and into his car, Doyle sat in the backseat next to Riki. Doyle gave the kind of instructions Kenny Brennan's father would have given.

Watch out for that truck. Slow down. Careful on this ice.

Despite everything that had happened in the past few hours, Kate had to smile. Brad Doyle was the ultimate backseat driver.

The boy had taken them back to the Dan Ryan and then thirty miles along a sand-covered icy highway.

Now they were on a two-lane blacktop. The toll of the blizzard was easy to see. Every quarter mile or so, Kate saw a car that had spun out of control into a ditch or stalled along the edge of the road, emergency lights blinking in the lashing snow.

Kenny Brennan's car was a ten-year-old Ford badly in need of a tune-up. Wind whistled coldly through the windows. The defroster didn't work properly, so half the windshield was lost in a coating of ice.

She was cold and afraid. She kept waiting for a glimpse of an escape route. As yet, she hadn't seen any.

Once, Kate turned around and looked at Riki huddled in the backseat. Both Riki and Kate wore jeans, winter boots and winter jackets. Now Riki looked like an angry but beautiful little girl, huddled up sullenly in the corner, staring out at the passing farmhouses distant on the hill, and the sad slow cows finally heading into shelter.

When Kate and Riki made eye contact, Riki nodded at Doyle and gritted her teeth. Kate had rarely seen Riki as angry as she looked now.

Doyle caught their silent message.

He grabbed Riki by the wrist, twisted her frail arm back against the seat and shoved her deeper into the corner.

"Turn around!" he snapped to Kate.

"You're such a bastard, Brad, I can't believe it," Riki said. She abruptly broke into tears.

Doyle let go of her arm.

She continued to cry, choking, angry tears.

"All I need," Doyle said to himself, settling back in the seat. "Crying."

Fifteen minutes later, Kate said, "You're doing fine, Kenny."

The poor kid was trembling. His whole body. Once again Kate wanted to gather him in her arms and hold him tight and comfort him.

"I'm sorry I'm not doing so good," the boy said, obviously ashamed of his fear.

"You're doing just fine."

Doyle leaned over the back of the seat and grabbed Kenny's ear. He twisted it hard. The kid yelled.

"I want you to shut up and watch the road, all right?" Doyle said.

The boy had tears in his young, scared eyes again.

Kate wished she were a man. Someday she'd grab Doyle and . . .

They drove on into the storm . . .

22

RICHARD Conroy had twice picked up then set down the telephone receiver.

All he could think of was high school, when this had been a nightly ritual.

He'd decide to call a girl, then sneak upstairs to the TV room where there was a phone. He'd look up the name of the girl's father in the phone book, get the number and then lift the receiver. Sometimes, he'd get as far as actually dialing a few of the digits. Once or twice, he'd even heard the phone ring once, twice, three times before slamming the receiver down in blind panic.

What if she answered?

What would he say?

Or what if one of her parents answered and he had to identify himself?

He would then run from the TV room straight into his bedroom, close the door and lie in the dark thinking of what a sad and foolish boy he was. He liked girls too much—he was obsessed with girls—yet he couldn't do anything about it.

Not even make a phone call.

He recalled all these things this snowy afternoon as he first lifted then replaced the receiver.

All these years later, he was doing it again.

He wanted to call Jenny, place the same kind of "surprise"

call to her that she had to him a few hours ago, yet he couldn't.

What would he say when she answered?

He knew he'd only stammer and sound foolish, and then manage to embarrass both of them.

He was just about to give it a third—and perhaps successful try—when he heard the car approaching.

The snow was coming down so hard there was no way he could see the car from this distance. Only hear it.

His mechanic's ear told him that the vehicle was old and in need of a tune-up.

He wondered who would be driving out here at this time.

He was coming out from behind the desk and walking to the front door when he saw an aged, faded green Ford emerge like a mirage from the blizzard and stop a few feet from the big front window. One headlight burned. The other was apparently out. Wipers slapped angrily and uselessly at the heavy, damp snow on the windshield. The whole chassis shook. That tune-up had probably been needed for the last twenty thousand miles.

At first, nobody emerged from the car. It just sat there. The windows were ice-covered, so Richard Conroy couldn't see anybody inside. For a moment, he had an eerie sense that this was some kind of phantom vehicle, with a specter for a driver. Then he smiled. Too many *Outer Limits* episodes lately. They'd started rerunning the darn things again and Richard loved them.

Two minutes went by. Richard finished the dregs of his coffee.

Nobody left the car. The one headlight continued to burn. The wipers slapped ceaselessly.

Shrugging, wondering if perhaps somebody was sick in the car, Richard went over and took his green parka down from a line of empty pegs and then went outside.

He was almost knocked over. The headwinds were getting vicious. His cheeks were immediately numbed by the cold. His eyes were immediately blinded by the stinging snow.

He walked over to the car.

The closer he got, the more he heard the car. The muffler, badly in need of replacement, rumbled. He hoped these folks kept their windows open a crack. Otherwise, they might get asphyxiated.

He was two steps from the hood of the car when the back window started to roll down.

He walked to the rear of the vehicle. The window was now halfway open.

He saw a male face watching him. He was startled when he recognized the man, the same man who'd often chartered Conroy's plane for his performer friends.

"Why, hello, Mr. Doyle."

Doyle smiled. "When the hell are you going to start calling me Brad?"

Richard blushed. "Oh, that's right. I forgot."

In the front, behind the wheel, sat a teenage boy. Next to him was a very pretty young woman. They both looked tense.

In the backseat was not only Brad Doyle but . . . Riki herself.

What would a world-famous rock-and-roll star be doing in a beat-up Ford like this?

He was about to say something when Brad Doyle said, "C'mere a minute, Richard."

Richard Conroy took two steps forward.

The gun came up fast. Nothing dramatic. Brad Doyle simply put it in Richard's face, even with his eyes, and said, "Richard, I don't play bad guy, all right? You going to do what I say?"

Richard Conroy nodded.

"We need a plane big enough to carry four of us and we need it now. All right?"

"You can't fly in this weather."

"Don't give me the official line of bullshit, Richard, okay? You can fly above the storm and by the time we reach Los Angeles, there won't be any trouble landing."

"But there's so much that could go wrong—the mountains in a storm like this—"

Brad Doyle opened the door and got out of the car carefully.

"Now isn't a good time to fly," Richard Conroy said. "Believe me."

Doyle waggled his gun inside the car, totally dismissing Conroy, and said, "All right, start getting out of there one at a time. You first, Riki."

All Richard Conroy could think of was that maybe it would be more humane to have Doyle kill these people right here.

An airplane crash would be a much worse way to die.

"What could possibly be that important?" Conroy said.

As she stepped out of the car, Kate looked up at him. "There's a box he needs to open and I have one of the keys."

"Shut up!" Doyle said as he came out of the car behind her.

Kate looked at Conroy but kept quiet. There was no sense in angering Doyle further.

Conroy led the way to the offices.

23

DAVID Greene's public relations office was in a new brick building not far from the Newberry Library. With a lot full of BMWs and other expensive foreign cars, and very well dressed men and women entering and leaving the wide glass front doors, the feeling here was one of success and prosperity. A fierce yellow snowplow scraped away the tumbling snow.

Inside, walking along the quiet, carpeted hallway, Helman and McGivern noticed secretaries and receptionists hurrying to get the offices closed up for the day. The earlier you got on the expressways, the better your chances of getting home.

They took an elevator to the third floor. Greene's office was in the center of the east corridor.

A bell tinkled as Helman opened the door and led the way in.

As McGivern closed the door, and the echo of the bell began to fade, the men heard the unmistakable sounds of a woman sobbing.

McGivern walked past the reception desk to a partially open office door. So far as he could see, the entire office consisted of three rooms.

The woman continued to sob for some time, as if she had not heard him, or did not care if he heard her.

He knocked again, gently.

"Yes?" she said between sniffles.

"Police."

"Oh."

"May we come in?"

"Let me blow my nose first."

"All right."

She blew so hard the sound was almost comic. McGivern recalled a particularly funny Three Stooges bit involving Shemp blowing his nose. Shemp was his favorite Stooge.

McGivern and Helman waited patiently at the door as she blew her nose a second and then third time.

"You'll just have to excuse my nose and eyes," the woman said from behind the door. "I know that sounds vain at a time like this but that's just how I am—vain, I mean."

McGivern and Helman went into David Greene's private office. For a man who promoted rock stars and politicians, his digs were surprisingly bookish. A huge Renoir print dominated one wall while a large bookcase filled with older hardbacks dominated another. Bach played softly on an AM-FM tuner. A bust of Socrates sat atop a small stand.

The woman sitting in the executive chair behind the desk was a beauty. Even with her eyes and nose tainted with red from her tears, her soft features were classically perfect. Shining blond hair was pulled back to the nape of her neck in a loose chignon. A white silk blouse and a dark skirt with a large dramatic black belt revealed a fetching body. She smelled of a perfume that was both exotic and erotic.

"I'm Detective McGivern. This is Captain Helman."

"I'm Dori. Dori Townes. David's secretary."

She started to cry again, then put a Kleenex to her nose. "Sorry."

"That's all right," McGivern said. "This is a time for tears."

She looked up at him and smiled miserably. "Thanks for saying that. You seem like a fine man."

McGivern nodded, not quite knowing what else to do with such a compliment.

"We need to ask you some questions, Ms. Townes," Captain Helman said.

"Of course."

"Are you acquainted with a man named Brad Doyle?"

"Yes." She paused. "My God, you think he killed David?"

Helman said, "It would seem so. At least for now."

"He's a crazy man."

"How so?"

"Just the way he is about Riki."

"And how's that?"

"He never wants anybody to be alone with her, never wants anybody around her who is closer to her than he is."

McGivern spoke now. "What's his business relationship to Riki?"

"Well, supposedly he's her manager but he's a lot more than that. He's her boss."

"How did that come about?"

"He discovered her. He never let go."

"I see."

"Anyway, he's very possessive." She made a face. "He's a hood. He really is." She sniffled. Daubed at her perfect nose with a tattered Kleenex. "I know that's a corny word— 'hood,' I mean—but that's just what he is."

McGivern said, "What was his relationship with Greene? Why would he want to kill him?"

She glanced at the drawers on the left side of the desk, then quickly brought her eyes back to the detectives. "I don't know."

McGivern said quietly, "We can only do our jobs if we know the truth."

Her eyes strayed momentarily to the desk drawers again.

"He sent David an envelope every month."

"An envelope?" Helman said.

"Yes."

"What kind of envelope?"

She shrugged nice shoulders. "Just an envelope."

"Did you ever see what was in the envelopes?" McGivern said.

She hesitated. "I cared about David very much. Not sexually or anything. To be honest, we spent a weekend together one time but the guilt really ate him up. I think he thought a lot about firing me. I reminded him that he'd been unfaithful. He had a hard time living with that. He was pretty much a straight arrow."

McGivern said, "What about the envelopes?"

"I always figured that was his business."

"Meaning what exactly?"

"Meaning that we all have dark sides. You seem like a very nice man but if I got to know you—you know what I mean."

"Are any of those envelopes around here now?"

Her eyes went again to the line of desk drawers.

She looked up at him. She seemed even sadder than she had a few moments ago. "It's all going to come out, isn't it?"

"Isn't what?"

"What David was doing." She pulled out the center drawer and reached down and took out a white number ten business envelope. There was a window in it, the name and address being that of David Greene.

She handed McGivern the envelope. "He didn't always use them right away. Only when he had cash problems. Keeping offices both here and in Los Angeles—well, cash flow got to be a problem sometimes. The envelopes really came in handy for him."

McGivern peered inside. A heavy white piece of paper was triple-folded. He removed the paper, unfolded it.

He stared at its contents and then raised his head and met Helman's eyes.

On the other side of the desk, the woman said, "It's going to be in the press, isn't it, what David was up to?"

24

ALL the time he was doing his preflight in the hangar, Richard Conroy kept looking over his shoulder.

Brad Doyle held the gun on the two women and the boy. They were in the corner, watching Conroy go about his work.

Before coming to the hangar, Conroy had checked the weather one more time. The ice storm had quit, as had the blizzard winds. All they would likely encounter was heavy snow. Given the capabilities of his Cessna 340, Conroy felt that they had a good chance of reaching Los Angeles, which Doyle had given as their destination.

Conroy tried to explain the danger of flying in such weather—and at roughly fourteen thousand feet—without adequate instrumentation, and without filing a flight plan. In weather like this, chances for collision were already high. Without filing a flight plan—without air traffic controllers and other pilots even knowing they were up there—those chances quadrupled.

All the time he did his preflight, Conroy thought of Jenny Stivers and their date Saturday night. He wanted to take her out no matter what. He didn't care what happened to him in the meantime, whatever fear or suffering he might have to endure, as long as this miracle date (he still remembered how exultant he'd felt when he realized that she was asking him for a date) took place.

Preflight consisted of draining the sump to make certain there was no water in the fuel; checking to see that all control surfaces were free and working, including the rudder, ailerons and elevator; and checking the electrical system and the radio, plus everything else on the preflight checklist.

When he was finished, he walked over to the others, his footsteps loud in the large, nearly empty hangar.

"I want to tell you again that I don't think this is a good idea," Conroy said to Doyle.

"And I want to tell you again that I don't give a damn what you think, friend. All I want you to do is fly the plane."

He waved his gun at Kate and Riki. "You two go over there and take your seats."

Kate said, "What about the boy?"

"I'll worry about the boy. You get in there and sit down."

Riki touched her arm. "C'mon, Kate. Do what he says."

But Kate was adamant. "What about Kenny?"

"He'll be fine. I'll tie him up and leave him here."

Kate didn't trust him. "Then tie him up in the hangar here where I can see him."

"You seem to forget who's holding the gun, Kate."

"I don't want him hurt."

Doyle stared at her, then threw Conroy two lengths of rope. "Tie him up, Conroy. Tight."

Conroy took the rope and walked over to Kenny, who looked happy to comply. Better tied up than shot.

When his hands were cinched tight, Kenny sat on the floor. Conroy wound the second length of rope tight around the boy's ankles.

Doyle went over and checked the knots. "You must've been a Boy Scout, Conroy."

"I was."

Doyle smiled. "Figures." He turned to Kate. "Do these slipknots meet your approval, Kate?"

She nodded to Kenny. "Somebody will find you soon. You'll be fine."

Doyle pointed to the Cessna with his gun. "Kate, you come over and stand right here. I'm going to use that phone. Then we'll get in the plane and take off." He waved the gun at Riki and Conroy. "You two stay where you are."

There was a wall phone in one corner of the hangar. Doyle led Kate over there—close enough so he could grab her if she tried to run away, not close enough so she could hear anything he said.

25

"LINE one, Frank."

"Thank you."

Frank had the phone to his ear in less than two seconds.

"It's Brad," Doyle said.

"Where the hell are you?"

"At an airplane hangar."

"The story about David Greene is national news. The cops are looking for you everywhere."

"I'll be in L.A. later tonight."

"What the hell happened?"

"He came over to my place and said he needed a lot more money than we'd been giving him and that if we didn't pay him right away, he'd take those papers he found to the press."

"So you shot him? In cold blood?" Sayler said.

"Calm down, Frank. He had a gun and I was afraid he'd shoot me. It was self-defense, believe it or not."

"What about the papers?"

"They're in a safe-deposit box in L.A. He gave one of the two keys to Kate. She's with me right now."

"Does she know what's in the papers?"

"No. David didn't tell her that."

"God, Brad, if those papers ever got out we'd be ruined. All of us."

"That's why I'm coming to L.A. I'll get the papers and destroy them."

"I need your assurance that nobody will ever find out what's in those papers."

"You've got my assurance, Frank. Everything's going to be fine."

"What about you?"

"After I get the papers, I'll call you. Then you're going to help smuggle me out of the country. I know some people in your area who can handle that sort of thing, but I'm going to need you to do some running around."

"I've got a meeting with the boss man in a little while," Sayler said. "He'll want to know how all this will affect Riki's record sales."

"That's your department, Frank. Right now, I've got to get out of here. I'll check in when we land."

"I'll talk to you soon."

Brad Doyle hung up.

26

KATE had never liked flying. The times she'd gone from Chicago to Los Angeles, she'd always swallowed a Valium before taking off. And sometimes, usually the night before the flight, her dreams were troubled with TV images of plane crashes.

Now that they had been in the air for forty minutes, Kate didn't know which to be more afraid of, the way the twin-engine Cessna was being tossed around by 200 mph headwinds, or Brad Doyle, his gun and his irrational temper.

Richard Conroy had explained that they'd flown out of the bad weather surrounding Chicago and had enjoyed a ten-minute respite from turbulence until he saw another storm front starting to form farther west.

Kate sat in the copilot's seat, next to Conroy. In this particular craft, the pilots were separated from the backseats by a few feet.

Doyle and Riki sat in back. Riki had slid into one of her silences again, her head tilted as if she were sleeping, and her eyes closed.

Kate had never flown in such a small craft before. This was an impressive one. What seemed to be dozens of gauges and controls were displayed before her.

"Why the hell can't we see anything?" Doyle said.

"It's called a whiteout," Conroy said.

Because they couldn't see anything except snow out the

cabin windows, Kate had the sense that they were in this little toy craft, lost in a foggy netherworld filled with monsters they would soon encounter.

"For now, everything's going all right," Conroy said. "Relax."

Kate admired the way Conroy stayed calm and steady. He spent all his time and energy on flying, disregarding Doyle's frequent outbursts of anger.

"It's also too damned cold. What's wrong with the heater?"

"Nothing's wrong with the heater. Between the headwinds and the snow, it's going to be cold up here."

For the next twenty minutes, the plane bucked headwinds, engine droning, cabin getting colder and colder.

Richard Conroy regularly checked the wings. He had explained to Kate about temperature inversions and how melting snow can turn into rime ice, the same kind of ice you find in a freezer, robbing the plane of its natural lift.

If that happened, he hinted, they would have big problems. Better that the temperature stayed cold and the snow on the plane hard. That way there would be no significant icing problems.

They were headed for the mountains where the winds were frequently dangerous at any time. In weather like this, those winds would be deadly.

Conroy did not want rime ice to add to the difficulties of flying over the mountains. But the mountains offered him one advantage. He'd have to take the plane way up—and when he did, there was a good chance they'd be discovered on radar.

"Are you warm enough, Kate?"

Kate's mind had been drifting to McGivern again. She

wanted to be within the circle of his arms, talking about marriage and children and growing old together.

Riki's voice startled her.

She turned around.

The singer was holding up the blue V-neck sweater she'd been wearing.

"You really look cold, Kate."

"I'm fine. Really."

Riki smiled. "Take it. Please. I'm plenty warm. I really am."

Doyle said, "Why the hell give it to her? Why not keep it on for yourself?"

"Because she's colder than I am. I can tell that even from here." She glared at him. "I mean, if it's any of your business in the first place." She leaned forward and handed Kate the sweater.

Kate couldn't deny that she was trembling from the seemingly endless drop in temperature.

"You sure?" she said to Riki.

"I'm sure, Kate. Take it. Please."

Kate took it and less than a minute later was tugging the sweater down over her shirt. She put her down-lined jacket back on immediately.

Then she felt something fall from inside the sweater to her lap.

She almost started to tell Riki that she'd left something inside the wool sweater, but then she realized that was why Riki had offered her the garment—to pass something over.

Kate tried to sound casual. Instead she sounded strained, frightened. All she could hope was that Doyle didn't sense anything going on.

"Thanks, Riki," Kate said.

"My pleasure."

Riki fell into her depression and silence once again, lost in her thoughts.

Kate sat completely still, wanting to touch the object in her lap but afraid to. She was very conscious of how quiet everybody was suddenly—just the steady burrowing sound of the engines.

She was also aware of how close Doyle was, even with the separation between pilot and passengers. He could easily lean over and see what lay in her lap.

After a few more moments of debating with herself what to do, Kate dropped her gaze to her thighs.

A long switchblade knife had been wrapped inside the sweater, a long switchblade knife that was now lying in Kate's lap. With its mother-of-pearl handle and its concealed four-inch blade, the knife was certainly dramatic-looking. Kate's experience with knives was limited to the blades the Sharks and the Jets carried in *West Side Story*, one of her favorite musicals.

When she looked up, she found Richard Conroy staring at the knife, too.

They looked at each other, saying nothing.

Conroy went back to his flying.

Kate quickly put the knife in the right pocket of her down jacket.

27

BY 1:58 P.M., CST, the temperature in the Chicago area had risen six degrees. The National Weather Center was now downscaling its predictions of a full-scale blizzard. They were issuing bulletins that said that, for much of the plains states, the worst of the snow was over. Flurries were expected to continue into the evening but the predicted six inches would not be reached. Much of the city had already shut down, however, and the majority of the residents were in their homes, enjoying some leisure time with their families.

By 2:19 P.M., CST, the description of Kenny Brennan's car and its license number were on the Chicago police radio. Two calls came in quickly, both reporting a similar vehicle seen headed out of the city.

By 2:43 P.M., CST, Tom Warner was on the phone, describing to police how he'd found young Brennan bound with rope in his hangar. Warner also reported that his Cessna 340, the best plane in his fleet, was gone. On the phone, Kenny Brennan told police how Doyle had nearly killed him and how Doyle had commandeered the Cessna and Richard Conroy to fly it.

Police officials wanted to know if a flight plan had been filed. After checking, none was found.

Just before three that afternoon, McGivern parked his police vehicle in a prosperous Chicago suburb where most of the houses ran to half-million-dollar refurbished Victorians. The snow and the dusk-like sky lent the lighted windows a rich and welcoming warmth. Most front doors boasted massive holly wreaths and most front yards were guarded by plump snowmen with tilted black top hats and red woolen scarves swung festively over their shoulders. Tiny children in awkward snowsuits tottered down the walk, running after sleds being steered by older brothers and sisters.

He thought: This is the kind of neighborhood I always hoped Kate and I would live in. With the kids. One boy, one girl.

He went up the walk and pressed a doorbell.

As he waited, he thought of what Dori Townes had told him. Greene had kept his family here, in a Chicago suburb, so they would have a chance for a normal life. Despite the fact that much of his business was on the West Coast, Greene preferred relentless commuting to making his family live in the Third World city of Los Angeles.

The door was opened by a tall, striking woman whose classic features were framed by a dark page boy. She wore a kind of old-fashioned jumper and white turtleneck sweater, with a style that made them seem special. Her makeup was fresh but no amount of makeup could hide the sadness in her brown eyes.

"Mrs. Greene?"

"You're the detective who called?"

"Yes, ma'am."

"Come in, please."

She stood back and let him walk in.

He had not quite crossed the threshold when he smelled the fresh sweet scent of baking.

The interior was shadowy except for the front room, where a fire cast warmth and light across a hardwood floor made colorful with occasional hook rugs. Books filled one wall, collectibles from miniature dolls to Victorian antiques another. On a long couch before a TV console sat two children watching a Deputy Dawg cartoon. When he came into the room and looked closely at their faces, McGivern saw that while both children were staring in the general vicinity of the picture tube, neither one of them was actually paying any attention to the flickering lights of the animation. They were staring at something else, some wraith, some sorrow they were too young to understand. The little girl, who was perhaps two or three and wore tidy blond pigtails, had a round face slick from her tears.

The mother went over to the TV and stood next to it and said, "Grandma's just about finished baking those cookies. Why don't you go ask her if she needs any help?"

The boy, who was perhaps seven, said with heartbreaking solemnity, "I'll bet she's still crying. Gramma, I mean. She told me not to cry any more but then she started crying herself."

Then he took his sister's hand and escorted her to the kitchen.

McGivern was rocked by the tenderness he'd just seen. It was some kind of confirmation—a kind of confirmation a cop rarely had in his line of work—that there was still purity and grace and dignity and hope in this weary old world, after all.

"Would you care for some hot cider?" the woman asked.

"No, thanks."

There were two rocking chairs facing the fire. Each had a shawl set over its back.

"Would you like to sit down?"

"Thank you."

They sat down.

"My name's Linda."

"My name's Robert."

She looked at the crackling flames and then at him. "Do you know who killed him?"

"We think we do. A man named Brad Doyle."

Something changed in her expression. He wasn't sure what. He certainly had no idea why. But merely by his mentioning the name, Linda Greene had been altered in some way.

"Do you know him?" McGivern asked.

"Doyle?"

"Yes."

She nodded.

"Do you know why he would want to kill your husband?"

"No." But her face remained changed. There was an uneasiness in her dark gaze now.

McGivern thought of the envelopes, the monthly envelopes, with the money in them.

"I have to ask you a terrible question, Mrs. Greene."

"Please. Call me Linda. Really." She smiled sadly. "I'm a pretty informal person."

He wanted to sit here and have some of her cider and be warmed by this cheery winter fire. He wanted to think of how moved he'd been when her son took her daughter's hand and led her off. That was the world as it should be, not monthly payments trading on somebody else's secrets and shame.

"This afternoon," McGivern said, "I went to your husband's office and met a woman named Dori Townes."

"Oh, yes. Dori."

He couldn't quite read her inflection. Did she know that her husband had once spent a weekend with Dori Townes?

"I'm sure Dori was helpful. Dori always tries to be— helpful."

This time there was no mistaking her inflection.

"She showed me an envelope," McGivern said.

"I see."

"A white envelope."

"A white envelope?"

He paused. "I think you know what I'm talking about, Linda."

She stared into the fire for a time. "It was so unlike him. When I found out what he was doing, I was shocked."

"He told you?"

She shook her head. Tears glistened in her dark eyes. "I was taking one of his suits to the cleaner's one day and I found an envelope in his pocket. With money in it. I asked him about it. He wouldn't say anything for a long time and then he said, 'Why should they get it all, Riki and Doyle and Frank Sayler? I built her, too. I'm entitled to a share of the spoils, aren't I?' That's how he justified it. His share of the spoils."

She turned her eyes back to McGivern. "I don't even know what it was about, what Doyle was paying to keep secret, I mean."

"But you did know for sure that your husband was blackmailing him?"

"Oh, yes. One night in the garage, I heard the two of them arguing. It was late at night. Doyle had pulled up in one of his new convertibles. We were sitting out on the screened-in porch in the back. Doyle was very drunk and abusive. He talked David into going into the garage and he really beat him then. Very, very badly. David had a knot on the back of his head for two months and two or three times he urinated blood. I was terrified. I said that whatever it was Doyle wanted, give it to him. But he just looked at me—I'll never forget how he looked—and said, 'Honey, if I gave it to him, we could never afford to live out here and raise our kids. I'm doing it for them, honey, for the kids. Not for us.' "

"Did Doyle ever beat him again?"

"No."

"And you don't have any idea what any of this was about?"

"No—just that David saw it as a way to keep our daughter, Alana, at home with us—she has Down's syndrome. And as a way of keeping us all together in this nice big house. David was very foolish with money."

McGivern looked up as the boy led the girl back into the room.

The boy came up to McGivern and held up a small plate. Two huge cookies encrusted with chocolate chips sat in the center of the plate.

"My gramma said to give one to my mom and one to you."

McGivern smiled. "Why, thank you. A cookie sounds real good about now."

The little girl said, "She wanted us to leave, my gramma did, and you know why?"

"No," McGivern said, "why?"

"Because she was starting to cry again," the little girl said.

McGivern felt a little like crying himself.

28

THE Cessna 340 was now two and a half hours into its flight. It was presently approaching a mountain range. The headwinds were getting worse, the plane bucking every few minutes. Icing was also becoming a problem. Richard Conroy had once been copilot on a small Piper that had become covered with rime ice. Despite the expertise of the pilot, the plane had nearly crashed.

Conroy should have been concentrating all his attention on weather conditions. Instead, his mind kept flashing back to the switchblade knife he'd seen in the lap of the woman half an hour ago.

Conroy wanted to warn her off doing anything impulsive, but how could he say anything with Doyle only a few feet away?

The cabin was still very cold. Conroy's nose was running. He could feel his throat grow raw.

As the plane bucked again, his grip tightened on the wheel.

In a few minutes, the plane would begin passing directly over the mountains. The turbulent winds they would encounter would test all of Richard Conroy's skills. He had no problem admitting to himself that he was afraid. Any good, practical small-craft pilot would be.

Big commercial jets often plunged thousands of feet in such turbulence. Imagine the plunge in a Cessna 340 . . .

His mind drifted back to Jenny Stivers and their Saturday date. He'd been worried about his shyness silencing him, but now he knew he'd have plenty of good conversational material. Being kidnapped and forced to fly dead into a blizzard was a tale worth repeating. Especially when a famous rock star was involved. Maybe all the fear of these past few hours would prove worthwhile for something.

"What the hell's going on?"

Conroy looked over his shoulder. "I'm not sure what you mean."

"The turbulence," Doyle said. "It's getting worse."

"We're approaching the mountains."

"Are we going to be all right?"

Conroy sighed. "That's something you should have thought of before we took off."

"That isn't an answer."

Conroy shrugged. "What can I say? I'll do my best but these aren't exactly optimum conditions."

Next to him, Kate tensed in her seat as the plane bucked once more. She wasn't much of a flier to begin with. This entire journey had been unending terror for her, he could tell. He wished there were some way he could ease her fear.

"Riki's getting sick," Doyle said.

"I'm sorry, Riki. There's a plastic bag back there."

"Thanks," Riki said weakly.

Conroy noted the expression on Doyle's face just then. As he looked at Riki, concern showed clearly in his eyes and on his nervous mouth. There was a tenderness in Doyle's gaze that was almost unimaginable to Conroy. Who would have thought that a man like Doyle could so obviously care about somebody?

Doyle reached over, snatched up the barf bag and handed it to Riki with no time to spare.

The young woman was sick immediately.

Conroy turned back to his flying, the sounds of retching filling the cabin.

When Riki was finished, Conroy heard Doyle say, "Are you all right?"

Riki's whispered response was lost in the drone of the engine and the headwinds slamming into the plane.

Kate had also noticed the tenderness Doyle showed Riki.

It was long rumored, in the upper echelons of the music business, that Doyle was hopelessly in love with the beautiful young woman he'd discovered, which was why he guarded her so jealously, which was why he managed to end every romantic relationship she'd ever had. He wanted her for himself, all for himself.

Kate wondered what lay in the safe-deposit box in the Beverly Hills bank.

In the reflection of the cabin window, Kate watched as Doyle reached across and touched Riki's hand.

Riki jerked away from him, turning to her own side of the aisle. Even though she could see nothing but the whiteout, she stared out the window.

Doyle hung his head, looking profoundly sad, looking profoundly different from the angry man he had been just a few moments ago.

What was going on here? Kate wondered.

For the first time, she found herself curious about the real relationship between Doyle and Riki.

The beauty and the beast?

Kate certainly sensed that dimension in Doyle, an almost pathetic jealousy and twisted love for the diminutive singer whom he seemed not simply to love but to idealize in some sick way.

In the cabin window, Doyle's reflection sat back in its seat, turned to its own window and began staring outside, much as Riki's reflection was doing.

Kate kept touching the switchblade knife she had tucked in her jacket pocket.

She wondered if she would get a chance to use it.

She wondered if she would have courage enough to use it.

She was just starting to think about Robert McGivern again—what he'd be doing right now, if he'd be thinking of her, too, right now—when she felt the nose of the craft suddenly start to tilt down steeply.

"What's wrong?" Doyle shouted, panic clear in his voice.

"The winds!" Conroy said. "We're over the mountains now and with all the ice and snow on the plane, we're very vulnerable."

"Can you get the plane steady again?" Doyle said.

His answer was the right engine, which started to splutter. His answer was the nose that was now pointing down at an even steeper angle. His answer was the sharp scream that was coming from Riki in the backseat.

"Hold on!" Conroy said. "We're going to crash!"

29

HIS name was Mr. Nakagama and he was actually a decent guy. He had been Frank Sayler's boss ever since the Japanese corporation had bought out Scimitar Records.

He sat in a large but very simple office at a large and very simple wooden desk, one that was usually clean of everything except a black telephone and a small white writing tablet and an expensive gold ballpoint pen.

Mr. Nakagama never forgot a birthday, an anniversary or a holiday. He had been to Sayler's house for dinner several times, and Sayler had just as often been to Mr. Nakagama's house. Sayler always liked to think of them as friends but somehow they weren't. They were exceedingly polite and deferential to each other, Mr. Nakagama never failing to compliment Sayler, and Sayler never forgetting to compliment Mr. Nakagama. And yet . . . they weren't friends because Sayler could never forget that first and foremost, Mr. Nakagama was his boss.

Sayler and Bryce Conlon were shown in one minute before the meeting was scheduled to start. As usual, the trim Mr. Nakagama wore a dark suit, white shirt and dark tie. Despite the fact that the company had recently helped him celebrate his fiftieth birthday, his silken dark hair, unlined face and wry dark gaze made him seem much younger.

Sayler and Conlon sat down, nodded good morning in a

vaguely ceremonial way and waited for Mr. Nakagama to begin.

"I just spoke with Henry Fowler," Mr. Nakagama said to Sayler. "He said that Riki's new album is doing very well on the East Coast." Fowler was one of Scimitar's major East Coast wholesalers. When Henry Fowler, a wily old bastard who'd been hustling records since Elvis Presley was singing to his hound dog—when Henry Fowler had reason to be happy, so did Scimitar.

Sayler smiled, appreciative that Mr. Nakagama had elected to start the meeting on a positive note.

"I'm told the other news isn't so good, Frank," Mr. Nakagama said.

"No, I'm afraid it isn't."

"I'm speaking of course about Chicago."

"Yes."

Mr. Nakagama looked first at Conlon and then back at Sayler. "I'm wondering about the impact of the shooting on Riki's career."

"That's what we're all worried about."

"For her to be involved in violence of this sort . . ." He looked at Conlon again. "When I spoke to you earlier, you told me that you had an idea of how to handle this situation, Bryce."

Bryce Conlon smiled his cold glib smile. "I'll defer to Frank on this one, if you don't mind."

"You are, are you not, our corporate troubleshooter?" Mr. Nakagama said, not willing yet to let Conlon retreat from his responsibility so easily.

"True enough," Conlon said, sounding nervous for the first time. "But Riki is Frank's discovery."

Sayler smiled. "I'm willing to take the responsibility here." He wished he felt half as confident as he sounded. "There's going to be a press conference."

Bryce Conlon stared over at Sayler as if Frank had just announced that he'd recently been abducted by a UFO.

"A press conference?" said Mr. Nakagama.

"Someplace impressive. All the networks there. And Riki surrounded by well-wishers and fans as she tells her story."

"And what exactly will her story be, Frank?" Mr. Nakagama said.

For this, Sayler had to stand up. Pace the room. Use his hands theatrically. Try to paint a picture with his words.

"A deranged manager. A man who both loves and hates her. And Riki always trying to get away, get away. Then one insane night, the manager accuses her of having an affair with David Greene. She denies it because it isn't true. But her manager is adamant. In a jealous rage, he kills Greene and then abducts Riki and her friend Kate."

Sayler paused in front of Mr. Nakagama's desk. "And you know what? This young woman who is so beloved by her fans becomes even more beloved—and her records sell even faster. There's a big story about the murder in one of the weekly newsmagazines. Then a paperback. Then a TV movie. The result? Riki is bigger than ever."

Sayler glanced at Conlon. "You know how we were worried about getting her to the next level of public acceptance? Well, here it is." Sayler watched Mr. Nakagama again. "Now she's not just a singer—she's a heroine. Maybe even a role model."

Mr. Nakagama smiled. "Now I know how you get your clients to sign, Frank. You know how to get people worked up about your ideas." Then he was no longer smiling. "You know how much Riki means to our corporate profits?"

"Of course."

"If you can turn her into the heroine you claim, Frank, we'll all be happy."

"Yes, indeed," Bryce Conlon said. "Damned happy." He

was one of those men who didn't like to sit quiet for too long, apparently afraid people would forget he was in the room.

"But," Mr. Nakagama said, "if Riki was somehow involved in the killing—"

"She wasn't," Sayler said.

"You know that for sure?"

"Well, not for sure but—"

"If she's innocent," Mr. Nakagama said, "I like your idea of a press conference very much. So will our sales department, I'm sure. But if she's not innocent—" He smiled first at Conlon and then at Sayler. "There's a lot on the line here. For both of you. I don't care what happens to Brad Doyle. But I very much want a happy ending for Riki. And for Scimitar Records."

"I'm in complete control, I can assure you of that," Sayler said.

Mr. Nakagama stared at him for a time. "I hope that's the case, Frank. For all our sakes."

A minute later, Mr. Nakagama showed them to the door.

At the elevator, Bryce Conlon said, "I sure hope you know what you're doing."

Sayler tried hard to laugh. "So do I," he said.

Aboard the elevator, dropping the six floors to his own fiefdom, Frank Sayler wondered just how he was going to do it. How he was going to kill Brad Doyle.

30

EVERY few minutes, the Brennan kid would shake his head, run a hand through his tousled hair and say, "I can't believe how lucky I was." Then he'd shudder and make loose fists of his hands.

McGivern interviewed the young man in a small office just off the large hangar at Ames Flying Service. Tom Warner, the owner, had made a fresh pot of coffee and left the pot on the desk between McGivern and Brennan. All the time they talked, a civilian band radio quietly kicked out information about the diminishing storm.

McGivern, sitting on the edge of the desk, tried to be as gentle as possible with the young man. Kenny Brennan didn't need to be pushed around by anybody else today.

Still, there was an urgency, even a hint of desperation in McGivern's voice whenever he thought of Kate.

"So the last time you saw them, everybody was all right?"

"Yessir."

"Then they took off?"

"Yessir. Out the hangar."

"How long ago was this?"

"Four hours, I guess."

"Did they mention any destination?"

Kenny thought a moment. "I think Mr. Doyle said something about Los Angeles once."

"You're not sure?"

"Yeah, I guess I'm sure because then Mr. Conroy—you know, the pilot—said they'd have to fly over the mountains."

The boy rubbed at the deep red indentations in his wrists where he had been bound with cord. Likely they not only hurt but itched as well. His ankles were probably in the same condition.

"Did Doyle mention *why* he wanted to go to L.A.?"

Before the kid could answer, Captain Helman came in. He had been in the large front office talking to Tom Warner. He carried a cup of coffee.

"Excuse me a minute," Helman said, "Warner just picked up word on a small plane crashing in the Rockies. An aircraft spotted a plane going down. Maybe you want to come here a minute."

Kate, McGivern thought, and said something like a silent prayer. Kate.

"I'll be right back," McGivern said.

He followed Helman into the front office.

Warner was on the phone. All the time he listened and talked, he kept rubbing a wide, flat hand over the chest of his overalls. With his tanned red face and tanned bald head, he would have looked like a farmer except for all the grease smudges. McGivern guessed Warner was one of those men who took a small boy's delight in spending their time with engines and getting just as dirty as they could in the process.

"Get back to me as soon as you've got anything else, will you?" Warner said to the phone. "Thank you."

After hanging up, he lifted his coffee mug, sipped and said, "That was the Air Force Rescue Coordination Center at Scott Air Force Base in Illinois. Civilian authorities in Colorado don't feel they have the manpower to spare for a search like this right now, so they've turned the whole operation over to the Feds." He shook his head. Scowled. "I hope if it was our plane that went down that they're all all right. Except for that sonofabitch Doyle."

"What makes you think that the plane is yours?" Helman said.

"There was a cargo plane not far from where the smaller craft ran into trouble. The boys in the cargo plane got a glimpse of the other plane as it was going down. It sounds an awful lot like a Cessna 340 and it's blue and white, just like ours. Plus, the boys at Scott Air Force Base can't find a flight plan filed for a small plane that was supposed to be in that area at that time."

"How could the cargo plane see it in this kind of weather?" McGivern said.

"Well, a whiteout has pockets like any other kind of weather front. Every once in a while, things get clear for a little bit. Apparently that's what happened. The cargo plane radioed the other craft but by then it was too late. The pilot didn't answer. The small craft went into the mountains."

Warner walked over to a large map of the United States that covered half a wall. He pointed upward to the Rocky Mountain chain in Colorado. "Up here is where they went down, from the sound of things, anyway."

McGivern and Helman walked over for closer inspection.

"The Rescue Coordination Center will be dispatching a mission very soon," Warner said, tapping a blunt finger on Colorado as he spoke.

"Is it possible I could go with them?" McGivern said.

Helman and Warner both stared at him.

"The weather alerts are being canceled," McGivern said. "All I'd need is a ride to Colorado and I could go along."

"McGivern's lady friend is one of the people aboard the craft," Helman explained.

"Oh, I see," Warner said. "Sorry. Maybe I shouldn't have told you about it. I know this sounds like I'm only trying to spare you some grief, but we really don't know for sure that the plane that went down is our Cessna."

"I know. But I'd still like to be there on the chance that it is." McGivern tipped his coffee cup in the direction of the runway. "How long would it take me to fly to Colorado and meet the rescue team?"

"Few hours, I guess." Warner looked at him. "You sure you want to do this?"

"Yes," McGivern said.

Warner set down his coffee mug and picked up the receiver of his phone. "All right. Let me make a phone call and see what I can do."

Helman walked McGivern back to the office where Kenny Brennan waited.

"You sure you want to do this?" Helman repeated Warner's words. "If it is them and they did crash—" He paused, looked carefully and sympathetically at his friend. "It could be pretty grim."

"I know," McGivern said, and then went back into the smaller office.

"I need you to think hard," McGivern said.

"I'm trying. I honestly am."

"Think back. Did he give any reason for being so desperate about getting to L.A.?"

All energy had been blanched from the Brennan boy. His hair was still damp from fear; his skin was pale. His face was smudgy with dirt from falling over while bound and rubbing against the concrete floor of the hangar. Even several feet away, he smelled warm and sweaty.

"Oh," Kenny Brennan said. "I forgot."

"Forgot what?"

Kenny thought for a long time before speaking. "He said,

Doyle, I mean; Mr. Doyle said something about the woman Kate going in to open the box."

"Box? Did he say what kind of box?"

"I don't think so."

"Please, Kenny, think hard."

McGivern realized he was sounding too intense again. "I'm sorry. Just relax."

Kenny Brennan smiled at him. "I heard what Captain Helman said while you were out there. About Kate being your lady friend. I'd be pretty upset about this whole thing, too."

"Thanks for understanding, Kenny. I appreciate it."

"All I know is he said 'box.' I mean, I wish I could be more helpful."

"But your impression was that he was going to Los Angeles because of this box?"

"Right."

"And Kate had the key to the box."

"One of the keys."

"What?"

"One of the keys."

"One of the keys? He said that?"

"Yes." Kenny seemed baffled. "Did I say something important?"

"If he said 'one of the keys,' then I probably know what kind of box he was talking about."

"You do?"

"Right. Safe-deposit boxes generally have two keys. That's what Doyle must have been talking about."

"I hope I helped you."

"You helped me a hell of a lot, Kenny. A hell of a lot."

McGivern pulled out his notebook and flipped through a few pages. He pulled the phone toward him and dialed a number.

"Mrs. Greene?"

"Yes."

"This is Detective McGivern again."

"Hello."

"I'm really sorry to bother you again."

"That's all right. How may I help you?"

"Did your husband do most of his banking in Chicago?"

"I think so."

"Any at all in L.A.?"

"I think he kept a small checking account there."

"How about a safe-deposit box?"

"I'm not sure."

"Is there any way you could check?"

"I could try the desk in his den."

"Would you, please?"

"Would you like me to call you back?"

"I'll just wait on the line if you don't mind."

"You sound excited."

"Maybe some of this is starting to make a little sense."

Tears filled her voice suddenly. "I wish it made some sense to me."

Then she went away from the phone, soft retreating footsteps.

He wished he hadn't made the remark about things starting to make sense. Maybe to him they were. But not to the widow, nor to the two small children. Your daddy being murdered made no sense at all.

"I found billing for a safe-deposit box," she said when she returned to the phone.

He tried not to sound delighted. Any kind of delight right now would sound obscene.

"A savings and loan in Beverly Hills."

He took down the name and address of the S&L.

"Do you think you'll catch him?" she said.

"Doyle?"

"Yes."

"I hope so."

"I've never thought of myself as a vengeful woman. But now—maybe it's the only way I can deal with my loss. I really want you to catch him and then I want something really bad to happen to him." Pause. "I hate to hear myself like this. I was raised to be forgiving."

She started crying then.

She didn't say goodbye.

She simply continued to cry, soft but anguished grieving, and then gently replaced the receiver.

McGivern tried hard not to gloat over the information he'd just been given.

He did not want to be too cocky.

He might soon find himself mourning the loss of Kate just as Linda Greene was now mourning the loss of her husband.

When McGivern walked into the outer office, Warner gave him the thumbs-up.

"I'm getting a plane ready. I'm flying you to a base just outside of Colorado. The rescue boys agreed to let you go along."

31

THE Cessna 340 lost altitude just after entering that part of the Rockies known as the Sangre de Cristo Mountains. Earlier, Conroy had taken the craft up to fourteen thousand feet so that the FAA Flight Following Center would pick him up . . . but only moments later, the plane had fallen into trouble.

As the plane fell, Richard Conroy instructed his passengers how to prepare for a crash. Little could be seen out the windows. The whiteout continued. As the plane tilted downward, the one functioning engine began to splutter, just as the other one had done before quitting altogether. Wind whistled against every inch of the plane.

Kate tried hard to gather herself. Her mind was bombarded with images. She saw quite clearly a golden collie she'd had the summer of seventh grade. She saw the anniversary cake she'd made her parents during her senior year in high school. She saw Robert McGivern asleep, somehow both a boy and an old man at the same time.

Doyle shouted an obscenity.

Kate was conscious of being in the plane again.

Hurtling toward the mountains below.

Next to her, Richard Conroy went through what seemed like two dozen different motions. He flipped switches, knocked gauges with his knuckles, grasped the wheel.

"Put your heads down and tighten your seat belts as tight as you can get them.

"When we hit, we need to get away from the plane as soon as possible. Does everybody understand that?" Conroy said.

Doyle shouted another obscenity.

The cockpit window changed like a slide on a screen. Gone was the murk of the whiteout.

Now rushing toward the plane was the side of a ragged mountain. In the fog and overcast, the terrain was gray and threatening. Even the growth of scrub pine down the rough slope looked mutated and sickly, as if it would collapse under the whipping white snow assaulting it.

Kate turned once to see how Riki was doing.

The beautiful young woman had her hands folded and her eyes closed. She was praying.

Kate brought her head down, preparing for the impact of the crash.

The wind continued to scream. The plane continued to angle toward the mountainside. Richard Conroy continued to make last-minute adjustments.

Doyle screamed once more.

The plane roared into the side of the mountain.

Kate heard more screams—startled that one of them was her own—and then the sounds of metal grinding into rock and the smell of fuel leaking . . .

There was time enough to register the pain that the crash sent throughout her body—

And then darkness.

Forty-three minutes later, Kate returned to consciousness. For some reason, she could not get her eyes open.

At first, she had no idea of where she was, no memory of what had happened.

She felt something tear at her right arm every time she moved even slightly.

She opened her eyes.

She was hunched over in the front seat of an airplane that had been reduced to little more than scrap and safety glass.

She sat up. Darkness and heavy fog made seeing anything difficult. But gradually her vision adjusted to the gloom and she saw that she was alone in the craft.

She thought of Riki, Doyle, Conroy.

Where were they?

Close by, she heard the wind race through the wreckage, cold and sharp on ear and flesh alike.

Then she heard the lonely sound of a coyote. She'd spent two summers on her grandfather's Colorado horse ranch. She knew a great deal about this area.

So dark. So cold. So alone.

Where were the others?

Then she heard the voices.

At first they were only disembodied fragments of noise that occasionally penetrated the murk.

She wondered if they might not be part of the dream. Simply one more imagining.

She tried to move in her seat and found it nearly impossible.

She was encased in ragged edges of metal and safety glass. Even the slightest movement against these pointed surfaces tore into her flesh.

She reached down, grabbed a knife-like jut of safety glass and pushed it upward, out of the way. In the process, she savagely cut her hand. Warm blood streamed down the inside of her wrist. She didn't care. She wanted to keep moving. She wanted to turn back every surface that held her prisoner here. She wanted to find where the voices came from and to whom they belonged.

She smelled: cold mountain air, the tang of pine trees, fresh snow, her own blood. She froze and sweated at the same time.

In all, it took her fifteen minutes to extricate herself from her tiny prison. She suffered three more cuts, one across her inner thigh, one on her left cheek, one on the tender flesh just above her right breast.

But she didn't whimper, let alone cry. She just kept pushing back glass and metal until she could grab the top of the cockpit and pull herself to freedom.

She got up on top of the seat, finally, and jumped down to the ground.

She had little luck.

Instead of landing on her feet, she smashed facedown into the rocky soil.

She lay panting, in great pain, thinking again that this could be a dream. All the fog. And the deepening night. And the coyote.

Some netherworld.

And again: *Where were the others?*

Slowly, she got to her feet. The inside of her ski jacket was cold and wet with her blood but she didn't care. She drew the jacket tighter and set off across the rocky terrain toward the voices she imagined she'd heard.

Snow numbed her face. Darkness made the terrain treacherous. Even with a cushioning of snow, there was so much she could trip over. She could see nothing.

This really was a netherworld, a cold, frozen hell.

Stumbling, she grasped for a small tree to steady herself. But when her fingers touched the tree, the bark was cold and slimy, like the writhing oily feel of a serpent.

She shuddered, righted herself and continued on.

It was five more minutes before she heard the voices again. She was going around the side of the mountain, having found a crude and narrow path, when she saw something that stunned her.

Down in a kind of shallow valley burned the flames of a fire of some kind.

She saw two people huddled near the fire. One was Riki. The other was Conroy.

Where was Doyle?

She whirled around, aware suddenly of footsteps in the snow behind her.

"I've still got my gun, bitch. Don't think I don't. Now you go down toward that fire. I'll be right behind you."

Doyle was back in control of her life.

"I was going to come back and get you, see if you were conscious. You saved me the trip."

He came up behind her and shoved her. "Get moving, Kate."

32

THE Air Force Rescue Coordination Center, located at Scott Air Force Base, Illinois, was the single federal agency responsible for coordinating search and rescue activities in the forty-eight contiguous states, and providing assistance to Mexico and Canada.

The Center operated twenty-four hours a day, manned by military personnel trained and experienced in such work. Equipped with extensive communications equipment, including telephone, teletype and satellite radio capability, the Center also worked with the giant Space System for Search of Distressed Vessels satellite, which was put in orbit as a cooperative venture between the United States, Canada, France, the Soviet Union and other countries. This satellite was able to scan the globe for emergency signals from downed or lost craft.

The Center also actively participated in search and rescue missions, sometimes as part of a team comprised of planes provided by the individual state and the local Civil Air Patrol. Other times, weather conditions overwhelmed state capabilities and the Center was asked to conduct a search on its own.

This was the case this early evening as McGivern sat in a small office on a military base just inside the Colorado border. The snow had let up but darkness and the freezing temperature were still enemies in the attempt to find the downed craft carrying Kate and the others.

Colorado authorities had reported many road accidents plus three different plane accidents. They could not deal with this burden. Thus they called Scott and asked that a military rescue team be dispatched to look for the Cessna 340 from Chicago.

As McGivern sat and waited for the return of Lieutenant Colonel John Marsh, he stared out at the runway where a twin-engine helicopter known as the "Jolly Green Giant" was being readied for takeoff. McGivern had been reading a brochure about the big machine, how it had been configured for combat aircrew recovery missions, how it was specially equipped with various hi-tech rescue capabilities and how it was one of the few helicopters that had an external fuel probe for in-flight refueling, thus giving it an enormous range.

As he looked out at the runway, everything but a small portion of which was lost to tumbling snow, McGivern felt totally isolated, bereft. He was in a strange land with strange people and strange mechanical beasts. He wanted warmth and a familiar room and a sense of safety and security. He wanted the things most people wanted, whether they were young or old, rich or poor, black or white. But most of all, he wanted Kate. Gentle, loving Kate.

As wind whipped snow into the mercury vapor lights on the edge of the runway, McGivern watched as two members of the ground crew dipped their heads and ran into the wind.

In the next five minutes, the two ground crew members performed their mysterious last-minute ministrations on the giant green flying machine, and then ducked their heads down again and ran back toward the base buildings.

Moments later, properly suited up, Colonel John Marsh returned to the small office where McGivern waited.

"We're ready," Marsh said.

"Any more emergency signals?"

Marsh shook his head. He was a rangy man with gray hair, brown eyes and the kind of leanness that was most likely genetic. Ready for action this way, he would make a good recruiting poster.

"I think this Doyle guy is pretty smart," Marsh said.

"How so?"

"Remember how I explained the emergency locator transmitter?" Colonel Marsh said.

"Right. You said that there was one in every plane and if the plane went down, the transmitter automatically started sending out distress signals."

"Well, up to a point, that's right. In fact, when the Cessna went down this afternoon, a few pilots in the area did report an ELT signal. That's why we started searching that particular segment of mountain. But then the signal stopped."

"I'm not sure what you mean."

"I think our friend Doyle didn't want to be found. Wherever he's going, he's determined to get there and he doesn't want any interference from authorities. I think he knows enough about airplanes to have the pilot fool with the transmitter so it can't send out any more signals."

"So we don't have any sense of where they are now?"

"Oh, we've got a sense, all right, but at night this way and with this kind of blowing—and it's going to be worse the higher up in the mountains we go—it's not going to be easy to find them. We've had three other search planes out for the past four hours and they haven't had any luck."

McGivern nodded to the big green machine on the runway. "That's what we need, isn't it? Luck?"

Colonel Marsh smiled. "Well, a little luck certainly wouldn't hurt us, that's for sure."

They walked out the door, into the lacerating wind and snow, heads tucked down as they trotted toward the waiting steel beast.

33

TWO hundred fifty million years ago it began, the formation of the Rockies. Some of the mountains were once volcanic plateaus. Over hundreds of thousands of centuries, glaciers, rain and wind cut the mountains into their present shape. From an airplane, the mountains look barren, little more than jagged granite and snowy peaks, yet actually the clear mountain streams yield up grayling and rainbow trout and cutthroat trout and the land in the lower regions is rich with grains and potatoes and plump red sugar beets.

But the mountains are deceptive. Their beauty hides the cruelty they engender. In these mountains, winter is a harsh mistress. The pastures that are green in summer are furious, blinding white in winter and the starved corpses of elk and deer can be counted in the dozens. In the spring, predators such as wolves and coyotes will eat the frozen corpses, but since the number of elk and deer is generally decreasing, soon even the predators will go hungry and starve to death.

The mountains are defined by the timberline. Below it, human life can be pleasant, enriching. Above it, human life is virtually impossible, especially in winter.

Doyle nudged Kate again with the gun, hurrying her down the snowy trail to the overhang of rock. Beneath it, the fire still flickered and the shapes of both Riki and Richard Conroy could be made out in deep shadow.

Doyle marched her up a slope. Halfway up, she slipped, grabbing onto a jut of rock that tore a long, bloody line in the palm of her hand.

Doyle helped her by grabbing the back of her ski jacket and jerking her to her feet.

He pushed her into the small encampment. The fire made her almost idiotically happy, the prospect of light and warmth having never been so important to her as now.

There was a cleared area on the rocky ground. Doyle had dragged cardboard and paper from the plane to get the fire going. Small branches, now shorn of fir, had been added to keep the fire going.

It should have been a cozy little scene, a detail from a painting by Frederic Remington, Riki and Conroy crouched near the fire for warmth.

But then Kate saw why the two people seemed so still.

They were bound, wrists and ankles, with some kind of rough dark rope that must have been on the plane.

As she crouched on the other side of the fire, Conroy said, "We were worried about you." He explained that the plane had crash-landed in a valley rich with firs, pines and spruces and that these had helped cushion the impact. He was too modest to mention that he was a good pilot, Kate thought as he spoke.

After the crash, Doyle had revived first. One at a time, he'd led Conroy and then Riki from the plane to this overhang. He had just gone back for Kate.

"Ordinarily, I'd say we could count on the emergency signal to help somebody find us, but Doyle here thought it would be a good idea to disengage it." There was a wry bitterness as he spoke. Richard Conroy had a very good idea of what freezing to death would entail—literally freezing to death—but apparently Doyle did not. "I wish I could offer you a cup of coffee, Kate."

She smiled and went over and knelt down next to Riki. The young woman's forehead was smeared with blood. From a distance, the wound looked massive and serious. Up close, in the revealing flash of the flames, Kate saw that Riki had done little more than bang her head. There was a lot of blood but her eyes looked good—no sign of concussion—and she seemed alert.

Kate leaned over and hugged Riki. The young woman's cheek was so cold it was like touching a piece of glass that had frozen overnight. There was no human texture or odor to her skin.

Kate stood up, walked to the edge of the overhang and looked out.

She felt the way the Navajo and Shoshoni and Ute must have centuries ago when they first came to this land.

The overhang was a small jutting roof of granite that overlooked a vast valley of tree and rock and snow, sloping down a good half a mile to a small, frozen creek. In the moonlight, it was a beautiful land of silver snow and deep silken shadow. There was no evidence of man in anything she saw, and for a moment this splendid sense of isolation made her giddy, as if she'd just stumbled onto one of God's secrets—that the planet could survive quite happily and well without the relentless, selfish intrusion of mankind.

The wind and the vast, empty night brought her back to reality. For all its splendor, for all its historical poetry, the land offered neither shelter nor succor. They were just animals, no better or worse than the sweet small deer or lumbering befuddled elk who would be found ragged with frost and blanched with death when soft green spring touched the land once again. No, the planet did not need them, nor would it mourn their passing.

She heard a footstep behind her, a rough step on ragged rock, and turned to see Doyle.

From his right hand dangled two long pieces of the same rough rope he'd used to bind Riki and Conroy.

"Get down there by the fire," he said.

Apparently, she hesitated too long for Doyle's taste.

He cracked her hard across the jaw with the butt of his gun.

Darkness rushed at her momentarily. She felt herself begin to pitch over backward.

Somewhere in receding reality, she heard Riki scream, "Kate, please! Just do what he says!"

Doyle grabbed Kate's arm and pulled her over to the fire. She still couldn't see, but the warmth, however fleeting, was welcome.

Doyle threw her to the ground and tied her wrists and ankles.

34

RUNYON had been hiking when he looked up and saw the twin-engine plane go down just below the timberline.

The blizzard had been harsh enough to make progress moving upslope difficult. Though he had lived in the mountains for the past ten years, and had hiked through every kind of weather, the snow and ice and wind had been too much for him.

Much as he wanted to reach the downed plane and see if he could help, he crawled into a shallow cave and waited for the worst of the weather to relent. Life in the mountains had taught him that most elusive of virtues—patience.

He smiled to himself, wondered what the people at his old ad agency would have made of Jeff Runyon now being a patient man.

He had spent fifteen years in the ad world, at some of the most fashionable agencies on the East Coast. He had been into, variously, money, women, drugs and sports cars. Shiny red sports cars. He had also been into playing the ad game as if it were a war. He took no prisoners. When he stole another agency's account, he did so without guilt. Indeed, he did so with a great deal of festivity. The celebration parties were something to behold, three-day shoot-outs in posh midtown hotel suites, with all the lubricated pleasures one might expect.

It was one such party that had ended his advertising career, in fact.

He'd been doing a little coke as well as a lot of champagne when his CEO's wife, who'd always made a point of telling him how handsome he looked, maneuvered him into a bedroom and proceeded to push him back on the bed, managing to lose her clothes as she did so.

He'd been too drunk, too stoned, too satisfied with his own powers, to understand how perilous this moment was.

A few minutes later, looking for the wife who was rarely faithful, the CEO knocked open the door and found his naked wife atop the semi-naked Runyon.

The CEO, enraged, crossed the room in two steps, threw his wife to the floor and then started slamming punches into Runyon's face. Runyon had no chance to even get up off the bed.

The CEO could punch. The fact that he'd broken knuckles and badly ripped the skin on his right fist didn't seem to deter him.

Runyon got hit just enough to sober up. He realized that the CEO planned to kill him. He had to get up off this bed. The wife was no help. She stood cowering in the corner, uselessly trying to cover her voluptuous breasts with the perfect, pampered hands of a rich woman.

"Think about your heart, man," Runyon said to the CEO. The man had had two heart attacks in the past eighteen months. He should not have been throwing punches at anybody.

Runyon only got one chance.

Out of breath, the CEO paused a moment to regroup, before he visited more fists on the younger man.

Runyon raised his right foot, planting it firmly in the center of the man's chest, and shoved.

The CEO was off balance. He went back faster and farther than he would have normally.

After several steps backward, the CEO stumbled and fell sideways against the edge of the low, three-drawer bureau.

Runyon knew little of death. Most upper-middle-class white men of his age had been carefully protected from the sights and smells of mortality.

But he knew, even dizzy, even half-blinded from all the punches, that what he saw before him—it seemed to happen in some agonizing slow-motion effect—was the demise of a man he had disliked not at all, a man who had indeed been very good to him.

"Oh, shit," the naked wife said, knowing at the same moment as Runyon what was happening. "Oh, shit."

The CEO made a kind of grunting noise and then his liver-spotted hand reached forth feebly for his wife. And then—

Runyon went to the man, dropped to a knee, began checking eye and neck and wrist and chest for any sign of life. But there was none.

The naked wife began sobbing.

Even if he wasn't charged with second-degree murder, he would most certainly be facing manslaughter, a charge even the most mediocre of district attorneys would be able to apply, what with adultery, drugs and the romantic world of advertising involved.

So he did the only thing he could do.

He snatched up his clothes and ran, out the back window, down the fire escape, into a warm, rainy, melancholy Indian summer night, leaving behind him, in the *clang-clang-clang* of his feet slapping against the metal rungs of the fire escape . . . leaving behind him two loveless marriages, enough stock options to retire when he was forty and a truly predatory hankering for the ad game.

In the next eighteen months, he lived in Mexico, Georgia,

Texas, Florida and Oklahoma. He was a dockworker, a short-order cook, a counter clerk at Wendy's. He went four months without a drink and six months without sex. He had nightmares so bad he was sometimes afraid to go to sleep. He found a lump on his inner thigh which he thought might be cancer. He was almost disappointed to learn that it was nothing more than a fat deposit. He didn't have the nerve for suicide but cancer would leave him no choice.

Then he answered an ad for farm workers up near the Rockies. He went. After three months there, his life changed just as profoundly as it had changed the night his CEO died. He learned about the mountains and the songs they sang and the secrets they whispered. He found an abandoned shack just below the timberline. He taught himself how to gather and cook the plants and roots and weeds of the area. He no longer ate meat. He did not believe that animals should have to suffer and die for his appetites. He was a changed man.

He knew peace, finally. In the mountains, he saw few people, and that was one kind of peace, to be free of man's pettiness and jealousies and despair. The other kind of peace was the mountains themselves, sunsets and sundowns, the flowers of summer and the aspens of autumn and the sun-dappled snow of winter.

He had not seen his reflection for ten years. He had no idea what he looked like, nor did he care. He was no longer ego and id—if those Freudian concepts were even true to begin with—he was simply a sentient being who was deeply appreciative of what the gods had given him.

Now, huddled in the small cave that had been befouled by some poor frightened beast crawling to the back and dying, he thought of these things and waited.

Wind and snow were beginning to wane.

Soon, he would go upslope, not so far from his cabin, really, and see if he could help any survivors of the plane crash.

35

THE machine was darkness and wind and roaring relentless noise. The machine was arcing power and swooping grace and soaring screaking splendor. The machine was one-fourth swan and one-fourth hawk and one-half eagle.

The last helicopter McGivern had been in was a traffic chopper used by the Chicago police. The Jolly Green Giant was a different animal completely.

"How you doing?" Lieutenant Colonel Marsh said.

"Good, thanks."

"I've got a good feeling about this. About finding them, I mean."

"I appreciate you saying that."

For the past hour and a half, McGivern had felt himself become part of this machine. He imagined, had he not been so worried about Kate, that he would be feeling pretty god-like right now. That was how this incredible machine made him feel.

Presently, they were skimming over a wide valley. In moments, they arced upward, climbing up over the foothills, moving up toward the timberline. This terrain was too rugged to be ideal skiing territory, but that was what it reminded McGivern of, especially with the moonlight lending the snowy downslopes and the fir trees the painted aspect of a holiday card.

"Hold on," Marsh said, and went into the steep arc. This

was a maneuver they had been repeating since they first took flight, part of a shifting, integrating pattern of other planes and helicopters that were searching the area where the fleeting emergency signals had been noted earlier in the day.

The only light inside the machine was the soft red glow that outlined the various gauges and dials. Marsh continuously made notations on a long clipboard and went in and out of radio contact with others involved in the search.

McGivern tried to comfort himself with some of the war stories Marsh had told him earlier. Rescuing a critically ill Korean mountain climber at the fourteen-thousand-foot level of Mount McKinley. Taking a heart attack victim from a ship that was more than three hundred nautical miles from Iceland. Not only finding but saving a fourteen-year-old hiker who had been mauled by a rabid animal in the deep woods.

Marsh seemed to be saying that if he could find and save all these people, then surely he could find and save Kate and the others.

McGivern was still lost in his own thoughts when a new message squawked into the silence.

"Colonel Marsh, this is Tomlin with CAP."

"Yes, Tomlin."

"I may have found something, Colonel. I'm going lower to take a look."

Marsh glanced over at McGivern and smiled. "See, I told you we'd find them."

36

ROPE bit her wrists and ankles. But the rope did not bother Kate half as much as the cold. She had no feeling in her fingers or toes. Her nostrils felt as if they were glued shut.

Doyle had stamped out the fire, looking like some kind of demon as the flames leapt up his body and his right leg rose and fell, rose and fell as it trampled the flames to fleeing sparks, firelight painting his face a shifting mask of red and yellow.

Then there was only vast mountain darkness and vast mountain emptiness and vast mountain cold.

"There's a road down there somewhere," Doyle announced. "I'm going to check it out."

Kate watched him go downslope, slipping sometimes, half trotting others. He faded in and out of shadow pockets, boulders and firs and piñons, a silhouette-man who finally reached the moon-kissed creek far below, and then vanished completely.

"How's your head?" Kate said to Riki.

"Hurts a little, I guess."

Kate smiled. Riki was always so uncomplaining. No tantrums. No asking special favors. No pulling rank. Not even now.

"How are *you* doing?" Kate asked Richard Conroy.

"Feeling pretty lucky," he said.

"If you mean the crash, I doubt it was luck. More like good flying."

Shadows shifted across faces, moonlight only occasionally angling past the overhang.

"I wonder how far we are from a town or something," Riki said.

"I don't have a good sense of this area, I'm afraid," Conroy said. "But if Doyle thought he saw a road down there, then maybe we're not as lost as we think."

"You said Doyle did something to the emergency transmitter?" Kate said.

"Right. Smashed it so it doesn't work."

"Did any signals get out?"

"A few, I suppose. But whether they were enough to help anyone locate us—"

Kate tugged one arm then the other against her constraints. Doyle knew how to tie knots. These didn't budge.

"It's so beautiful out here," Riki said. "I keep wishing it were ugly. That would be more fitting. It's so beautiful—and yet there's nothing I want more than to be back in a dirty concrete city." She laughed softly. "So much for me as a nature lover, I guess." She paused. "Do you still have the knife, Kate?"

"The knife!" Kate said. She had forgotten the switchblade Riki had given her.

"I wondered if you still had it," Riki said. "I thought you might have lost it in the crash."

Riki was right. Maybe in the impact of the crash, the knife had fallen out of her pocket. Kate had no way of checking. Not with her hands bound this way.

"I'm going to crawl over there next to you," Kate said to Conroy. "Do you think you could work your hands so they could reach into my right-hand pocket?"

"I'd sure be willing to give it a try."

Reaching Conroy took more than ten minutes and was a most painful voyage. Her bottom was raw from tiny pinpricks of rock. She passed near the fire that was now nothing more than a few embers. The gray smoke seemed almost wistful to her, redolent of all that was safe and sane and civilized.

When she reached Conroy, she sat with her back to him, then lay on her side so that her right pocket was close to his fingers.

She'd had hopes that rescuing the switchblade would be easy. It wasn't. The first position didn't work. Conroy's fingers didn't even reach her jacket, let alone her pocket. They tried several positions before Conroy was able to start searching seriously for the knife.

"Anything yet?" Kate said.

"Not yet. I just now reached your pocket."

"Good."

"Darn."

"What?"

"Can you scooch a little closer?"

Kate scooched.

"Great. Thank you."

Conroy worked some more.

Kate could hear him exhale as his fingers strained inside her pocket.

"There."

"The knife?"

"I think so. I touched something, anyway." Pause. "But I lost it."

"I don't think I can get any closer."

"It's not you, it's me. I've got to stretch my fingers a little further and—"

Kate closed her eyes. Prayed.

"It's the knife," Conroy said in his usual low-key manner.

"I knew it would be there!" Riki said.

"Do you want me to move some other way?" Kate said.

"Just stay still. Just the way you are."

They were silent again. Only the wind; only the sad frantic noises of animals above the timberline.

Conroy kept working. "I—can't get it between my thumb and forefinger. Wait. There."

"You got it?" Kate said.

"Yes."

Kate allowed herself a laugh. "I've been meaning to ask you, Riki. Why does America's favorite singer of sad and vulnerable songs carry a six-inch switchblade?"

Conroy picked up the humor. "She's secretly the leader of a gang."

Kate laughed. It felt wonderful, forgetting utterly for a moment the pain she'd borne as a result of the crash, the anguish she felt over Doyle's murderous rage.

"In Florida once, a man came up and started to strangle me. He told the police later that one of my songs—actually one of the songs you wrote for me, Kate—had inspired his girlfriend to leave him."

"That's right. I remember that incident."

"After that," Riki said, "I went out and bought a switchblade. I keep it on me at all times. I don't even know if I'd have nerve enough to use it but it does give me self-confidence."

"Darn," Conroy said.

"What's wrong?"

"I got the knife out of your pocket, Kate, but I couldn't hold onto it. It's somewhere between us on the ground."

"I'll sit up."

Again, this was not as easy as she thought. Pain shot across her back and shoulders as she challenged her body to sit up. The crash had inflicted more damage than she'd realized.

Finally, she sat straight up, her back to Conroy's back. Her fingers waggled on the rocky floor in search of the switchblade.

"Any luck?" Conroy said.

"Not yet."

"Me, either."

Then, two and a half minutes later, Kate said, "I found it! I found it!"

She realized how young she sounded just then, the girl she used to be, exultant as she'd once been when playing hide-and-seek on a sunny small-town afternoon.

"I found it," Kate said again, as if she could not believe her good fortune.

37

FRANK Sayler enjoyed his drive to Brentwood. He supposed he could have simply called for the information but the day was too nice. He wanted to be outside.

With his Japanese employer mollified, at least temporarily, Sayler was able to slip into what he thought of as his "high school mode."

As the oldest of three boys in a working-class family, Frank had never been able to afford a car. And without a car, getting dates was made even more difficult for an unremarkable boy.

But as soon as he began to rise to prominence in the record industry, he learned that the best way to relax was to drive around the L.A. area in his expensive car wearing his expensive clothes exuding his important position in life.

And there was one more thing. He liked to think about the fates of three particular girls who'd spurned him in high school.

Though she'd once looked good in a bikini, Sandy Dobyns was now the two-hundred-pound mother of four.

Though she'd been the proudest girl in high school, Karen Tate was the wife of a man presently serving time for killing two little girls while driving intoxicated.

Though she'd been the richest girl in class, Trudy Baynes had been forced to watch her father's much-envied fortune wiped out in the 1987 stock market crash.

Frank Sayler knew about these girls and their fates because he'd hired a private investigator to keep him up to date.

Frank loved to drive around and daydream about how sick these women must feel whenever they saw his name in the gossip columns, involved with this or that rock star, this or that celebrity event.

Blue skies, a convertible with the top down, a one-hundred-dollar haircut and the certain knowledge that there were at least three women out there wishing that they'd given themselves to you back there in high school.

What more could a guy ask for?

The investigator's name was Ken Morrow. He'd spent twelve years with the LAPD, then quit to write novels. Like most police officers who take up the literary profession, his books were long on inside knowledge but short on such things as character, theme, story or the resonant phrase. Despite TV good looks and an insatiable desire for publicity—he was a tireless promoter of his novels—his income never rose above ten thousand dollars a year. Because he was a man who liked a splashy life-style, he soon relented and went into the private investigative business. He was smart enough to hire a sad little wife-left man named Silverstein who was one of those basement geniuses good at tinkering with electronic gear. Give Silverstein half a chance, and he could plant a microdot microphone in one of your molars without you having any idea at all what he was doing.

Thanks to people like Frank Sayler—who wanted mistresses checked out for HIV, coworkers checked out for loyalty and clients checked out for solvency—Morrow, Inc., prospered . . . as Frank was reminded when he pulled his Mercedes in between a red Ferrari and a silver Rolls.

Last spring Morrow had built his own office building, one of those small glass and steel structures that resemble a piece of modern sculpture. Most people seeing it for the first time were taken with its sharp angles and flashing, reflective surfaces and towering central spire. The only problem they had was that they weren't sure where the front door was.

A quiet decorative receptionist told Frank to take a seat in the quiet decorative waiting area. Two other clients waited to see their respective investigators from the Morrow staff—a plump matron with a sleek new mink stole who kept daubing her tears with a frilly handkerchief; and a most effeminate man who kept sighing with great and forlorn drama. In a way, it was like a psychiatrist's office, with none of the clients wanting to acknowledge the others, each trying to guess what had brought the others to be sitting in the waiting area of a private investigative office.

When Frank's turn came, he half leapt to his feet and followed the receptionist, who had quite nice ankles and an even nicer pneumatic behind, down the narrow carpeted corridor leading to Morrow's office.

The quiet decorative receptionist knocked discreetly on her employer's door, was given a muffled "Come in," swung the door open and then stood back to allow the client to walk in.

Frank walked in.

The next minute was pure ritual. Morrow, who looked like central casting's idea of a blond second lead in a cop series, came around the desk in his dark Armani suit and seized Frank's hand and crushed a few knuckles to demonstrate that his masculinity was above reproach, and then slapped Frank on the back so hard he seemed to be trying to dislodge something caught in Frank's throat.

Then it was around-the-desk, open-the-drawer, pour-the-brandy and, finally, sit back and give Frank a gander at the capped teeth that had suddenly and brilliantly appeared six months ago.

"How's it going, babe?" Morrow said.

"Some real problems."

"Sorry to hear that." Then he snapped his fingers. "Hey, before we begin, I've got a question for you. I mean, you know all this stuff. That new musical group, the Muggers?"

"Right. The Muggers."

"You know anything about them?"

Here we go, Frank thought. Different group every time, but same question. "A little, I guess. I mean, the usual industry gossip."

"That lead singer?"

"Right."

"The pretty one? Hair down to his ass?"

"Right."

"Is he gay?"

Is he gay? Morrow always asked that question and lately Frank had begun to get curious about it. Is he gay? Why would Morrow be so interested?

"Not that I've heard."

"He sure looks it."

Then Morrow shrugged, sipped some more brandy and said, "Okay, babe, lay it on me."

Frank decided to be dramatic. What better way to get Morrow's attention?

"You said Silverstein came up with the name of a savings and loan where Greene had a safe-deposit box."

"Right."

"I need to know the name of the place. Brad Doyle's going to try and get there very soon. I need to be waiting for him."

"What're you going to do?"

"I'm not sure yet," Frank said. "I wish I was."

• • •

Six months earlier, Frank had noticed an increasing anxiety on the face of Brad Doyle. This, in turn, made Frank nervous. As the manager of Frank's most valuable singer, Doyle must be anxious about only one thing. Riki's contract was up after the next album and Doyle was probably shopping her around. Of course, he did not want Frank to find out. Frank would be included in the bidding but only after Doyle had secretly contacted three or four other record labels and gotten his asking price way up in time for an auction.

Frank contacted Morrow, on whom he'd called a number of times over the past few years. Personally, Frank thought Morrow was a male version of one of those beach blondes you saw prancing around in string bikinis, but he had a lot of faith in Henry Silverstein. Henry had been a great help to several of Frank's best friends and would no doubt be a big help now.

He was.

He found that Doyle wasn't shopping around for labels. He was being shaken down by, of all people, David Greene. The publicity business hadn't been kind to Greene of late—too much overhead, too few new clients—and so Greene decided to turn some secret he'd been keeping into cash.

Good as Silverstein was, various as his microphone plants had been, he hadn't been able to turn up the nature of the blackmail.

All he knew was that on the second of every month, Brad Doyle sent David Greene a hefty check.

What the hell was going on here, anyway?

Silverstein and his men began tailing David Greene. They learned that, unlike most men in his profession, he (a) had no girlfriends on the side, (b) had no boyfriends on the side, (c) did not take dope, (d) did not use alcohol excessively and

(e) spent every possible moment with his nice little family in his nice little suburb outside Chicago.

What the hell kind of blackmailer was he, anyway?

Frank Sayler had been told all this in a presentation a few months back.

He spent a long weekend with his girlfriend's new silicone breasts brooding about what to do.

On Monday morning, he called Brad Doyle and suggested lunch. He met him at the Polo Lounge, where, three tables away, Julia Roberts also happened to be lunching. Frank tried not to think about the three girls who'd dumped him in high school. Wouldn't they love to be lunching three tables away from Julia Roberts?

"David Greene's blackmailing you."

When he got down to it, which was right after his chef's salad, Frank went right at it. No mincing of words. No sparing of feelings.

"I don't know what the hell you're talking about."

"Sure you do."

"Blackmailing me?"

"Yes, and I want to know why."

"I don't know where the hell you'd get a dumb-ass idea like that, Frank."

Frank, very much out of character, slammed his fist so hard against the table that all the fine china jiggled. And everybody in the near vicinity looked at Frank, including Julia Roberts.

"I'm in no mood for bullshit, Brad. No mood at all."

Doyle started to protest again but then gave it up. "Yeah, he's blackmailing me, all right, Frank."

"About what?"

"You really think I'd tell you?"

"Maybe I can help."

"You can't, Frank. You can't."

But now, as he sat facing Morrow, Frank Sayler did know what was going on, did know what David Greene had had on Doyle.

"I want to be there waiting for him."

"How will you know when he gets to the city?" Morrow said.

"He'll tell me. We're in phone contact."

"You're sure he'll go to the savings and loan?"

"He's got to get his hands on that safe-deposit box before the press does."

"So do you, Frank."

He nodded his head. "That's why I want to be there waiting for him."

"I've been listening to the news. Maybe the cops'll get him before you do."

"Not Doyle. He's just one of those guys."

"One of those guys?"

"One of those guys who's more animal than human. You'd have to know him to know what I mean. You'd have to see him around Riki—he'd destroy anybody who tried to hurt her. He loves her in some sick kind of way that's pretty spooky to see."

"You want me to bring Silverstein in and tell you where this savings and loan is? I mean, he's a little more familiar with this thing." Morrow's standard cop-out. "A little more familiar" meaning that he hadn't been paying attention at all.

Henry Silverstein came in. He shook Frank's hand and got down to business, telling him the name of the savings and loan and its location.

Unlike Morrow, Henry Silverstein was worth every penny Frank paid him.

38

SEARCHLIGHTS played over the rugged side of a snowy ravine. One of the lights belonged to a small army helicopter from a nearby base, the other to the Jolly Green Giant carrying McGivern and Colonel Marsh.

The rotors of the hovering machines whipped the ground snow into a tumbling, blinding frenzy, but even so it was possible to see that what the CAP had reported as the possible wreckage of Kate's plane was nothing more than a car that had been wrecked and pushed over the side of the ravine long ago. There were no windows left in the automobile, and two of the four doors had been removed.

Colonel Marsh pulled his helicopter up and away from the scene, stirring up the snow into an even greater frenzy.

The helicopter then angled away from the steep rock cliff on the other side of the ravine road.

Once again, the Jolly Green Giant was a bird of night, ineluctable as the moon and the racing clouds.

In the red glow of the instrument panel, Colonel Marsh's lean face showed tension and disappointment.

He looked over at McGivern. "I'm sorry, McGivern. But they have to report everything they even think might be wreckage."

"Just doing their job," McGivern said, trying not to sound unduly grim.

The helicopter roared away into the darkness.

39

THERE was once a Cleveland cop named Haney and there was really nothing remarkable about him—he was fat, had flat feet, his daughter drove him nuts with her Beatles records, he was a member in good standing of the Knights of Columbus—except that he once tried to get an arrest warrant on an eight-year-old boy. The judge said, An eight-year-old boy? Get outta here, Haney. Why'd they ever make you a detective, anyway? My good looks, Haney said.

For the next two years he kept gnawing at the case, kept trying to figure if there was some way he could prove to somebody other than himself that this kid had killed his old man by pushing him down the basement stairs in a wheelchair, just like Richard Widmark had done right after World War II in *Kiss of Death*. (Ask Haney what he had done *during* World War II and he'd proudly tell you he'd been a member of the Marines' V Amphibious Corps and had helped storm the beaches on Iwo Jima.) The kid's old man, drunk as always and a real mean bastard according to all the neighbors, had snapped his neck when his head collided with the concrete basement floor. At least that was the coroner's version of it.

But Haney knew better. He could tell by the kid's face. Every time the handsome little boy spoke of his father's death, his mouth broke into a smile. Couldn't contain his joy. Just couldn't do it. The mother was just as obvious. Oh, she put on a good show of poor hardworking Fred, first he gets into an accident at the plant that crippled him five years ago and now he gets drunk and falls down the basement steps. Boo-hoo-hoo-and-please-hand-me-that-box-of-Kleenex-thank-you-so-very-much-you're-so-very-kind. But when she thought Haney wasn't looking, she'd glance over at her son and they'd smile at each other. Real proud-like. Real satisfied-like. A job well done.

Hemingway once said that if you took any story far enough, it ended in death, and Haney's story was no different. He never forgot the kid or the mother—he spotted them for Oedipal right away, the way her hands clung to the boy, the way the boy obviously both loved and despised his mother; Haney had once read a tabloid article titled "Mama's Boys: Is Your Child Safe?" and ever since had considered himself an expert on the subject—he never quit believing that the kid had killed the old man. Never.

In 1971 Haney went to the doctor one day because he thought he had a cold, the cough and all, and the doctor said why don't we just get an X ray of your chest to see if there's any pneumonia in there. Three days following the X ray the doctor called Haney and asked him to come in. And when Haney did come in, the doctor told him that there were two spots on Haney's left lung. And Haney knew. Right then, right there, no mistaking it. He was hearing his death sentence. There was surgery and there was chemo and there were endless beseeching prayers, but Haney went and went fast, less than ten months following the diagnosis, and it was a miserable way to go. In effect, with lung cancer, you drowned.

He died at home as he'd requested, with his wife and kids on either side of the bed. After he told them how much he loved them and after they all (including Haney) cried at the prospect of the great sad journey he was about to make,

Haney took his wife's sweet hand and held it tight and looked up into her melancholy Irish face and said, "Brad Doyle, that little bastard, he killed his old man and don't forget it." These proved to be Haney's last words. None of his family had any idea what he was talking about. They assumed he'd been hallucinating. Who was Brad Doyle and why was he a little bastard and why would he want to go and kill his old man? Haney was buried with his secret.

Brad Doyle was a popular boy. He had good looks, easy charm, and he was ruthless about getting his way. In high school and two years of college, he specialized in breaking up couples. He'd see a fine-looking woman with a good-looking guy and he'd say to himself, I'll bet I can break them up. I'll bet I can break her heart and bust his balls. And then he'd proceed to do just that.

Also he was into rape. Nothing excited him as much as stalking a girl down a dark street then vanishing suddenly, making her think she was safe, and then appearing from nowhere and raping her. Afterward, he would inflict a savage beating. He loved the smell and taste of blood spilled violently.

He lived at home all this time, a commuting student who took the city bus to the college campus, a fact he always found humiliating. He wanted money, power, he wanted to matter to the world.

Among his crowd was a young man obviously gay and obviously taken with Doyle. The young man was rich. Doyle found the young man pathetic and disgusting but he remained friends because the young man was always buying Doyle presents. Eventually, other people on campus became aware of this relationship. They were already whispering about the young man. Now they whispered about Doyle, too. When he became aware of their hints about his nature, Doyle became uncontrollably violent. One night he went to the young man's lavish apartment and beat him so badly the young man lost permanent use of his right arm. The young man's father being wealthy and powerful, Doyle was soon arrested, charged with attempted murder and sentenced to prison.

In the spring of Doyle's third year in prison there was a fire in the cell block above him and three guys were so badly burned one of the guards puked all over himself when he made his way through the smoke and saw the charred human statues on the floor before him.

As a result of this fire, there was some rearranging of cellmates and that was how Doyle came to meet Neary.

Doyle's previous cellmate had been an auto thief who'd been paroled a week before the fire, a big angry Mexican who never ceased arguing with the guards. Because of this, he'd served two years longer than the parole board had earlier mandated.

Neary was the polar opposite, of course, a handsome but almost frail twenty-year-old who was doing five-to-ten for his part in a series of convenience store robberies. He had been part of a trio. He'd been the driver, waiting in the car. On the night of the last robbery, he'd gotten spooked by a prowl car coming around a corner and had taken off without his friends. When they were arrested, they were only too happy to steer the cops to him.

Neary was an intellectual. At least Doyle considered him one. Neary read books every chance he got. All kinds of books, from poetry to novels to biographies. He was like a vending machine for facts. Press Cuba, say, and he'd give you twenty minutes on how the Spaniards first colonized it in the 1500s and how America seized control of the place in

1906. And on and on. The same went for Mozart, Mickey Mantle, Cary Grant and Mother Teresa. Name it and he'd give you twenty minutes.

At least this was how things went the first three months. By this time, well into his sentence, Doyle was a trusty, and Neary, naturally, worked in the prison library. At nights, after lights-out—though just as there is no such thing as privacy in the joint, neither is there such a state as true darkness—Doyle would lie on the bottom bunk and keep coming up with subjects that he hoped would stump Neary. But they never did. No matter how arcane the topic, Neary was ready with his twenty minutes.

Then, late at night, Neary began crying. Doyle had never heard anybody cry like that. Soft but unceasing. Long, long hours of tears. He felt sorry for the guy. By now Neary was the best friend Doyle had ever had. He'd say, there in the shadows of their cell, "What's wrong, Neary? What's wrong?"

He never found out what was troubling Neary, at least not that first spring.

The other prisoners weren't as fond of Neary as Doyle was.

One spring a convict in the next cell block accused Neary of informing on him to the warden. He cut Neary severely. Neary lived.

Doyle waited a reasonable amount of time then caught the con in the library, where he put a homemade ice pick right through the man's eye and into his brain.

No charges were ever brought. There had been no witnesses.

Doyle had never felt protective of anyone before, not even the numerous pets he'd had as a child, so watching out for Neary was a new experience.

When Neary got into an argument with a guard and swung

at the man, Doyle stepped in before the punch landed—and decked the guard with his own punch. He wanted to take the blame for the incident. He knew that the sentence for this would be solitary confinement. He also knew that Neary was not strong enough to survive "the Hole," as the cons called it. But Doyle was strong enough. Plenty strong enough.

Neary got out eight months before Doyle. They were the worst eight months of Doyle's life.

Neary wrote him every week and Doyle, not much of a literary man, wrote back.

Neary described how nice things were on the outside and always told Doyle that soon all these pleasures would be his.

Some of Neary's letters were kind of spooky, though. The old depression—confusion, rage, suicidal notions—could be heard in Neary's letters. And Doyle would get scared.

What if something happened to Neary . . .

When Doyle was paroled, his mother came to pick him up. Now a stout, drab woman in a faded housedress, she thanked the warden for all his help—even though he was black and Mrs. Doyle had never cared much for the "shiftless" black race—and then she escorted her son through what seemed to be a dozen different electronically operated doors, each with a solemn gun-toting guard, each with clanking iron bars that closed coffin-tight behind them.

At home, his mother gave Doyle three ultimatums: he was not to have any more of those nudist magazines she'd once found in his bureau; he was to attend Mass twice a week in addition to Sundays; and even though he had a full-time job at Penny's on the loading dock, he was to help her scrape and wash the dishes each night after dinner.

This went on for three and a half years, until his parole had ended and he was then truly a freeman.

The night after his parole abated, he packed one lone battered suitcase, went downstairs to the living room and kissed the sweet old family dog, and then went over to where his white-haired mother sat in her rocking chair and spat hard and hateful into her face.

"You fucking bitch," he said, "if I had any balls I'd cut your throat."

That was the last time he ever saw his mother.

Doyle found no road. He was sure he'd seen one, but he could not find it.

He cursed and started climbing back upslope to the overhang where he'd left his three prisoners.

During the long walk downslope, he'd thought of the past ten years of his life, prison, and meeting Riki and the incredibly good fortune that had suddenly become theirs.

Now all that was being threatened.

He had to get to that safe-deposit box before anybody else did.

Had to.

He kept climbing, climbing on the moonscape of mountain before him.

Climbing.

40

WHEN he got back to his office, Frank Sayler called the branch of Fidelity Savings and Loan where David Greene had his safe-deposit box.

"I'd like to speak to somebody about a safe-deposit box."

"Your name, please?"

"My name?"

"It's just a formality, sir."

"Oh. Right. Kenyon. Harvey Kenyon."

Kenyon was the bully who used to snap his towel at Frank's bare ass following ninth-grade gym class.

"One moment, please, sir. I'll let you speak to Mr. Mocher."

"Thank you."

Frank still couldn't decide if the operator was man or woman. This was, after all, L.A.

"Mr. Mocher. How may I help you?"

"I'm inquiring about safe-deposit boxes."

"Your name, please?"

What was it with these people? "Kenyon. Harvey Kenyon."

"Thank you, Mr. Kenyon. Now, how may I help you?"

"Do safe-deposit boxes come in different sizes?"

"Indeed they do." He described the three sizes.

"Are they safe from fire?"

"Completely. The entire building might burn down—not that it ever would, of course—and your safe-deposit box would be safe. The paint might have peeled and there might be some gray ashes on it but your box would be totally intact. Totally."

"Who would be permitted to get into the box?"

"Only you, sir. Our rules are very strict. When you come in and reserve a box, we take your photograph."

"My photograph?"

"Yes, sir. Your photograph. That way nobody else could come in here pretending to be you."

"I see."

"Every time somebody asks to take out the box with your number on it, that person is compared to the photograph we keep on file. If that person is lying—well . . ."

"Well, what?"

"Well, our president—who, between us, can be a real maddog when somebody is being dishonest—our president would see that the person was detained and then arrested and then prosecuted to the full extent of the law."

"So I had a safe-deposit box—"

"—yes—"

"—and somebody came in claiming to be me—"

"—umm-hmm—"

"—but he wasn't really me—"

"Right. Not really you."

"Then there would be no way he could get into the box and take something out."

"Absolutely not. I mean, absolutely not could he get into the box under any circumstances. Did I say that right?"

"You said it perfectly," Frank Sayler said, slamming down the phone.

So much for his plan that he'd hire some woman to saunter into Fidelity pretending to be Kate Evans and try to persuade the manager to open it. There were some good actresses in L.A.

But take a photograph of you!

The nerve of those bastards.

41

KATE bit her lip, afraid if she told Richard Conroy that the switchblade was cutting into her wrist, he'd be too intimidated to keep working. She could feel the rope starting to give. Even though he had cut a one-inch slash above her wristbone, she wanted him to keep going.

The icy wind had started up again. Silver sprays of snow touched Kate's face every few minutes. The coyotes above the timberline seemed louder, almost crazed now, and the downslope shadows of pine and fir trees had taken on an ominous quality, as if monsters, human or otherwise, hid in them.

"Am I cutting you?" Conroy said.

"No."

"You sure?"

"Positive."

"Can you feel the rope starting to give?"

"A little bit."

"Good."

He cut some more. She knew how hard it must be for him. How numb his fingers must be from the cold, how tired his wrists must be from supporting the knife and cutting. She just couldn't tell him about the warm blood flowing from her wrist as the wound got deeper.

"I don't see him yet," Riki said.

She had appointed herself lookout. Every few minutes, she gave them an update on what she saw downslope.

At several points since being taken from her apartment this morning, Kate had wanted to ask Riki what this was all about. Obviously, Riki knew. But Kate was well aware of Riki's shyness. She'd never talk about anything intimate with Richard Conroy present. Not even when their lives were at stake.

Richard Conroy kept cutting.

Doyle took a wide path on his return from the valley floor, up into several stands of fir that made him virtually invisible.

He was past being cold. His nose ran, he had to bite down on his fingers to keep feeling in them, and he had to stop every five minutes or so and urinate. Freezing temperatures had always had such an effect on him.

As he stood now, watching white steam rise from the yellow stream of his urine, he remembered reading an article about a guy who stayed alive in the wilderness by drinking his own urine. Doyle shuddered at the thought.

Then he was moving again, higher, higher, up toward the overhang.

His mind returned to L.A. and the safe-deposit box. One way or another, the contents of that box would soon be his.

"Does it feel any different?"

"A little bit."

"I wish I could get better leverage. I could cut that rope in no time."

"You're doing fine."

"Well, here goes again."

"I don't see him yet," Riki said, scanning the downslope.

• • •

Amidst the noise and flash and power of the Jolly Green Giant, Colonel Marsh told McGivern a story about how he had once saved a whale that had beached itself six miles off Key West. The whale was near death, so the colonel and his men picked it up, set it aboard an HH-3 helicopter and flew it to the Miami Seaquarium for intensive medical care. The whale was set on a four-inch-thick mattress and kept moist. It was given blood tests, medical exams, antibiotics, and force-fed. Marsh, who had to fly back to base, kept phoning the Seaquarium every three hours to see how the whale was. The mammal had become very human to Marsh. Two weeks later, the Seaquarium staff gave the whale a birthday party and Colonel Marsh was happy to attend.

Colonel Marsh always told this story to people who looked as if they were about to slip into despair. The story was great therapy. Hell, it had everything a good tale should have—a unique premise, a race against the clock with lots of suspense and a happy ending. It hadn't really happened, not to Colonel Marsh, anyway, but he felt justified in telling it because it always lifted people's spirits. Sometimes that was the most sacred task of all, giving people hope and faith to keep going no matter how grim things seemed at the moment.

In the red glow of the panel lights, Colonel Marsh studied McGivern's face as he told his spectacular whale tale.

For the first time in half an hour, the Chicago detective seemed interested in something other than his own dark and brooding fears. He watched and listened with interest.

"That's a hell of a nice story," McGivern said when the colonel had finished.

"Thank you."

Then McGivern surprised the colonel by smiling.

"I have a story like that myself," McGivern said, "that I tell to people who are starting to get depressed."

Colonel Marsh laughed. Their lines of work probably weren't so different, after all.

"So what's your story about?" the colonel said.

"About this poor little kitty who was on the sixth floor of a burning building and then jumped out on a utility pole and saved herself."

"Is that a true story?"

"I like to think of it as a parable about keeping hope alive."

"Well," Colonel Marsh said, "that's how I like to think about my whale story, too."

The two men grinned at each other as the Jolly Green Giant pushed into the night.

42

KATE felt the rope give. Her first impulse was to try and jerk her wrists apart. But loose as the rope felt, it would not give enough for her to free herself. Not yet.

By now, she had forgotten about the cuts and the blood. Well worth the price for freedom.

"I'm sorry this is taking so long," Richard Conroy said.

"You're doing a fine job."

"No sight of him," Riki reported.

"I'll try and hurry," Conroy said.

Kate imagined that Conroy's arms and hands were nearly numb by now. But there was a boyish determination about him she found endearing. He was one of the good ones, she thought. No hatred in him, no bitterness. And a real sense of principle, too.

Conroy angled the knife against Kate's restraints and started cutting again.

She was sitting there, her face wind-chafed, her nose running, thinking about McGivern again, forgetting about Conroy and his desperate attempts to cut her free, when suddenly—

"You did it!" she said.

She brought her arms up in front of her, held them up to the moonlight as if they were gifts from God. She did not mind that her hands ran with the blood from the cuts on her wrists.

Arms. Hands. Free. Escape.

She sat there exultant for a long moment.

She quickly set about unlashing her ankles, taking the knife from Conroy and slashing the rope in half.

She turned then to Conroy, tightening her bloody grip on the knife and sawing through the rope on his hands.

"Any sign of him?" Conroy asked Riki.

"All clear. And it's stopped snowing, so I should be able to see him."

"I'll hurry," Kate said.

Conroy was free. He took the knife from Kate and worked through the rope lashing his ankles.

Under the shadow of the overhang, the fire little more than ash now, the three people were silhouettes moving about frantically in the wind and the night.

Conroy bent over Riki, undid her ropes.

"Which way should we go?" Kate said as Conroy was helping Riki to her feet.

Conroy walked to the edge of the overhang, eyes scanning downslope and to the right. "There should be some roads around here, logging roads and old gold mine roads." He pointed to trees neither Kate nor Riki could see, somewhere to the right. "Let's try over there."

Conroy was still under the edge of the overhang. He could not see directly above him.

Kate saw snow suddenly drifting down from the top of the overhang, falling like tumbling diamonds in the moonlight. She had a sense of somebody crouching up there, accidentally kicking snow down.

She started to warn Richard Conroy but he stepped out from beneath the overhang and started trotting rightward across the slope to freedom.

Three shots cracked across the frozen night air.

Kate's eyes at first refused to believe what they saw. She

knew she screamed, muffling the sound in hands pressed tight against her mouth.

The top of Richard Conroy's head was blown off. He had been jogging to the right, still a silhouette figure in the moonlight, black against the sparkling white of the snow, when suddenly the top of his head was lifted off like a bad toupee caught in the wind, and then there was a splatter of blood and brain matter, and Richard Conroy fell face-forward into the snow. Dead. Unmistakably dead.

Doyle was on top of the overhang. Waiting. Playing some sadistic game with them.

"So much for the Boy Scout," he shouted down to them. "You want to try it next, Kate?"

Riki grabbed Kate's arm. "Don't."

Kate and Riki embraced, holding each other like young sisters in whose shadowy room the bogyman had suddenly appeared. Though Kate had initiated the embrace, it was Riki who put her head to Kate's shoulder and began crying. "There's something I should tell you, Kate, something you should know—"

But Kate quieted her, wanting to hear what Doyle was doing up there.

More snow was scraped down from above, spraying over the two women in a fine sparkling mist.

For the second time in less than two minutes, the seemingly impossible happened.

Kate was holding Riki when she heard a breathless grunt, as if great pain had been inflicted upon Doyle. Then a body fell down from the lip of the overhang and crashed into the snow no more than four feet from Kate.

The body, black on white once more, landed face-first and sprawled unmoving.

Kate, caught up in the madness of her abduction, first

wondered if this might not be some sort of trick, Doyle playing with them some more.

But then reason slowly returned. Why would he intentionally throw himself from the overhang? While it wasn't more than a five-foot fall, it was enough to at least cause him to lose control of the situation for the moment. At worst, he could break a leg or an arm.

Doyle lay flat, facedown, unmoving, arms spread out.

No, Doyle wasn't playing with them. Kate was sure of that now.

Then what had caused him to fall? Heart attack? Simple accident? Had something—some half-frozen and crazed mountain animal—suddenly appeared and frightened him, causing him to tumble over the edge?

"What's going on?" Riki whispered.

Kate only shook her head, pushed away from Riki.

She watched as a fine mist of snow was once more knocked from the edge of the overhang.

Somebody else was up there now. But who? And why wouldn't he identify himself?

Before she could puzzle through all this, the man was there, tramping down the side of the overhang.

He stood before them, the details of his face lost in the furry frame of his parka hood, a big, seemingly capable man with a strong confident voice.

"My name's Runyon," he said. Even in the shadows of his parka hood, they could see his wide white friendly grin. "You ladies look as if you could use some help. That's why I knocked your friend out."

He nodded to Doyle there on the ground.

Then he looked back to the women. "Let's get out of here."

43

AFTER lunch, a glad-handing hour at Spago, Frank Sayler decided to check out the branch of Fidelity Savings and Loan where David Greene's blackmail material was being kept.

On the drive over, the temperature just above eighty, Sayler started worrying again. Could he really go through with his plan? Could he really keep everything under control?

Fidelity proved to be a small red-brick building on a busy corner choked with cars and exhaust fumes. There was a parking lot on the west side and a drive-through teller window on the east side. And there were a couple of gargoyles squatting on the roof, watching everything with their evil immortal eyes. Gargoyles had always spooked Sayler.

Frank parked his convertible across the street and tried to get some sense of the place by watching customers going in and out. He had no idea what he was doing, really. He was afraid he was going to have an anxiety attack.

Most of the customers looked like nice, clean-cut middle-class people. At one point a gigantic limo pulled up and a big strapping white guy in livery jumped out and held the door for a tiny little old lady carrying her tiny little old Pekinese. The lady handed the dog to the chauffeur and then went inside, pecking out her steps with a rubber-tipped black cane.

Frank wanted to watch more, but a patrol car came along, giving him a suspicious eye.

He felt like a ten-year-old who'd been caught sneaking a peek at his older sister in the bathtub.

He put the convertible in gear and left.

Half an hour later he was in a dark, air-conditioned bar on Melrose.

He had two quick bourbons straight up.

"Another one, pal?" asked the bartender, who reminded Frank of Jackie Gleason in his Ralph Kramden role.

Suddenly Frank Sayler realized that his fingers were trembling.

In pitching Mr. Nakagama, his plan to turn this whole terrible incident into a great publicity triumph for Riki had sounded so easy.

But now—

"No, thanks," he said, and left.

This year's mistress was named Stacy.

Frank kept her in a four-room apartment not far from the ocean.

She was an actress, which meant that she never worked and let Sayler worry about how she supported herself.

When he got to the apartment, Stacy was out on the veranda, "taking the sun" as she liked to say.

She saw that he was a mess—he was frequently a mess, so nervous—and she knew exactly what he wanted.

She jumped up from the chaise lounge. He took her place. She deftly got him unzipped and ready, but it was no good, as it was frequently no good when he got this uptight.

"Talk to it," Frank said.

"Talk to it?"

"Yeah, you know how you do sometimes."

She looked at the limp little penis she held in her beautiful slender hand. "Don't little Roger want to get up and have some fun? Like that, Frank?"

"Yeah. Like that. It's worth a try."

So he lay back and closed his eyes and thought about how his entire world, how his entire frigging *universe*, could come crashing down around him. And while he thought about it, Stacy talked to Roger, which is what she had always called Frank's penis.

"I've got a real nice present for Roger if he's a real good boy today," Stacy said, addressing Frank's privates.

Frank opened one eye. "Tell him he's being a bad boy."

"You mean scold him?"

"Yeah. Scold him."

Stacy's eyes found Roger again. "You're being a very bad boy, Roger."

"And tell him he's ungrateful."

"Ungrateful, Frank?"

"Yeah, ungrateful."

"And you're being ungrateful, too," she told Roger.

Frank's eyes were closed again. He was starting to think about everything again, about Doyle and Riki and the Japanese, when he realized that Stacy wasn't saying anything.

He opened one eye again. "What's wrong?"

"I think we hurt his feelings."

"Huh?"

"I think talking to him that way really hurt his feelings. Now he won't do anything at all."

Frank jerked himself to his feet, tugged up his trousers, zipped up his fly and got the hell out of there.

Hurt his feelings. God, Stacy was the dumbest mistress he'd had in the last three years.

In the car, he started shaking again and asking himself the same question over and over. *Could he really do what he needed to do? Could he really kill Doyle?*

44

FOR centuries Indians had hauled supplies across this rugged mountain pass. Not until 1916 had a bright young engineer finally figured out how to build a highway on an ascent so steep. Travel got a lot easier except in bitter winter.

There were three of them, Kate, Riki and the man named Runyon, and they kept climbing, up past dark green spruce and up past trees turned a sparkling crystal by ice and up past the sad stiff corpses of deer and elk and antelope. It seemed they would soon be high enough to reach up and pluck the moon from the sky, like a fruit that had ripened and awaited picking.

Kate twice tumbled facedown into the snow because it was thigh-deep and all but impossible to walk through. Riki, exhausted, frustrated and afraid, burst into tears. Kate went to her and held her, saying, "It's all right, it's all right," over and over.

For his part, Runyon said nothing. Because of his parka hood, neither woman had had a good look at him as yet. He was just this lean, expert presence several yards ahead of them who kept looking back to make sure they were all right.

When they finally reached the road, Kate had an image of herself falling to the blacktop and kissing it, the way dignitaries sometimes did when they at last reached their homelands. She smiled. Her lips would stick to blacktop this cold.

She knew why she was trying to joke with herself. She kept trying to forget the sight of Richard Conroy's head exploding. She kept trying to forget her sorrow and rage. He had been an innocent, a gentle and decent man, and in a just world Runyon would have killed Doyle, not merely knocked him out.

The road wound through shadow and moonlight, vanishing around the bend of a steep varicolored cliff, atop which were more dark green spruces.

Here the women caught up with Runyon. They walked as a trio, breath ghostly in the air, footsteps echoing off the canyon wall.

"Do any cars ever come along here?" Riki asked.

"Not very often. Especially in winter," Runyon said.

"Do you have a car?" Kate asked.

"I have a beat-up old truck. When it starts, that is."

"Any chance it might start tonight?" Kate said.

"I sure hope so," Runyon said.

They walked another half mile without saying anything. Every twenty feet or so they saw another dead and frozen animal. One young deer looked especially grim in death, and Kate had to look away quickly, thinking of Conroy again.

To reach Runyon's cabin, they had to leave the road again. As they did so, Runyon nodded to a small frozen animal on the edge of the blacktop. "That's a prairie dog. Believe it or not, at the turn of the century, ranchers around here killed and dressed and shipped them to restaurants back East. They told the restaurant owners that the meat was 'mountain squirrel' and that it was very popular in Colorado. Took the restaurant folks a long time to realize that mountain squirrel was a hoax. All those fancy folks in New York and Boston had been eating plain old prairie dog all along. They didn't think it was very funny."

"You must have made a study of this area," Riki said. She

had stopped crying when they reached the road. Even so small a symbol of civilization as the blacktop had seemed to buoy her.

"When you don't have a phone or a TV set or a radio," Runyon said, "you have a lot of time to read."

There was a snowy straight-up hill and both women took turns falling down when they reached thigh-deep snow again. There was a stand of dark spruce that formed a long wall, so thick the women could see nothing beyond it.

Runyon led them through the spruce, the boughs slapping snow in their faces, filling their nostrils with the sweet scent of resins.

When they emerged on the other side of the spruces, they stood on the top of a hill. Below them, in a valley, was a small cabin crudely made of native wood. In the moonlight, the cabin looked very dark. Only the curling gray smoke from the chimney offered invitation.

"Home sweet home," Runyon said.

"You weren't kidding about not having a phone?" Kate said.

"Afraid not."

"You haven't asked us about what happened," Riki said. "The crash and all. And the shooting."

Inside the furry frame of his parka, Runyon smiled. "Figured I'd save that till we were all huddled around the wood-burning stove with cups of hot tea in our hands."

The women didn't need any more encouragement than that to follow Runyon down the steep, snowy hill.

45

THE wreckage of the missing Cessna 340 was found by a military plane that had flown over the same section earlier without sighting the downed craft.

The pilot of the CAP plane immediately contacted Colonel Marsh, and Colonel Marsh immediately informed the Air Force Rescue Coordination Center at Scott Air Force Base in Illinois.

The contact was made while Colonel Marsh pushed the Jolly Green Giant full out toward the crash site.

Finding a place to set down was difficult. The downslope was approximately a forty-degree slant. Even the Jolly Green Giant had trouble accommodating it.

Before the craft was discovered, the radio had been still most of the time. Now it was busy constantly, Colonel Marsh talking and responding to others.

When the searchlight came on, illuminating the angles and juts and raw torn metal of the wreckage, McGivern's jaw tightened and he shook his head. Who could survive such a crash?

A part of him wanted to leap from the helicopter even before it set down—leap from it and run to the crash and see if he could find Kate somehow alive inside.

Another part of him wanted Colonel Marsh to pull the big

machine back up. This part of him wanted to go no closer. He was terrified of what he would find.

By now, two more helicopters had appeared. The rescue mission was in full operation.

Searchlights played across the ragged rock and blowing white snow as if a Hollywood premiere were taking place.

McGivern glanced up at a small chopper that made a very different sound from the others. He saw the logo of a local TV station on the dark bubble enclosing the craft.

Great, he thought. We don't even know if anybody's alive and the press is already here.

Colonel Marsh had been watching him. He smiled. "Necessary evil in a democracy like ours," he said. "The press, I mean."

"I guess I forget that sometimes."

"Yes," Colonel Marsh said, "so do I."

He took the Jolly Green Giant down to a small flat area just above the overhang where Kate and the others had been tied up.

Before the colonel had time to kill the engines, McGivern was out of the machine, making his way through the deep snow to the wreckage.

It was very cold and the way through the swamp of snow was difficult. But McGivern didn't notice these things. His only awareness was of Kate. Somewhere, she was alive. She had to be.

46

IN the record business, a surprising number of people carried handguns, including some of the stars who feared that one of those strange, kinky kidnap threats just might come true.

Guns scared the hell out of Frank Sayler but in order to overcome this fear, he'd bought a membership in a gun club and started taking lessons.

Standing in line on the practice range, big-ass ear guards making him look like some kind of moonman, Sayler always tried to feel macho—but never did. Because the jerk of the gun always knocked his arm back. Because no matter how long he practiced, he never quite got the hang of it all. Oh, by this time he could hit the target all right but he only rarely hit the bull's-eye.

The parking lot of the Rochester Gun and Saddle Club could have doubled for Spago's. Three silver Rolls-Royces, two red Ferraris, one beautiful antique blue Porsche. The clubhouse itself was a rambling wood and glass structure. The bar overlooked rolling green hills that had been planted with Kentucky bluegrass. Sleek horses the color of saddle leather ran the hills. Every once in a while you saw a young colt walk on tender legs into the presentation area near the track, cute and gawky and heartbreaking all at the same time. The sight always amazed Frank—how vulnerable and fine life was as represented by colts. If only there were time to appreciate all life this way, Frank invariably lamented. To see how gawky and heartbreaking *everybody* was when you took the proper time to see them for what they really were, scared souls in a dark and terrifying universe.

He fired three clips, smiling every once in a while at the nice little blonde Beverly Hills housewife who stood two slots away and nailed the bull's-eye virtually every time. She had one of those droopy middle-aged asses that Frank had curiously come to appreciate with the onset of his own middle age. But he sure wouldn't want to make her mad. Not the way she handled firearms.

When he'd used up the clips, he walked back to the clubhouse and the bar. He didn't own a gun, felt that he didn't want the responsibility. The owner, a Greek named (unimaginatively enough) Gus, always let Frank use one of his. Gus had a frigging arsenal in a small room off his cushy office, an arsenal so vast many Third World countries would envy it.

Frank had a bourbon and branch water and talked to the bartender, a nice kid he'd seen a few times on various TV shows. But the kid had gotten married a while back and now, with a baby on the way, had taken a job at the club here full-time, acting being way too risky for a new father. He was clean-cut and manly and polite, a trio of virtues you didn't find all that often in L.A. Sayler, out of some kind of guilt, always left him lavish tips. When the baby was born, Frank planned on giving the kid five hundred dollars.

"Gus around today, Greg?"

"Afraid not, Frank. He's looking at some property over in the valley. His son's a contractor."

"Uh-huh," Frank said. God, the day finally comes when he's ready to buy a gun and then Gus is gone.

"Is there a waiting period in L.A.?"

"Waiting period?" Greg said. He was sandy-haired with altar-boy good looks and a trim but not narcissistic physique.

He wore a blue short-sleeved dress shirt and tan slacks and a very clean white apron. All Frank could hope was that his own son ended up half as decent as Greg here. Not that Frank had contributed a hell of a lot of time or energy to that end.

"Yeah. Waiting period for buying a handgun."

"Oh. Right. Fourteen days."

"Oh."

"Something wrong, Frank?"

That was another thing about Greg. He could read people like a telepath. Some little thing wrong with your mood and Greg spotted it like radar. Very handy attribute in a bartender.

"I need a gun."

"God, Frank, is everything all right?" Greg sounded concerned.

"Weird phone calls. They're starting to bother me. I'd just feel safer with a gun."

"You can borrow mine."

"You have a gun?"

"Sure. Nothing fancy. An old Smith and Wesson .38. My uncle used to be a cop."

"And you'd let me borrow it?"

"Sure I would, Frank. You're one of my favorite customers."

Greg seemed ready to say more but a customer came in, walked to the far end of the bar and ordered a bottle of imported beer.

While Frank waited for Greg to come back, he looked out the window. There was a horse on a distant hill rearing on its hind legs and it looked so beautiful and mythic, Frank felt his throat constrict. That's what he wanted to do. Get a horse like that and ride off to some faraway land where nobody knew him and where he could feel some self-respect and where he could love a woman in some unfettered way, not as husband, not as sugar daddy, not as powerful record magnate, but just as man. Man. Yes, Frank liked the sound of that. Man. Because deep down he'd never really felt like a man. Like most male Americans of middle age, he was nothing more than an aging boy. But "man." Yes, he really liked the sound of that.

"It's out in my car."

"Huh?" Frank pulled himself from his thoughts.

"It's out in my car. The .38," Greg said.

"Ah."

"If you'll watch the bar here a sec, I'll run out and get it."

"Hey, I'd really appreciate it."

"I'll load it for you."

"You're a great guy, Greg. You really are."

Greg went out of the bar. Frank sat finishing his drink. He glanced down at the bar's only other customer, the man who'd ordered the imported beer.

"Hot one," the man said.

"Very hot."

"Imagine what the summer's going to be like."

"A bitch," Frank said. "That's what the summer's going to be like. A real bitch."

The man nodded and went back to his beer.

Frank, now in a gloomy and philosophical mood, realized that many, too many, conversations in his life had been like this one. Forced, rote, empty. Even conversations with his wife and growing children were like that. Again, he let an impossible Technicolor movie play out in his head. Frank on a steed. Frank in the arms of a woman who knew him intimately and found worth in him despite all his flaws. Frank feeling like an adult for the first time in his life.

"Here you go," Greg said when he got back.

Frank had been ready for him. Two crisp green hundred-dollar bills.

"Oh, no; no, sir, Frank. I don't want any money and I mean it."

Frank smiled. "You take that money and you take that wife of yours out to some fancy restaurant. I'll bet she's a hell of a woman, your wife."

Greg nodded. "She sure is. God, I love her even more now that she's pregnant."

Frank wasn't sure why but he felt tears in his eyes.

Hey, that's all he needed, some gossip about how he'd been sitting in the clubhouse bar the other day with tears in his eyes.

He wrapped his hand around the cold hard metal of the .38, dumped it into the pocket of his sport coat, gave Greg a parting nod and left the bar.

But he couldn't quell the urge to cry a bit, not even when he was on the Santa Monica and hauling ass at well over a hundred.

He kept thinking about how the kid had looked and sounded talking about his pregnant wife. So warm, so loving, so proud.

Not even at the zenith of their love had Frank ever spoken about his own wife that way and now he knew why he wanted to cry. Because he was ashamed of himself for having been such a shit all his life. He had never been a good husband or a good father, just some dreamy aging boy pursuing fleshy fleeting starlets and the kind of ruthless business triumphs that made him feel adult and manly despite a lot of evidence to the contrary.

I'm sorry, honey, he said silently to himself, knowing that he would somehow never say this to her face.

I'm sorry.

47

IN the center of the one-room cabin squatted a bulbous wood-burning stove that cast off heat and light and shadow. The cabin windows were covered with burlap, the splintery wooden floor with a large grubby hook rug, and the walls with various rock and roll posters from the psychedelic era, faded images of Jimi and Janis and the Quicksilver Messenger Service. Simmering atop the stove was a battered pan filled with a stew that smelled good. Vegetarian stew, Runyon had explained. He did not think that any animal should have to lay down its life for his stomach. There was a wobbly bookcase overburdened with paperbacks that ran to sixties cult novels such as *Been Down So Long It Looks Like Up to Me* and *Beautiful Losers*. Against one wall was a spavined cot piled high with faded but warm-looking cotton blankets. Set on the back of the stove was a teakettle that had whistled a few moments before.

He served them steaming peppermint tea in big ceramic mugs. As they drank it, the three of them sat before the stove, getting warm and letting the heat dry their clothes.

"His name's Doyle?"

Riki nodded.

"And he's your manager?"

She sipped tea, nodded again.

"Did you ever think he was capable of killing somebody?"

She took a long time to respond. "I knew he was violent. I didn't think that—what he did to Mr. Conroy, I mean—I didn't think he was capable of that."

"I didn't either," Kate said. "Not until this morning."

Kate shuddered and raised her eyes to Runyon. Once he had been a handsome man, she could see. He had good bones and startling brown eyes. But time and weather had dried and lined his face harshly so that there was an almost simian tightness to his cheeks and jaw. The rock posters on the wall would mark him as being fifty or so. Some of those years appeared to have been very, very hard ones.

"Are we anywhere near Denver?" Riki said.

"A few hours away."

Kate and Riki both stared at Runyon. Ever since Kate had brought up the truck, he'd become nervous.

"Is everything all right, Mr. Runyon?" Kate said.

"Sure, uh, everything's fine." He stared down into his mug. "Well, I guess there's one thing."

"What is it, Mr. Runyon?" Riki said.

He raised his head, his eyes meeting Kate's. "The law."

"The law?" she said.

"I don't want to get involved in this."

"I see."

They sat silently for a time. The warmth of the stove and the warmth of the tea replenished Kate. She wanted to get to civilization and phone McGivern and tell him everything was all right. She wanted to sic the police on Doyle. But she kept thinking of poor Conroy.

"Mr. Runyon," Riki said, "there's no reason you need to get involved. If you'll just give us a ride into town."

"That I'll be happy to do."

"Then there's no problem."

"You won't mention me to the police?" Runyon said.

"No," Kate said.

"I know how ominous this all sounds," he said. "I was accused of something I didn't do."

"You don't need to explain yourself," Kate said.

He jumped suddenly to his feet. "Why don't I see if I can get that old truck running."

"We'd really appreciate that," Kate said.

He went over to the cot and picked up his parka and shrugged into it. Once again, his face darkened by the frame of the hood, Runyon became a mystery man.

He walked over to a toolbox by the door. He spent two minutes searching through unseen tools that clanged and clanked as he tossed them around. Finally, his hand reappeared. It was filled with a long, greasy wrench and a hammer.

Lofting the wrench, he said, "This is what I use when I try and finesse her." Then he lofted the hammer. "This is what I use when finesse doesn't work."

He went to the cabin door, opened it. The wind was calmer now. There was just the still white silence of the mountains and the mad luminous eye of the moon.

He went out, closing the door behind him.

"I wonder why he's so afraid of the law," Riki said.

"I'm willing to take his word that he's innocent."

"I guess I am, too."

They were quiet. Kate sipped her tea. She was trembling. She wanted to ask Riki what this was all about.

She had just started to speak when Riki said, "When Brad Doyle discovered me, I had already signed a ten-year contract with another manager."

In the soft yellow glow from the stove, Riki looked younger and more frightened than ever. "He used to book me into places like Vegas. Me, Vegas, if you can believe that." She shook her head. "Anyway, Brad really came after me. He even offered to buy my manager out but Andy wouldn't sell.

He had a bunch of low-level rock acts and he could never book them into 'decent' places. I could go into those decent places, not because I was so good, but because I was quiet and respectable. You know? Brad came to every show I ever did. He started to show me the plans he had for my career. I was impressed. Even though he hadn't had any experience at being a manager, I saw that he knew what he was doing.

"Then something happened to Andy. He was an alcoholic, a bad one. He was found dead in his car one morning, in his garage. The police ruled the death accidental asphyxiation. I wasn't sure I believed that but I didn't say anything. I mean, I didn't have any proof or anything. After the funeral, Brad went to Andy's widow and made her an offer on my contract. She accepted. Brad started managing my career."

Riki set her mug down, put her small hands very near the stove, massaged warmth into them. "I've never known how David Greene came by it, but somehow he turned up something that proved that Brad actually murdered Andy. I'm not sure of that, of course. But I think that's what David had on Brad. And Brad paid him a lot of money. The trouble is—" She hesitated, rubbing her hands together again. "The trouble is, you can push somebody like Brad only so far. He has a violent temper anyway. When the resentment and rage build up . . . And I think that David recently asked for even more money. Otherwise he was going to take his evidence to the Japanese. Given everything they've got invested in me—well, it would have been a terrible situation all around."

As she listened to Riki speak, Kate thought of her friend David. No matter what she heard about him, she couldn't bring herself to hate him. With the burden of his daughter, with wanting to give his entire family a safe haven from an increasingly violent world, David had turned to blackmail. No, despite her disappointment and her anger with David, she could not bring herself to hate him. Like all human beings, he was flawed. Like many human beings, he had rationalized and justified and become a criminal. She couldn't even hate him for dragging her into the situation. Obviously, he'd never thought she would have to risk her life holding the second key to the safe-deposit box.

"Did Doyle tell you all this?" Kate said.

"Not much of it. But when you spend as much time with somebody as I do with Brad—well, it wasn't hard to figure out what's going on."

"So in the safe-deposit box—"

"In the safe-deposit box, Kate, is the information David used to blackmail Brad Doyle with. I don't know what it is, or what form it's in, but Brad knows he has to get it before Mrs. Greene opens the box and turns the information over to the police."

"And that's it? That's everything?"

For just a moment, Riki averted her gaze from Kate's. For just a moment, she unwittingly gave Kate the impression that she was keeping back some other piece of information.

"That's it," Riki said. "All of it."

She quickly turned her eyes to the stove. "Thank God for Mr. Runyon. I don't know what we would have done if he hadn't come along."

Kate wanted to ask her more—given the circumstances, she felt she was entitled to know everything that was going on—but then they heard the truck motor turn over and burst into shaky life.

"It's running!" Riki said.

She struggled to her feet, ran to the door, threw it open.

In the frozen silence of the mountain night, the sound of the truck motor, however tentative, brought home images of the life Kate was familiar with—shelter and warmth and safety.

Soon they would be out of these mountains and back to civilization.

She only wished that David and Richard Conroy would be there when she returned.

Runyon came to the doorway. He threw his parka hood back and shot the women an exultant grin. "It sounds a little rough but I think it'll get us to town." He laughed. "I wasn't sure the goddamn thing was even going to start. Excuse my French."

Riki laughed, exultant as Runyon. "Use all the French you want, Mr. Runyon. Use all the French you want!"

By now, Kate was on her feet and grabbing her coat. She had forgotten her sense that Riki was withholding something and joined in the spirit of the moment. "That's right, Mr. Runyon. Use all the French you want!"

Kate and Riki got ready for the cold weather again, then followed Runyon out to the ancient black panel truck. Even in the midnight shadows, rust showed clearly along the lines of fenders and doors. The right windshield panel had long ago been shattered and was now little more than a silver spiderweb. The tires looked low. The radio antenna had been snapped in half. But none of this mattered. The headlights burned with triumphant ferocity and the motor, despite the fact that it sounded about to shake and shudder its way into death at any moment, throbbed with stubborn life.

"Get in!" Runyon shouted above the engine.

Kate sat next to the door, Riki between them. Kate couldn't see much in the back except for deep shadow. There was a dash ashtray that smelled of ancient dead cigarettes and a floor transmission with a hula-girl gearshift knob jammed atop it and a heater that roared tinnily and poured forth only flesh-numbing cold air and a floorboard that trembled with every pulsating stroke of the engine.

Runyon cranked the stick transmission into first gear.

"Hold on," he said, nodding to the small hill they would have to climb before reaching the road. "I always make it up there but it takes a few tries."

Kate leaned her head back, felt a girlish rush of pure pleasure. Soon she would see Robert McGivern, hold him, tell him that they'd waited long enough to get married.

She was thinking this when Brad Doyle came up from beneath the tarpaulin in back and put the gun flush against the back of Runyon's head.

"Let's go," Doyle said. "I want to be in Denver for the first flight out."

48

ON a fishing trip when he was seven years old, McGivern had seen the aftermath of a bad car wreck when his father pulled off the highway to see if there was any way he could help.

Curiously, what McGivern remembered most clearly about the wreck were the smells, so many different odors filling the air when a complicated piece of machinery like an automobile was torn apart.

Now, standing downwind from the plane wreckage, he recalled that long-ago day. The debris of the Cessna offered a similar variety of odors—oil, gasoline, lubricating fluids.

As he looked at the wreckage, McGivern could imagine the terror Kate must have felt as the plane tore into the mountainside.

He took several steps forward, wind flapping his trench coat. The impossible thing was that everybody aboard had survived. Or presumably so, anyway. While he'd found some blood inside with his flashlight, the passengers had walked away from the crash.

But where had they gone?

By this time, the mountainside was well lighted. Two additional helicopters had appeared, adding their searchlights to the wide sprawl of ragged rock, deep snow and twisted debris.

A young man appeared and jarred McGivern from his

thoughts. "Sir, I'm Corporal Chaney. The colonel asked me to show you something." Chaney, who was dressed in fatigues and parka, glanced down at McGivern's feet. "There's an extra pair of buckle boots in our helicopter, sir. If you'll wait a minute, I'll get them for you."

"We're going where exactly?"

Chaney, a young man with a brown crew cut and an eager, midwestern face, pointed upward and into the darkness. "There's an overhang up there I thought you might want to see."

McGivern nodded. "Thanks."

"I'll be right back, sir."

Chaney ran back to the second Jolly Green Giant to put down on the mountainside tonight. He returned in less than a minute bearing a pair of black rubber boots.

When McGivern leaned very close, he could smell the remnants of the fire that had been built beneath the overhang.

He stood up, checked the shale around the fire carefully. The ground was filled with footprints. No doubt about it, they'd only left here a while ago.

But where had they gone? And why?

The beam of his light paused on several small worms of rope. He bent down, picked up two pieces. They'd been sawn with a knife of some kind—not cut clean and quick, but sawn, indicating that the task hadn't been an easy one.

"Sir."

McGivern looked out to the right. In the moonlight, Chaney, downslope, appeared to be bent over something in the snow. Chaney had his flashlight beam trained on the white ground.

"You'd better come down here, sir."

"Be right with you," McGivern called.

The pines smelled fresh. The night was beautiful. McGivern made his way carefully. He could only envy Chaney. The kid took to these hills like a strong young mountain lion.

Even with the buckle boots, the deep snow managed to fill up McGivern's shoes and dampen his socks. He held a momentary image of himself and his brother as youngsters sledding out by the old baseball stadium and its endless succession of hills.

All his nostalgia died as soon as he saw what Chaney's flashlight revealed in the snow.

The top of the man's head was gone completely. Blood and brain matter had turned the surrounding snow a deep red color. The man's gloved hands were claws, as if he'd been trying to crawl away in the last moments of his life.

"Know him, sir?"

"I'm not sure."

Much as he didn't want to, McGivern knelt down next to the man and rolled his body over several inches for a better look at the face.

"Richard Conroy," McGivern said, remembering a framed photograph he'd seen earlier back at the flying service. "He was the pilot."

McGivern stood up. His eyes scanned the moonlit snow. The tracks were unmistakable. Three sets of them leading west, to the small forest and beyond.

"You see these tracks, Chaney?"

"Yessir."

"I'm going to follow them. I need you to call Colonel Marsh and tell him that."

"Yessir."

Chaney got on the radio mounted on his belt. He raised Colonel Marsh and conveyed McGivern's message.

"Tell him to wait there for me," Colonel Marsh said.

"Yessir."

After Chaney clicked off, he said, "Did you hear that, sir?"

"Yes, I did. And thank you."

Chaney's eyes moved once more to the body in the snow. "He sounds like a bad one, sir. This Brad Doyle, I mean."

"He's that, all right," McGivern said.

"I hope you get him."

"Yes," McGivern said, thinking of Kate. "So do I."

Five minutes later, Colonel Marsh was there. He took his turn examining the corpse and shaking his head.

He came over and stood by McGivern and Chaney. "The way the snow has started to drift over the footprints, I'd say they've got about a ninety-minute start on us."

"Then we'd better go," McGivern said.

Colonel Marsh nodded, gave Chaney some instructions. Then he said, "You ready?"

"I'm ready."

They set off.

49

THE first time he ever slept with her, he was twenty-six years old and he was having some erectile problems. He wasn't sure why. There was this great loneliness in him and suddenly all the little chickies always available looked foolish or cynical or sleazy. What did they know about loneliness? Before he could enjoy sex again, he had to unload his loneliness. It was like excising a tumor.

He got in bed with her one night and he couldn't do anything. He was fine right up until the last moment, but then . . .

This was only their third date. He was mortified.

After a long silence, she said, "It's my fault."

"Huh?"

"You know. What happened."

"Don't be silly."

"I've seen some of your girlfriends."

"You have?"

"Oh, sure. You're in the tabloids with them."

"Well, I—"

"I'm not up to standard. That's all."

"You're very attractive."

"Yes, attractive. But not beautiful. Not glamorous."

"This is crazy."

"If I was better-looking, this wouldn't have happened."

"You're wrong. This isn't your fault at all."

"They have beautiful faces and beautiful bodies and beautiful voices and—"

"You're very good-looking. You know you are."

"But I'll bet there's one thing I have over those girls."

"There are a lot of things you—"

"How much I care for you."

"Huh?"

"How crazy I am about you."

"Crazy? About me?"

"From the first time we met."

"Really?"

She laughed.

"I'm in love with you and you don't even know it, do you?"

"You're in love with me?"

"See, I told you you didn't know it."

No woman had ever told him she loved him. He'd had flings but love wasn't a part of flings.

"You really love me?"

"Umm-hmm."

"Why?"

"Because we're alike."

"We are?"

"We're lonely people."

And the moment she said that, the moment she identified what was in his most secret heart, he loved her, loved her more deeply and more truly than he'd ever loved any other human being before.

She'd reached across the darkness and touched him and he was instantly erect. He never had the problem again. Ever.

But he didn't even care about that. He just cared that he had found somebody who knew what it was like not to fit, not to be fashionable, not to be sought after.

"I love you, too," he'd said in the sweet spring darkness of that long-ago night. "I love you, too."

Now, all these years later, she stood in front of her husband, Frank Sayler, on the flagstone walk surrounding their Brentwood swimming pool.

He was stretched out on a chaise lounge. His two daughters were in the pool. Their laughter was as silver as the water they swam in. It was dark. Japanese lanterns swung in the gloom like red and yellow and blue cartoon fireflies. An illegal alien named Maria poured Frank another bourbon and water. She had a nice bottom, did Maria.

"I'm over here, Frank," his wife said.

"I can see you fine." And he could. She wore some kind of gold lamé outfit. She looked good in it. She was trim and tight and if no longer quite vivacious, she still had that sad killer smile of hers, half sister, half lover. She wore her hair short and bobbed in the fashion of the season.

"You can't see me when you're staring at Maria's tush."

He immediately repaired his eyes to his wife's face.

Impossible to believe this was the same woman with whom he had shared that special darkness that night of so many years ago when she'd identified them both as lonely people. The first five years had been so good. God, he hadn't been able to get enough of her in any sense. Hell, he even resented their first daughter because she deprived him of his wife. Frank had the first affair and a shabby little one it was, too, a Venice cocktail waitress who gave him the clap. He'd wanted to make sure that he didn't fall in love. He certainly picked the right one for that. He had twenty-one affairs (he kept count) before his wife had number one. Her first set the pattern for all the others. She was forever taking college courses, everything from astronomy to Zen, and most if not all her lovers were professors. As she got older, they got younger. In recent years, she'd been doing associate professors and teaching assistants. It was only a matter of time before she turned her sad and somewhat frantic lust on students who were not much older than her own children.

She stood before him, sixteen years his wife now, the sum of such parts as three face-lifts, a five-day-a-week aerobics class, a three-day-a-week session with a lesbian psychotherapist, an inclination to tears and belligerent drinking on the occasions of their wedding anniversary and her own birthday and a benumbing guilt for her quite real failures as a mother. She didn't see the girls much more than Frank did.

"You're going out?" he said.

"Meeting."

"Ah." They almost never had sex—indeed, she seemed to have a real aversion to being touched by him in any way—when she was in the first sixty days of a new affair. There was an almost painful restlessness about her when it was fresh and good with a new man. He saw that restlessness in her face now. Even though he was long past loving her in any way, he felt sad looking at her now. Sad . . . but he had no idea why.

He nodded to the sweet noisy girls in the pool. "Do you think they'll ever forgive us?"

"I doubt it. And I don't blame them." She paused. "I'm afraid for you, Frank."

"Afraid for me?" Her words startled him. "Why?"

"Tonight, when you were taking a shower, Maria was setting your sport jacket on the laundry hamper and she found a gun in it. And then at dinner—"

She nodded to his hand.

His eyes followed her gaze.

His hand. Wrapped around the drink. Shaking. All the way up his goddamned arm he was shaking.

"Are you going to tell me what's wrong?"

"Just some business things."

"The Japanese?"

He shrugged. "Things will be fine."

"Is that why the gun? What the hell's the gun all about, Frank?"

"Do you suppose you're looking for your son?"

"What?"

"They get younger and younger, Ann. You shouldn't take those goddamned Polaroids all the time." She always had her men pose outside of places they went, theaters, the beach, art galleries. "You know how you always wanted a son? Maybe that's what the young men are really all about."

She smiled. There was a melancholy in her eyes now, one almost painful to see. "If I'm looking for a son, then you must be looking for a daughter, Frank. Even though you've got two perfectly wonderful ones right here." She leaned forward, all high hypnotic perfume and clacking wooden bracelets, and kissed him gently on the cheek. "I don't love you anymore, Frank, but I still worry about you. Be careful, all right? Everybody you know is a ruthless bastard, Frank, a lot more ruthless than you'll ever be." She smiled, and in so doing resembled the tender young woman who'd so long ago recognized the loneliness in each of them. "You just *think* you're a ruthless bastard, Frank."

Then she was gone and for the first time in twenty years, he found himself with that old raw loneliness again. He'd pissed it all away . . .

When the phone rang, he reached for it abruptly, the hand lifting the receiver trembling badly.

He listened, muttered something, cupped the phone and then said, "Darcy, it's for you."

Darcy came over shaking off water like a young collie.

He just sat there numb, looking at the empty space where his wife had been. He felt a vast and abiding loneliness . . .

50

"I want the knife."

"The knife?"

Doyle put the gun to the back of Kate's head and said, "You used a knife to cut your ropes in the mountains. I want it."

She'd had no choice but to give it to him.

This had been five minutes ago . . .

Several times Doyle told Runyon to drive faster. His command did little good. Flat out, the truck went 46 mph.

For all the noise it made, the heater was little help. Kate sat huddled against the front door, shivering. Her nose was plugged. Her throat was starting to feel raw. Her job was to work the yellow plastic scraper. Every few miles, the windshield would be covered with a furry silver frost. She leaned over and cleared as much of the glass as possible and thought of how ridiculous it was. Despite the fact that she was in real danger of losing her life, what really bothered her at the moment was the discomfort of it all—the truck interior that reeked of gasoline, the fingers and toes in which there was no feeling, the flu-like achiness that was starting to spread throughout her body. And then on top of all this, the true problem, that Doyle was a real killer. She could not stop thinking of Richard Conroy.

"What time is it?" Doyle said from the back.

"Nearly midnight," Riki said.

"How much farther to Denver?"

"An hour or so. If the truck makes it," Runyon said.

"What the hell's that supposed to mean?"

"Well, if you've been paying any attention, Mr. Doyle, you've probably noticed that this isn't the most reliable engine a guy could have. It's starting to overheat pretty bad."

"It better make it," Doyle said.

Kate looked out the window. Two or three times she'd wondered about escaping by opening the door and tumbling into a snowbank. The mountain road was narrow and buffered on both sides by walls of snow. In the moonlight, the snow appeared white and festive, perfect for skiing, sledding and building cute plump snowmen. But she knew better. It would be covered by a glaze of ice and when a human body was hurled against it at forty-some miles per hour—

The narrow blacktop road wound continuously downward. Runyon was a good driver. Only rarely did the rear end slide on patches of ice, only rarely did he have to apply the brakes when heading into a deep curve.

"Pretty soon I'm going to need a gas station," Runyon said. "It's really overheating—"

"Wait till we get to Denver."

"That's my point. We won't make Denver if we don't get some water in the rad soon."

"Maybe you're lying."

"Maybe I am, Doyle, but it won't do any of us any good to get stranded in these mountains."

Doyle cursed again. "Where the hell would we find a gas station out here, anyway?"

"Down in the foothills. About twenty minutes from here there's one."

"Open all night?"

"Right. Open all night."

"I still think you're lying."

"Well, I guess the only way I can prove I'm not is for the truck to stop running."

They drove two more miles. Riki sneezed several times. Twice she gripped Kate's hand and squeezed. Kate squeezed back.

After another mile or so, Kate raised the yellow scraper again and sheared the ice into a crystal version of wood shavings.

As she worked, she glanced at Runyon. He didn't even seem to be watching the road. He looked lost in thought. Kate wondered what he was thinking about.

Either way he went, Runyon thought, he was in mortal danger. On the one hand, he fully expected Doyle to kill him as soon as he felt Runyon was no longer of any use. Runyon had snuck up behind Doyle on the overhang just as Doyle had shot and killed Richard Conroy. Doyle had grunted "You sonofabitch" just as the top of Conroy's head flew into a dozen pieces. Runyon had no doubt he was dealing with a sociopath.

But even if he did manage to escape somehow, he would inevitably be drawn into the police investigation that would follow. And a police investigation meant that he would be found out as the man he really was—the runaway advertising executive accused of killing his boss. Runyon would end up in prison.

There was only one hope. The more he considered it, the more impossible it sounded. But what choice did he have?

As he drove, the freezing temperature causing him to cough, Runyon began refining his plan.

If he could just lure Doyle into the combination gas station and convenience store down in the foothills . . .

Next to him, the two women looked miserable, frozen, terrified, hopeless.

He wished there were some way he could tell them about his idea.

If nothing else, it might give them a few moments of false hope.

Right now, even false hope was better than nothing . . .

"How you doing?"

Doyle's voice brought Runyon from his revery. At first, he wasn't sure who Doyle was addressing. His voice was different somehow, almost tender.

"I want you to let them go, Brad."

"I can't, babe. You know that."

"Then there's nothing for us to talk about, Brad. Nothing."

A few times tonight, Runyon had noticed that Doyle had looked almost longingly at Riki. He'd wondered what their relationship was all about. Now, given Doyle's gentle tone of voice, he wondered again.

The truck wound down the mountain blacktop.

Runyon kept the gas pedal flat to the floor. He was eager to get to the gas station and see if his plan would work.

51

HE stood in the doorway of the TV room watching his two daughters giggle over the new Elton John music video. MTV had premiered it yesterday and had immediately put it into heavy rotation. In this one, Elton did a soft-shoe with the cartoon characters Tom and Jerry and the result was an inspired and very funny video.

"Hi, Dad," Kerry said, glimpsing him over her shoulder.

Darcy didn't even turn around. Just waved backward.

Darcy was older by a year, just about fifteen. Both girls had dark hair cut short, both girls wore the colorful tunics over stretch pants popular this year and both girls were heartbreakingly cute. Not beautiful but the next best thing—engagingly, entrancingly cute.

After Elton John came Paula Abdul and after Paula came Guns n' Roses, a group he despised. Kids came by prejudice naturally, usually passed down by a parent. They didn't need any help from an overpaid and overpriced group of mediocrities like this one.

He walked into the room and sat on the edge of the leather couch. The room was large and box-like, its walls covered with autographed celebrity photographs. The girls were too young to be impressed with the people shown in the glossy pictures.

"Hi, Pop, everything all right?" Darcy said, turning to him now that they were into a commercial break. She always called him "Pop," the way daughters always did on those old black-and-white sitcoms she loved so much.

"Just thought I'd come in and see how my girls are."

Kerry looked at Darcy and laughed. "Something *is* wrong."

"Yeah, imagine Pop coming in and sitting down with us."

"Very funny," he said, a bit more defensively than he'd intended.

"Well, you don't exactly spend a lot of time with us, you have to admit," Darcy said.

"You're busy. And so is Mom. We understand. That's just how it is," Kenny added.

"I try to be adult about it," Darcy said. Then she smiled. "I heard that line on *Father Knows Best* yesterday. Betty was trying to explain to Bud how she felt about getting turned down for the prom by this real hunky football star." She giggled. "Well, hunky by 1954 standards. By today's standards, the guy was actually a geek."

Kerry laughed, too.

"So," Frank Sayler said, "how's it been going?"

"How has what been going?" Kerry said.

"You know," Frank said. "Things."

"Things?" Darcy said.

"School. Stuff like that."

"Oh, God," Kerry said to her sister. "Do you know what this is?"

"Huh-uh."

"It's Dad's annual attempt at having a heart-to-heart talk," Kerry said. "Cloris Leachman did the same thing on an episode of *Phyllis* once. It was pretty pathetic."

"He wants to tell us how much he loves us."

"And how he wishes he had more time to be with us."

"And how when he was a kid, his pop didn't have much time for him, either."

"And how sometimes he wishes he could just load us up

in his car and drive us far away where we could spend the rest of eternity together."

"And," said Darcy, deepening her voice in imitation of her father, "I want to see what my two little daughters are doing in school."

"Shouldn't I be interested in how my daughters are doing?" Frank said, a certain desperation in his voice. When they mocked him this way, he realized how transparent and clichéd he'd become to them. And to himself.

The doorbell rang.

"Want me to get it, Pop?" Kerry said.

"That's what we have Maria for," Frank said.

Darcy giggled. "So *that's* why we have Maria. I knew there was some reason." Her sister started giggling, too.

Frank consulted his Rolex. Near midnight. Who the hell would be at the door near midnight?

Distantly, he heard the front door being opened and Maria showing somebody in. Again he wondered, *Who would be here near midnight?*

He heard Maria's wide fat feet slapping the tiled hallway leading to the TV room.

She put her brown head mere inches inside the door and said, "Mr. Sayler. You have a visitor."

"A visitor? Now?"

She nodded. "Yes. His name is Grogan and he's from the Los Angeles Police Department."

The girls looked at each other and laughed. "Looks like Pop is in big trouble," Darcy said.

"Sounds like he's going to get the chair."

They laughed some more.

Frank got to his feet.

His stomach was suddenly in terrible condition. Bile rose in his throat and for a terrible moment he was afraid he was going to vomit on the spot.

52

MCGIVERN and Colonel Marsh found Runyon's cabin at 1:37A.M. They had had a relatively easy time of following the footprints through the snow.

Though the cabin was dark, both men drew their weapons before entering.

Once they got the kerosene lantern lighted, they examined the one-room cabin carefully. A fire still burned heartily in the stove. They found three different sets of footprints on the wooden floor, presumably belonging to the same three people they'd followed through the snow.

McGivern looked carefully for any signs of struggle. He found none. He tried to take some hope from this.

"They had some tea," Marsh said, pointing to three ceramic mugs. "But I wonder where the hell they went."

"I'm going back outside. Why don't you keep looking around in here?"

"Fine."

The heat of the cabin had started to slow McGivern down. He was grateful for the harsh cold air of the outdoors.

He took his flashlight and started walking around the cabin. It didn't take him long to find the tire prints of the vehicle, the wide tracks indicating that it was a truck of some kind.

In one spot he found drops of motor oil tainting the snow.

A few feet away he found where the tire marks were very deep, indicating that the truck had been parked here for some time.

In all likelihood, the truck belonged to the owner of the cabin. Had the man—or woman?—used his vehicle to take Kate and Riki to safety?

McGivern looked around some more, his footsteps the only sound in the vast white night.

It took him several minutes to realize that there were not three but four sets of footprints. The fourth came up a small slope, coming at the cabin from a different angle. The tracks led to where the back of the truck must have been resting.

The tracks did not lead to the cabin, which McGivern found most curious. Why wouldn't the fourth person have gone into the cabin? Why would he stop at the truck?

McGivern looked for the fourth set of prints to lead away from the area of the vehicle. If he hadn't gone inside, maybe the fourth person had walked back the way he'd come.

But McGivern found no tracks leading back to the slope.

So the person had come up to the truck and stopped.

But why? And what had he done, simply stood outside in the raw night cold?

A terrible image came to McGivern. What if the fourth person did not want the others to know he was out here? What if the fourth person had climbed inside the truck to surprise the others when they came out?

Was the fourth person Brad Doyle? Had Doyle somehow gotten separated from the others and then ambushed them in some way?

"Couldn't find anything else," Colonel Marsh said, coming out of the cabin. The windows were dark again. He'd turned off the kerosene lantern. He closed the door snugly behind him.

"Something odd went on here."

"Oh?"

"Over here."

McGivern walked Marsh through everything.

"You think the last set of prints belonged to Doyle?"

"Probably."

"You've got a point."

Cold snow sprayed in McGivern's face, the residue of an idle wind. He walked to the edge of the hill and pointed to the blacktop road. "Where does that lead?"

"To a few villages. Nothing special."

"How far away from Denver are we?"

Colonel Marsh told him. "You think that's where they went?"

"I imagine. If they were healthy enough to travel any great distance."

Colonel Marsh patted his walkie-talkie. "I can have somebody start checking the hospitals. See if they're there."

"I hope that's where they are." McGivern raised his eyes to the starry night. Up here you had the feeling you could talk directly to God. No intermediaries to make up their own rules for you. Now he spoke directly to God. Asked Him to spare Kate's life.

Colonel Marsh spent the next few minutes on the walkie-talkie. Its crackling transmission noise seemed almost obscene in these pristine mountains.

"They're checking all the area hospitals and the Highway Patrol," Colonel Marsh said as McGivern walked over to him.

"Then alert the airports at Denver, Colorado Springs and Pueblo. Denver is farthest away but he might use it, anyway, to throw us off."

"The airport?"

"Yes," McGivern said. "Doyle seems desperate to get to Los Angeles. There's at least a small possibility he'll try to get the first plane out."

Colonel Marsh nodded and thumbed his radio into squawking life again.

53

"YOU know Mr. Doyle, then?"

"Of course."

"You work with him?"

"He's Riki's manager."

"Riki being the singer?"

"Yes."

"You know what happened in Chicago—" The detective consulted his wristwatch.

"Yes, unfortunately. David Greene was a very decent man."

"Everybody seems to agree on that." Pause. "Do you know why Mr. Doyle would want to shoot somebody as decent as David Greene?"

Frank Sayler listened hard for any trace of sarcasm in Detective Grogan's voice. He couldn't find any.

They sat out by the pool. The girls had gone to bed—reluctantly. His wife wasn't home yet. He felt utterly alone, Frank did. Utterly.

Detective Grogan was apparently unfamiliar with the concept of lung cancer. He had been here twenty minutes and had already smoked two cigarettes. He was just now lighting his third. He was big, even chunky, and balding. He looked uncomfortable in his dark suit, like a blue-collar man dressed up for a funeral.

There were birds in the warm California night. Sayler

wished one of them would swoop down and sweep him away.

"I guess I don't know of any reason Brad Doyle would have killed David."

"They got along?"

"As far as I knew."

"We've been led to believe that Doyle is coming here."

"Really?"

"Yes. Would you know why?"

"Why he's coming here?"

"Right."

"I guess not."

"Do you know Mr. Doyle well?"

"Not well, I suppose. But well enough."

"How about Riki? Do you know her well?"

Sayler shrugged. "Probably about as well as I know Doyle."

"Have you ever looked into her background?"

"Sure. When we signed her to a contract. The recording company, I mean."

"What did you find?"

"Not much. Nothing untoward, if that's what you mean."

"Then you did better than we did."

"Pardon?"

"We couldn't find much at all."

Frank Sayler realized that Detective Grogan had begun to study him very closely.

"Have you been in touch with Mr. Doyle?"

"No."

"You're sure?"

"Positive."

Frank knew he was sweating. He imagined that his entire body was glistening. He imagined that even a child could tell he was lying.

"You're not under oath, Mr. Sayler, but it sure wouldn't look right if we found out later that you were lying."

"I'm not lying."

"You haven't heard from Brad Doyle since the shooting yesterday morning in Chicago?"

"No."

"You're sure?"

"I'm sure."

The detective exhaled a great deal of smoke. He nodded to the pool. "That's always been a dream of mine. A pool like that."

"The funny thing is, I rarely use it."

His eyes rested on Frank again. "They don't have pools in prison."

"That's not very subtle."

"No, I don't suppose it is. But then neither is prison."

"I haven't heard from him."

"And if you did hear from him, you'd notify us immediately?"

"Immediately."

Detective Grogan stood up. Looked around the flagstone pool. "Bet you have some nice parties here."

"The recording industry's in a slump right now. Not as many parties as there used to be." He nodded to the gate in the terraced wall. "I can show you a shortcut to your car."

Detective Grogan smiled. "Are you trying to get rid of me, Mr. Sayler?"

After Grogan left, Frank went into one of the downstairs bathrooms and vomited.

54

RUNYON still liked violent movies. He couldn't understand it. He couldn't justify it, either. He'd lived in the wild for years now and had put away the things of the city—the greed, the jealousy, the pettiness, the constant, sapping anger. In his new and more mature incarnation, he preferred the soft blue breezes of spring to the adulterous kiss; and the chill pure beauty of spring water to the benumbing effects of gin. And yet . . . on those occasions when he packed himself off to Denver for a city day, he invariably wound up at one of the big mall cineplexes . . . and he invariably chose an action picture with lots of fistfights and gunfights and car fights, Gene Autry movies of his youth . . . only with blood and bare breasts and epithets so foul even he was sometimes shocked.

A year ago Runyon had seen a movie where the heroine had made a daring escape on the drive of a gas station.

Runyon was going to try and pull the same escape tonight, and his good, trusty, lovingly inscribed cigarette lighter was going to help him.

It was one of those convenience stores that only incidentally sold gas. Inside you could buy milk, eggs, shotgun shells, newspapers, condoms, microwaved hamburgers, and play one of three state lottery machines. On the graveyard shift, you often found a sad-faced man who had been a happily employed factory worker until six months before when the latest recession infected the economy like a virus. The guy would be sleepy because he wasn't used to staying up so late and he would be a little stiff because being sociable wasn't a part of his normal job and he would be a little slow in responding to questions because there was actually a lot to learn about the job and he made no claims to being a mastermind. He probably had a wife and three youngsters at home. He longed to be with them in that warm family darkness and not out here shivering through the night with drunken teenagers and stoned truck drivers and easterners crazy enough to drive through the winter night.

Symons, his name was, Donald Symons, and he was leaning on the register and smoking one of the Kents his wife was after him to quit when the ancient black panel truck pulled in.

He knew immediately that something was wrong. He didn't know how he knew. He just knew. He had been working at the convenience store three months and dreading this moment. You saw it on TV all the time. Some poor bastard on the graveyard shift in some convenience store getting his head blown off.

Maybe it was the way the truck just sat there for long minutes with nobody getting out. Maybe it was the way the driver glanced into the store every few seconds, his expression clearly troubled.

Something was wrong. Something . . .

There was a trooper named Malley who came in every night—he'd been in earlier this evening, in fact—and he was always telling Don the same thing. You think you got problems out here, you just pick up that phone and we'll have somebody here in five minutes. And that's a promise.

Don glanced down at the phone beneath the cash register.

Pick it up. Punch out a few numbers. A Highway Patrol car would come right away.

But what if he was wrong? What if nothing was going on in that old black panel truck at all? What if it was only some drunken teenager, or some couple and she wasn't quite finished with him yet (that had happened to him his second night here; he'd gone out on the drive to check out a car and he saw a very pretty blonde girl with her face buried in her boyfriend's lap). He'd feel embarrassed and stupid, calling for no reason like that.

His eyes returned to the drive. The black panel truck still sat there. Nobody getting out.

"I'm going to get out with you and I'm going to stand right at the front of the truck and watch you put the gas in and if you do one thing I don't like, I'm going to kill you on the spot. You understand me?"

To emphasize his point, Doyle jammed the pistol into the back of Runyon's head.

"I understand," Runyon said. In the palm of his hand, the lighter was getting warm with his sweat. He had persuaded Doyle that in addition to adding water they might as well get some gas, too.

"You two sit here and don't do anything," Doyle said, gesturing at the women.

Neither Kate nor Riki acknowledged him in any way.

Doyle crawled to the back of the truck, opened the door. Cold mountain wind clattered through the wide cavity of the panel truck. Doyle jumped to the ground and closed the door.

Runyon sat there, watching the drive.

A few moments later, Doyle appeared, standing in front of the truck, his gun obvious in the pocket of his overcoat. In the blanched light of the drive, he looked older and tired but still angry. Very angry.

"Wish me luck," Runyon said, and got out of the truck.
"Fill it up and let's get the hell out of here," Doyle said.
Runyon nodded and walked back to the gas pump.

Odd, Don Symons thought. The way the guy in the over-coat had gotten out of the back of the truck.
Why would a nice city-dressed fella be riding in the back of an old panel truck?
And why had he walked around the front of the truck to simply stand and observe the driver putting in the gas? Why hadn't the city-dressed fella put in the gas himself?
Don Symons glanced down at the phone again. Just a few numbers. Just a few seconds. And the Highway Patrol would be here. Checking these folks out.
He had just decided to pick up the phone when he saw the guy pumping gas do something unbelievable.
The guy whipped a cigarette lighter from inside his jacket and held the lighter perilously close to the gas tank.
He was about to blow up the entire drive.
Don Symons forgot about the phone. He ran around the corner and out the front door. He was already yelling for the crazy bastard to put his lighter away.

"Even if you shoot me, Doyle, you won't have time to run. You'll blow up along with the rest of us." Runyon nod-ded to Doyle's gun. "Now put the gun down on the hood there or I'll touch this lighter to the gas tank and—"
"You wouldn't kill the women."
"Wouldn't I? You're probably going to kill all of us, any-way, sooner or later. One way to die is as good as another. And this way, you go, too."
Runyon moved the lighter with its whipping flame an-other inch closer to the nozzle of the gas hose. He had origi-

nally hoped to spray gasoline all over Doyle, but Doyle was smart and kept his distance . . . too far away.

"You're not getting the gun, Runyon."

"Then we're all going to die together, Doyle."

From his left, Runyon heard sudden shouting. He saw the store attendant bolting through the door and running across the drive toward them. He was shouting for Runyon to put his lighter away.

In that moment, Runyon saw that Doyle was distracted, too. For a long second, Runyon saw his chance to jump Doyle.

Runyon flung the gas pump aside and started to dive for Doyle.

He was in midair, arms and hands outstretched for the wonderful collision that was about to occur, when the gunman turned back suddenly.

Doyle's eyes registered awareness instantly. Runyon was nearly on top of him. Runyon meant him deadly harm.

Doyle squeezed off three shots just as Runyon was about to slam into him.

Runyon didn't feel the pain. That was the curious thing. He continued flying through the air but now Doyle wasn't there to stop his flight. Runyon went right on past where Doyle was supposed to be, landing hard on oil-stained concrete that was now coated with frost and ice.

Then the pain came. And the rushing darkness. And the odd thoughts. Of boyhood. Of his parents. Of his first summer here in the mountains. And then the tears. At first he wasn't even sure they were his. But they were. Great hard convulsive tears. And the darkness rushing, rushing even faster now.

The bark of a gun. Once, twice, three times.

Who was being shot and why?

Darkness . . . death.

• • •

Doyle swung around as the clerk started running back inside. He put three bullets in the man's back. The man did not fall immediately. He merely stopped, frozen. Then, abruptly, with no sound, with no outsize motion of any kind, he fell straight down in a heap in front of the door, as if he hadn't quite known what else to do.

Doyle worked quickly then, hustling the women from the truck, forcing them to drag the two bodies around to the back of the store, and then to go inside and get a bucket of hot water to throw on the bloodstains. The snow would take care of the rest. He made Kate drive the black panel truck around back, too, where nobody could see it.

He took them inside. He told them to pick up head scarves and dark glasses and a Denver Broncos hat for him.

He forced them outside again, into the eight-year-old Ford that had belonged to the clerk. Doyle had found the keys in the dead man's pocket.

Just before dawn, they pulled into a breakfast restaurant packed with truckers.

55

"ARE you all right?"

"Can't sleep."

"I'm sorry."

"Can you see the clock?"

"Four-sixteen."

"Thanks."

Frank Sayler closed his eyes. When he was young, he sometimes thought of himself as a corpse. No more disappointment, no more fear. All he had to do was close his eyes and pretend that his entire body was shutting down, even his autonomic nervous system, and then everything would be fine. He would be dead and either there would be a heaven—he could not imagine God sending him to hell, he had not been a bad boy—or there would be nothingness. Either one was fine with him.

"Maria was in the kitchen when I got home. Sneaking in a little whiskey for herself, I think."

"I told you, I think she's an alcoholic. She's always sneaking a drink."

In their bed of darkness, there was only their voices, almost as if they had no bodies at all.

"She said the police came tonight."

"You make it sound like there was a raid or something. It was just one detective."

"What did he want?"

"About Doyle. He was here about Doyle."

"They still haven't found him or Riki or Kate?"

"No."

"Don't they have any leads or anything?"

"You sound like a cop show. 'Leads.' God."

"It's a little late for your sarcasm."

"I'm sorry. No, they don't have any leads."

"Why did they want to talk to you?"

"Just routine."

She was quiet for a long time. "Are you in trouble, Frank?"

"What's that supposed to mean?"

"Don't be evasive."

"No, I'm not in any trouble. The cop wanted to know if I'd heard from Doyle."

"Have you?"

"No."

They were silent again. Gradually, he became aware of her body. They so seldom made love that he was surprised by this. She kept herself in shape, and while he couldn't be said to ever feel outright lust for her, there were still a few times when he wanted her, when he remembered how good it had been back there in the beginning, back then when the world was so different a place and they were so very different people.

"You were pretty late tonight," he said.

"Frank the scoutmaster."

"I just thought I'd point that out."

"Do I ever 'point it out' to you when you're late?"

"You're always this way when you've found a new one."

"So are you, Frank. The time you discovered that black bimbo in the Valley, you didn't get home till nearly dawn. Several nights running."

Frank sighed. "I guess I shouldn't have brought it up."

"No, you shouldn't have."

Silence again. Just house noises. Creak and crack of timber; thrum and thrust of the electrical system, kicking in, kicking out.

Then her hand found his groin and his first reaction was one of utter surprise.

They used to do this back in the beginning, find each other in sleepy darkness in the middle of perfect loving nights.

He was scarcely aware of what was happening, it began so quickly, her drawing him closer, hands silken and warm, and taking him inside her and making a love that was meant to communicate tenderness, meant to communicate thoughts and feelings that somehow neither of them could utter. It was about love, lost love perhaps but love nonetheless, and not at all about lust.

Then they were done, and separate once more there in the shadows, separate but for the small hand she slid into his larger one.

"I'm afraid for you, Frank. I know you're in trouble."

"It'll be all right."

"He's coming here, isn't he? Doyle, I mean."

Frank Sayler said nothing.

"Maybe you should be honest with the police, Frank."

"If I was, I wouldn't have a job. The Japanese would get rid of me."

"Why is he coming here?"

"There's something he needs. And I need it, too. But I'm going to surprise him. I'm going to take it from him."

"You're scaring me, Frank. I don't like to hear you like this."

But he did. Frank liked to hear himself angry and threatening. It made him feel purposeful, manly.

He squeezed her hand, thinking of what morning would bring.

Doyle would reach L.A. somehow and he would call, not knowing that Frank knew where the safe-deposit box was, and then Frank would move in and get the contents of that box—

And then Frank would be in control. Total control.

"I'll be fine," he said, thinking about the gun. "I'll be fine."

56

THE cab smelled of cigarette smoke and cold air. Kate, Riki and Doyle sat in the backseat, several spots of which had been torn and covered with silver masking tape now tugging free and curling in the winter weather.

"You got a charter flight, huh?" the cabbie asked. He wore a white Stetson, a suede western jacket with fringe and a Navajo clasp at the top of his black string tie. He had teeth so bad they looked rusted.

"Right," Doyle said, "charter flight."

Kate could only guess what Doyle had in mind. Once they'd reached the Denver city limits, he'd dragged them to a phone booth, where he earnestly looked through the yellow pages. Then he called the cab.

As the cab rounded the bend of an industrial park—the first day-shift workers just now pulling into the various lots adjacent to several new, small plants—Kate saw in the distance a small private airfield. On the other side of Cyclone fencing there must have been a half dozen planes parked.

Five minutes later, the cabbie stopped in front of a one-story concrete-block building. Adjacent to this were two hangars. Doyle tipped the cabbie enough extra that the man grinned with his rusty teeth and said, "Yessir, and thank *you.*"

Doyle nodded for the women to get out. A minute later, the three of them stood behind the cab as it pulled away, driving back toward the city. The smell of its exhaust was sour on the clean, frosty air.

There was a phone booth outside the gate. Doyle led them over there, then went in the booth and made a collect call to Frank Sayler.

"God, Brad, let's get inside where it's warm," Riki said, shivering when Doyle stepped from the booth.

"Not going inside."

"Where are we going, then?" Riki said.

"After her."

Doyle nodded to the section of landing field where several planes were parked. A woman in a heavy but fashionable winter coat marched sturdily toward one of the planes. She carried in her gloved hand what appeared to be a quite formidable cowhide briefcase. She moved without pause toward a large Beechcraft.

Doyle hustled the women in through the gate and out to the landing field. They marched several yards behind the woman. The sun was starting to make everything bright, the purple shadows of dawn leaving the surrounding mountains now.

They passed four planes, each empty, each clean and precise in the strong clean light.

"Ma'am?"

Apparently the woman hadn't heard Doyle. She kept walking to the Beechcraft, not hesitating in the slightest.

"Ma'am?" Doyle called out again.

This time, she turned and looked back at them. She was six feet tall at least and possessed of a fine, strong, vital prettiness. The blue eyes bespoke intelligence, the full, comely mouth hinted at irony. Dark hair was cut short and complemented nicely the black turtleneck sweater she wore beneath her light blue down jacket. She wore a pair of gray, pleated slacks and western boots. "May I help you with something?"

she said. Her tone carried both irritation and impatience. Whoever she was, she had an obvious belief that she was somebody special.

The four of them stood between planes. Nobody in the office back down the strip would be able to see what was going on here.

Doyle took the gun from his coat and put it right into her face. "You're flying us to Los Angeles."

"Who the hell are you?"

Kate half expected what happened next. This woman was strong enough to intimidate Doyle. He would need to establish his superiority.

He raised his hand and brought it down swift and hard on the left side of her mouth. She mewled with pain but kept both her poise and her temper. "You're supposed to be a tough guy, I suppose."

"Just get in the plane."

A tip of pink tongue tasted the blood on her lower lip. All the while she continued to glare at Doyle.

Riki said, "I'm sorry about this. But he isn't kidding, ma'am."

The woman did not even try to conceal her disgust with Doyle. She shook her head. "No, I don't suppose he is."

"You're going to get in that plane and you're going to fly us to Los Angeles and if you try anything funny, I'm going to kill you on the spot. And don't give me any bullshit about taking us all with you, because I don't care," Doyle said. "I'm ready to die just as long as I can take you with me. Do we understand each other?"

Two minutes later, the twin engines on the Baron 58 were firing, and Doyle was getting comfortable in the backseat next to Riki. Kate was up front with the pilot, who said her name was Christa Everson.

Ten minutes later, the plane took off.

57

HE wasn't sure who she was, but she was young and fetching and found him endlessly attractive and amusing.

And then the clock radio went off. Some banjo tune on the Easy Listening station his Junior League wife preferred.

Out of bed he got, long of limb, stiff of joint, weary of mind. Hell, even if he did happen to meet a nice young thing, he wouldn't know what to do with her. He'd be too worried about the federal regulators to think of anything else.

God, it was barely dawn.

In the old days, back when savings and loans had been really humming, he'd never gotten up before 8:30 A.M.

But now—

In the shower, Ralph K. Thornton, MBA, president of Fidelity Savings and Loan, remembered how it used to be. For one thing, you got community respect. S&Ls weren't nearly as splashy as banks, but they paid a higher rate on their passbook accounts and they were generally considered much safer risks for large investors. And why shouldn't they be? When you invested in an S&L you were really investing in nothing less than the American Dream itself—the houses of the great expanding middle class that emerged from World War II. All S&Ls had to do was sit back and collect perfectly respectable mortgage payments from perfectly respectable middle-class people. Then came deregulation in the early eighties, at the time good old Ron Reagan was tottering into the White House, and things were never the same again. At first, Ralph K. Thornton was a vociferous booster of deregulation. Jimmy Carter's inflation had virtually wiped out any competitive edge the S&Ls had enjoyed—how could people make money on an 8 percent passbook when inflation was running 23 percent? They had to figure out a way to be competitive with banks.

So it was that S&Ls went into the business of installment loans and took the first step on the road to utter catastrophe. For the first time in history, S&Ls lost money. Big money. Out of desperation, they convinced a corrupt Congress to let them make ever wilder investments with the hard-earned nickels and dimes and dollars of their customers. Hence the boom in shiny new condos in Texas and dazzling new office buildings in New York and Boston and Miami. S&Ls poured billions into projects such as these (many S&L presidents getting large kickbacks for doing so). But very soon they realized that the condos had gone unsold and that the office buildings had gone unleased. And then disaster. Oh, a good number of congressmen and FSLIC people were paid off to keep news of the disaster covered up, but that didn't last long. Soon enough a few brave men and women, bucking a Republican administration and a Democratic Congress, began talking candidly to reporters. And then, quite abruptly and most unceremoniously, the lives of such men as Ralph K. Thornton changed utterly. To be sure, they retained their membership in the city's most prestigious clubs, and their stock portfolios looked fine and dandy, thank you, and their quick annual European trips with wives or mistresses or boyfriends continued apace, but their image changed.

In the old days, reporters always sought out the opinions of such men as Ralph K. Thornton, MBA. As bona fide members of the carriage trade, their words on art museums, charity balls and community development were seemingly inspired and invaluable. No longer. Not if you were associated with S&Ls. The word was "bailout" and it was heard more and more now. High-living S&L presidents would have to be shored up by the taxpayers, perhaps for as much as three billion dollars ultimately. So what had once been a fine and honorable (if slightly stuffy) calling was now a most suspect one. S&L presidents, it seemed, were regarded as slightly more reprehensible than used-car salesmen and televangelists. When they were not being castigated, they were being snickered at.

And they had to get up early. Very, very early. The regulators liked to know that you were at work before 8:00 A.M.

Sour little men, they resented the fact that men like Ralph K. Thornton had once led imperious lives.

Showered, shaved, loaded up with vitamins and a bowl of bran, Ralph K. Thornton, MBA, set off for work, assuming it was going to be one more dull day.

58

THE call came at 6:22 A.M., Pacific standard time. Frank Sayler sat in the breakfast nook, watching a cute little robin perch on a branch of a lemon tree. The silver dew and the deep dawn shadows made him sentimental for his old Cleveland home. They hadn't had much in the way of love or money, but by God the Saylers had had a great backyard and how Frank had loved to stare at it.

The morning mayhem was beginning.

Maria was fixing three different breakfasts—the girls were into eating whatever packaged breakfast food was being heavily advertised on TV at the moment; his wife ate a plain piece of toast and an apple and a cup of hot water, because she'd read in *Mirabella* that this was how Jackie O. began her day; and Sayler was Sayler, screw all the reports about bacon and eggs and jam-covered toast, it was what he wanted for breakfast and dammit it was what he always had for breakfast—and a general din came from the back of the house as the girls ran showers, jerked open drawers, slammed doors and got two different CD players going, one booming out a rap song about how all white people should be sliced and diced; the other a bland Michael Bolton rip-off of a Ray Charles song.

A typical morning. Until the phone rang.

"For you," Maria said as she hustled about the stove and the toaster, getting everything ready.

There was a canary-yellow wall phone right in the nook. Frank grabbed it instantly. He had no doubt who would be calling.

"I'm glad you're up," Brad Doyle said.

"Up? You think I could sleep?"

"We're coming around ten your time. Then I'm going to the savings and loan and get that document. Afterward I'll call you. That's when I'll need your help."

"A detective was here late last night. He wanted to know if you'd been in contact with me."

"What did you tell him?"

"What the hell would I tell him, Brad? I told him no, that I hadn't heard from you at all."

"Good boy."

"I don't think he believed me."

"All I want from you, Frank, is a little help. And then you'll never see me again."

"What about Riki?"

"She can do what she wants."

"She's the only star I've got, Brad. Without her—"

"You should hear yourself, Frank. Those Japs make you whine, Frank. They take all your masculinity away."

"Thanks for the compliment."

Doyle sighed. "I've kept you out of this, Frank. You won't be implicated."

"I'm giving you a ride, aren't I? Isn't that being implicated?"

"At gunpoint. All you need to tell the cops is that I told you I'd kill Kate if you didn't come out here."

"How is Kate?"

"Holding up."

"I wish this was over."

"So do I."

"I'll see you in a little while, Brad."

● ● ●

Twenty minutes later the girls came in, all mousse and makeup and perfume and giggles. Usually he was happy to hear his daughters giggle, but this morning he almost resented the sound. Here he was, very much standing on a cliff above a chasm, and here were his two daughters having a wonderful time.

One daughter kissed him on the right cheek, one on the left. Quick wet girly morning kisses, he thought, holding them there longer than he usually did, holding them tight and remembering when they were babies. He'd been such a terrible selfish father, never home, never attentive to what they were doing, yet somehow he loved them, too, loved them deeply and truly and profoundly in a way he would never be able to love anybody else.

"My dad the lech," laughed Darcy.

"My dad the pervert," laughed Kerry.

He realized suddenly what they were laughing about. He was holding them too tight, mashing them.

Then they were off to Maria to receive from her, like a priest dispensing communion, their TV-advertised breakfasts, this particular thing being something that you put in the toaster and it popped up and when you forked a bite from it you found gobs of goopy stuff that was allegedly pure fruit, some kind of purple gunk that had undoubtedly been concocted in a laboratory and was rife with red dye and other world-famous carcinogens. They wore mini-miniskirts and blouses in bright girly colors.

They brought big white glasses of milk over and slid into the breakfast booth across from him and there in the sunlight through the window he saw how young and pretty and vivacious they were, and he felt terrified that he would never see them again after this morning.

"So what's up for you today, Pop?" asked Darcy.

"Why don't you sign Johnny Reb?" said Kerry. "He's dreamy."

"Yeah, Pop, why *don't* you sign him?"

"He's already with Columbia, honey. A long-term contract."

"I'll bet he'd break it if you told him he could have a date with both of your daughters."

Frank smiled at the silly notion. They were silly girls and how he loved them. He was almost in goddamned tears they were so silly and he loved them so much. "Would this be one at a time or both together?"

Darcy shrugged. "It'd be up to him."

"Just as long as he understands the cruel ground rules set down by our cruel parents," said Kerry. "You know, having to be in by nine o'clock on school nights and eleven o'clock on weekends."

"He's probably never been around girls as racy as we are, Pop."

He had determined long ago that they would not be typical Beverly Hills girls, into drugs and sex and decadence-for-its-own-sake, by the time they were fourteen.

The phone rang again. He let Maria get it, certain that it would not be for him.

He was starting to talk to the girls again when Maria said, "It's for you."

"Me?" He pointed to himself.

"You," she said.

He picked up.

"Good morning, Mr. Sayler."

The voice was not familiar.

"Good morning."

"I'm sorry. You probably don't recognize my voice. I'm the LAPD detective who was at your house last night."

"Oh."

"I know it's early."

"What can I do for you?"

"Well, I was just kind of wondering if you'd heard anything from our friend Doyle."

"No."

"You're sure?"

"I said no, didn't I?"

The girls had stopped talking. His tone of voice had silenced them. They were no longer sweet giggly girls. They looked not only concerned now but vaguely afraid.

"Mr. Sayler."

"Yes?"

"Lying to the police is a bad thing. A very bad thing."

"I haven't heard from him."

The cop sighed, sounding almost weary. "All right, Mr. Sayler. I thought I'd give you one more chance to cooperate."

"I haven't heard from him. Now, if you don't mind, I'm having breakfast with my daughters."

"All right, Mr. Sayler. Have a nice day."

Have a nice day, Frank Sayler thought, feeling as embattled as he had all his life. Right. He'd had so many nice days in his life and this was certain to be another one of them.

But then he remembered his plan. And his gun. By God, he was going to come out all right in this thing. He was sure of it.

"You have a nice day yourself," Frank said, and hung up.

"Now," he said to his two daughters, "I believe we were talking about Johnny Reb."

But they were past it, the early morning giggles. The girls were shoveling their food into their mouths, obviously wanting to get away from the breakfast nook as soon as possible, obviously sensing that their father's life had suddenly taken another wrong turn.

"Everything will be fine, girls," he announced in a splendid manly tone. "Everything will be fine."

"Right, Pop," said Darcy.

59

MCGIVERN was flown to Edwards Air Force Base on a scheduled transport flight.

After landing, he was taken by police vehicle straight to the precinct that was working on Brad Doyle's presumed arrival. He shared with them what he'd learned in Colorado. The LAPD shared with him what it suspected, namely that a man named Frank Sayler was most likely going to pick up Brad Doyle. During a police interview yesterday, Sayler's secretary had acknowledged that her boss had heard from Doyle around eleven o'clock, California time. This would put the phone call well after the time Brad Doyle was suspected of killing David Greene. The police had asked Sayler about having contact with Doyle, but Sayler had denied it. This made the detectives suspicious enough to put a tail on Sayler.

The detectives were telling McGivern about the tail that was now on Sayler when the Chicago detective was informed that he had a phone call.

It was Colonel Marsh. "Well, looks like Brad Doyle struck again."

"Where?"

"Near Denver. A convenience store. Two men were found shot to death and dragged around back. Bodies weren't discovered until early this morning when the man on the day shift came in."

All McGivern could think of was Kate. Doyle seemed to be getting more violent by the hour.

"Thanks for the call, Colonel."

"I wish it could have been better news."

McGivern hung up and told the two Los Angeles detectives what Colonel Marsh had told him.

"I have only one question."

"What's that, McGivern?"

"Where do I find the guy staking Sayler out?"

"Why would you want to know that?"

"Because I want to be in the car with him."

They knew about Kate. They nodded somberly.

"Come on," said the tall one, "I'll take you out there right now."

Only when McGivern reached the parking lot did he realize how warm it was already. At least it seemed that way to him. Six hours ago he'd been in the snowy mountains. In L.A. this morning, it was already seventy-eight.

He got in the car and five minutes later was on one of those killer L.A. freeways. The detective drove happily, smoking a cigarette. He didn't seem to notice that he'd pushed the Ford sedan right up near 100 mph.

60

CHRISTA Everson did everything Brad Doyle told her to, but she never once gave him the satisfaction of being dutiful about it. She kept her contempt easy to see.

Kate watched the big, competent woman fly the airplane with great skill and ease. As Los Angeles loomed to the west, the winds began to die down and the sun to beam.

Occasionally, Kate glanced at Riki in the backseat. Riki had gone into one of her tune-out modes, head set back, eyes closed, earphones from her small recorder filling her ears.

Doyle showed no signs of relaxing. He sat hunched on the edge of his seat, the gun a part of the hand that held it. He showed exhaustion and anxiety in his otherwise handsome face—but mostly he showed anger. Kate sensed that he would be happy if somebody forced him into violence.

For long stretches, there was just the steady sound of the engine. Doyle had told Christa to turn off the radio. The noise seemed to make him even more nervous.

"How far to go now?" Doyle said. Each time he spoke, he sounded a little more tightly wound.

"Half an hour," Christa Everson said. She looked over at Kate and snorted. "He's got nerves of steel, doesn't he?"

Kate nodded silently. She didn't want to bait Doyle.

Below her, she saw golden land. She wanted to be down

there amidst the warmth and life, hear birds and children and rolling white surf.

She had to hold on and hope for the best. Right now, there was nothing more she could do.

The plane pushed on toward Los Angeles.

61

"HERE'S our boy," the detective said.

McGivern had been in the man's car for the past forty-five minutes. They were parked down the wide street, approximately a half block from Frank Sayler's. This early in the morning, the only cars moving were the large fashionable foreign vehicles that belonged to the various small mansions along the street. Workmen and servicemen would come later.

Sayler pulled out and drove right past them without even glancing in their direction.

Detective Grogan gave him a few minutes and then made a U-turn and started following.

They passed a small Catholic church made of stone and brick. In the cool morning shadows, the church looked as immortal and inviting as a painting. On the adjacent parking lot, a nun garbed in white stood in the middle of a circle while half a dozen little girls played ring-around-the-rosy with her. Their laughter was like cool, clear water on a hot day.

"Any idea where he's going?" McGivern said.

"Can't tell yet. Right now, he could be going about anywhere." He grinned at McGivern. "Relax. I've got a good feeling about this one."

"That's what the colonel told me."

"The colonel?"

"Yeah," McGivern laughed, "right before we found the air crash."

"Air crash?"

"Never mind," McGivern said, "I'll tell you later."

Los Angeles was coming awake—school buses, milk trucks, UPS trucks, Federal Express trucks, lowriders, cop cars, vans with moms and kids, vans with plumbing supplies, vans with bread and doughnuts and cakes—all crowded the streets.

McGivern saw a sign indicating the freeway.

"Well, if he turns onto the freeway, he's not going to the airport," the detective said.

McGivern nodded. There was always the possibility that Sayler had made them, knew they were following him, and had decided to lead them around aimlessly. Tailing people was not a science.

They went another twenty minutes. Gray morning shadows were disappearing. Everything looked so vivid—trees, shrubbery, grass—that McGivern suspected a celestial hand had painted the entire city last night while everybody slept.

"Bingo," the detective said.

A half block ahead of them, Frank Sayler was putting his big car in a tiny parking space. He did so with great skill.

He quickly killed the motor and then proceeded to sit there and stare at the building across the street.

"That make any sense to you?" the detective said, finding his own parking space and pulling in.

"What's that?"

"Why our friend Sayler would park across the street from Fidelity Savings and Loan and then just sit there?"

"Yeah," McGivern said. "Yeah, that does make sense to me."

The two men sat also and waited for Frank Sayler to make his next move.

62

THE only time Christa Everson showed fear was right at the very end of the flight, as she was setting the plane down on the runway of a small private field not far from LAX.

Throughout the flight, she had kept up a steady stream of sarcasm and belittling remarks. But just as the Beechcraft began its descent, Doyle leaned forward and put the gun to the back of her perfectly coiffed head. "The ladies are very impressed."

Apparently sensing something new in Doyle's tone, Christa Everson chose not to respond.

"They think you're real brave for the way you've been doing numbers on me all the time. They're afraid of me so they don't say anything. But you—" He sat back and kept the gun on her and said, "Soon as we land, Christa, you and I are going to have a little talk."

Three minutes later, the radio on now and the landing field wanting to know who the hell she was and why the hell was she landing unannounced—three minutes later the wheels thumped the concrete and the Beechcraft rolled to a landing.

Riki was wide awake now, looking drained and frightened. Kate was turned around watching Doyle. She knew he was going to try something with Christa Everson. He was very angry.

Christa got the plane off the runway, over to where a row of other small craft were parked.

As soon as she shut off the engine, she turned around to look at Brad Doyle.

He was bringing his hand down in an arc, obviously planning to lay the butt of the gun hard along the side of her head. Given his strength, and his rage, he could easily kill her.

Impulsively, Kate pushed her arm between the gun and Christa's head.

Kate stifled a cry when Doyle's wrist slammed into her forearm. It was like a karate chop, a very violent one.

"What the hell are you doing?" Doyle said.

"I don't want you to hit her, Brad. You've hurt enough people already."

Doyle was about to argue with her until he saw a man in coveralls running down the landing strip toward them. The man looked angry.

Doyle said, "Out. Everybody. Now."

None of them, including Christa Everson, argued.

The man in the coveralls stood with his hands on his hips watching the four people emerge from the plane. He was obviously prepared to give them an epic chewing-out until he saw the gun Brad Doyle held in his right hand.

Doyle walked over to him and put the gun in his face. "I want a car. You understand me?"

The man who'd looked ready for rage didn't look so ready now. He stared at the gun as if he didn't quite believe what he was seeing.

Doyle herded them all toward the office.

Along the way, Doyle pointed to a brand-new Ford and told the man he wanted the keys. The man nodded glumly.

Inside the office, Doyle found ropes and rags. He bound and gagged Christa and the two airport employees.

Then he took the keys to the Ford and marched Kate and Riki out the office door.

Doyle, Kate and Riki went twenty miles in the Ford and then Doyle pulled into the lot of a country-western bar. Even this early in the morning the whine of beery jukebox tales and the stifling scent of hops were on the air.

Doyle found an old Chevrolet truck owned by a free-lance painter, the bed of the truck packed with ladders and brushes and paint-dappled tarpaulins. It took him less than two minutes to hot-wire it. Then they were back on the road. The police would be looking for the Ford Doyle had taken from the airport.

63

WHILE he waited for Doyle to show up, Frank Sayler picked up his cellular phone and called his wife.

Maria answered.

"Maria, I'd like to speak with my wife."

"One minute, Mr. Sayler."

Ann was there thirty seconds later. "Hi. This is a nice surprise. Hearing from you, I mean." Long pause. "Are you all right, Frank?"

"Fine."

"You sound—different."

"I'm fine. Really." He paused. "You'll never guess why I'm calling."

"Why?"

"Just to say hello. You know, the way I used to in the old days."

Long pause. "Something's wrong, isn't it, Frank?"

"God, can't I call my own wife and tell her I miss her and tell her I love her without getting the third degree?"

Long pause. "I had a nice time in bed last night, Frank. For a minute or two there, it was like the old days."

"I know. I felt the same way."

"Maybe we should talk tonight."

"Talk?"

"About seeing a counselor again."

"Oh, I don't know about counselors. I really don't."

"Couldn't hurt."

He sighed. "I guess not."

She laughed. "You think they're all diabolical lesbians. Even the male counselors."

"Well, the one we saw seemed to think that I'm the one who did in our marriage."

Softly: "You are, Frank."

"God, do you really believe that?"

"Yes. I didn't—seek outsiders—until many years after you did." That was how she always said it. So prim and sexless. "Seek outsiders."

"Do you think things could really be different?"

"If we tried hard enough."

"How about going out to dinner tonight?" he said quickly. He wanted to say, "We'll celebrate," but he didn't want to tell her about Doyle and everything.

"I—have a previous engagement."

"So did I. But I'm going to break it."

She giggled, sounding like one of the girls. "I probably shouldn't say this, Frank, but right now, right at this very moment, anyway, I'm very, very happy."

"So am I. Unfortunately, I've got to cut this short." Pause. "Is it all right if I say I love you?"

"If I can say it back."

"I love you, Ann."

"I love you, too, Frank."

He hung up the phone and started checking out his rearview mirror again. He wished he knew what kind of vehicle Doyle was coming in.

After a few minutes, he started biting his fingernails.

64

MCGIVERN and the detective did twenty minutes on Nam as they sat waiting across the street from Fidelity Savings and Loan.

Both men were veterans, both men still held a certain bitterness for those who'd managed to beat the draft by pulling various strings.

After Nam, they did cops. They allowed as how judges these days seemed at least a little more generally conservative than they had in the past, which was a good thing, but how the press was still as blindly liberal as it had ever been, which was, if you were a cop, not a good thing at all.

They were just starting to talk about the predilections of parole boards when McGivern jerked forward in his seat and said, "It's them!"

Doyle had parked in the rear of the building and had walked around front. He had his coat slung over his right arm. No doubt, the gun was beneath the coat.

Kate and Riki preceded Doyle through the glass door of the savings and loan.

"Let's go," McGivern said. "But we have to be very careful. Otherwise he'll kill them for sure."

65

ON this sunny and slightly lazy morning, Ralph K. Thornton, MBA, sat in his shiny new leather and cherrywood office at Fidelity and thought of the memo he would issue later this morning. More staff cuts. Three more, to be exact, though only he knew that in a month there would be another three. Until recently, he had imagined that the stories of men leaping from hotel rooms during the Depression were greatly exaggerated. But he had come to understand that impulse. Six months ago, the Feds had had to find a buyer for this S&L. In truth, the other S&L that took it over was not in much better shape than his own, but the Feds were desperate and would worry about the consequences later.

His was a cushy job no longer. In the old days, he'd come in around ten, look over all the pending loan apps, make a few calls, and then dispatch himself in his Lincoln to the Club. In the afternoon, he had often played golf. No more. Now, with all the staff cutbacks, he was little more than a teller himself. When Fidelity got busy, he frequently had to man a teller window, and even more frequently he had to take phone calls from nervous and surly customers who threatened to pull their money out if he could not reassure them that their life savings were absolutely safe. How he keened; how he groveled. In the old days, underlings would have keened and groveled, not he.

So it was on this sunny morning that Ralph K. Thornton

himself took the call from the receptionist out front. "There's a woman here who wants to get her safe-deposit box, Mr. Thornton."

He sighed. What next? Parking cars?

"All right," he said, "I'll be right up."

Before going, he stared up at the precious framed photograph above the mantel of his fireplace. The color photograph showed then-California Senator George Murphy with his arm around Bob Hope. On the other side of the comedian stood Ralph K. Thornton, MBA. He'd wanted to slide his arm around Hope's shoulder but he'd been afraid to, so he'd settled for merely standing there. Murphy and Hope had been playing golf and Murphy had recognized Thornton as one of his largest contributors and so had introduced the lean and hungry young man to Hope. There had even been, as if by divine providence, a clubhouse photographer around later when the three men had drinks. Ralph K. Thornton could actually *prove* he'd spent twenty minutes with Bob Hope.

Those were the days, by God. Those were the days.

Gathering what dignity was left him, Ralph K. Thornton, MBA, left his office and went up front to see some woman who wanted into her safe-deposit box.

Frank Sayler rushed across the street, dodging fast-moving cars as if he were immortal and death could not touch him. Several drivers honked at him. One even offered an obscene gesture. Sayler hardly noticed.

By now, he had only one thought: I need to get the document in the safe-deposit box. Nothing could dissuade him. Nothing could deter him. Nothing—

Sayler reached the door of the savings and loan. Grabbed the glass door bar. Started to open the door when—

A hand took his shoulder. An especially strong hand.

"Morning, Mr. Sayler."

Sayler was looking into the face of the detective from last night.

"Good morning," Sayler said, glancing at the man next to Grogan. Another cop.

"We'd like to speak with you a moment before you go in there," Grogan said.

Sayler became aware of his surroundings suddenly: rumble and thrum of traffic; chemical smell of exhaust fumes; glint and glisten of sunlight on chrome and glass of parked cars.

Sayler felt everything slipping away from him suddenly. The police would get their hands on the safe-deposit box and the contents would be leaked to the press and—

"Is that all right, Mr. Sayler?" Grogan said.

"Huh?"

"I asked if that was all right."

"All right?"

Sayler was dazed.

"All right if we speak to you a minute," Grogan said.

"Uh, sure," Sayler said, knuckles in his right jacket pocket touching the hard cold steel of his gun.

He would never have a chance to use the gun now. He would never have a chance to turn all this turmoil to Riki's benefit. Never have a chance to—

"So is that all right?"

"Sure," Sayler said, wanting to bawl right there on the spot. "Sure."

Inside . . .

Kate knew immediately that the man walking toward her would be no help. Everything about him suggested weakness, from his too-fussy tan to his too-fussy hairstyle. He wore a three-piece suit, a thumb cocked in one of the vest pockets, and new leather oxfords that squeaked with a kind of class-president pride. He had dark eyes whose meanness not even his quick empty smile could disguise, and a full, almost womanly mouth. In a movie, he would play the bully's best friend, a mixture of arrogance and cunning and sneering but unmistakable fear.

"Good morning," he said in an almost cooing way.

Doyle and Riki stood just behind Kate as she held up the key to the safe-deposit box. "I'd like to see this one, please."

"Of course," he said. "Oh, by the way, my name is Ralph K. Thornton. I'm the president of this branch."

"Nice to meet you."

"I just need to get my book. We keep photos on file, you know."

She nodded. He excused himself, smiling briefly in the direction of Doyle and Riki as he did so, and then stepped over to an unoccupied mahogany desk.

Kate looked over her shoulder. Riki appeared drained, about to drop. Doyle, as usual, seemed angry and impatient.

The savings and loan had been built in the heyday of the American financial industry, the decor being mahogany and oak. All the woodwork appeared to be hand-carved. The burgundy-colored carpeting was thick enough to break an ankle in. Overall, there was a hushed, almost smothering air about the place, like that of a church in which only the most important people prayed.

Ralph K. Thornton brought back a large three-ring black notebook. He opened it up, checked the number on Kate's key once again and then thumbed through the book until he reached the proper page. "Here we go." He turned the book for her to see. The page contained a key identical to hers and two color photos, one of Kate, one of David Greene. Ralph K. Thornton pointed to her photo. "That's you, all right. Quite an attractive woman, I might add."

"Thank you."

"If you'll follow me, Ms. Evans. The deposit boxes are in a locked room near the back of the bank."

She nodded and followed.

He kept several steps ahead of her. He didn't seem to notice that Doyle and Riki were following also. When he reached the room containing the safe-deposit boxes, he turned and looked surprised. "I'm afraid only Ms. Evans and I are allowed inside."

"You'll have to make an exception this time," Doyle said.

"I'm afraid I can't make an exception."

"Sure you can," Doyle said. He raised his arm. Beneath his coat, his gun was in evidence.

"God," Ralph K. Thornton said, sounding very young. "You have a gun."

"Open it up and get inside," Doyle said. "You understand me?"

Ralph K. Thornton looked at Kate as if she had in some way betrayed him.

Then he bent and opened the door. After two tries, that is. He was no more help than Kate had imagined he would be. His entire body shook.

The room was large. The soft ceaseless winds of air-conditioning blew. There were three walls covered with silver-faced safe-deposit boxes of various sizes. The floor was fuzzy with brown deep-pile carpeting. In the center of the floor was a chest-high table divided down the center by a shoulder-high piece of wood. This supposedly guaranteed privacy in case there were two different customers in the room at once.

"Open up the safe-deposit box," Doyle said. He pulled the door shut behind him. His gun was in plain sight now.

Ralph K. Thornton shook his head. "I just can't believe this."

"Believe it," Doyle said. "And get your ass in gear."

"He'll kill you if you don't," Kate said.

"Listen to the lady," Doyle said.

While Sayler and Grogan had their little chat, McGivern went inside the savings and loan. Just as he reached the lobby, he saw Doyle following Kate and Riki and a pompous-looking man through a large door at the rear of the office.

He immediately took off running, down the wide aisle leading to the rear of the place and the imposing vault that sat there like a massive religious icon.

"So you didn't see Doyle go in through that door a few minutes ago, Mr. Sayler?"

"Doyle? Through this door? No, I didn't."

"So this is a complete coincidence?"

"Coincidence?"

"Right. You just happened to show up here at the same time Doyle did?"

"I guess so."

"Do you have an account here, Mr. Sayler?"

"An account?"

"Right. You know. Savings. Checking. CD. Something like that."

"No, I guess I don't."

"So you don't have an account here of any kind but you just happen to show up at the exact same time Brad Doyle does."

"Well, like you say, a coincidence."

Right now that safe-deposit box was being opened up and—

• • •

McGivern grabbed the doorknob. Locked. Inside, he could hear voices. Kate's among them.

By now, he had an audience, a whole group of employees and customers who wanted to know why this crazed man was trying to rip the door off its hinges—

McGivern turned and shouted to a middle-aged woman in a blue Fidelity jersey, "Do you have a key to this door? I'm a police officer."

The woman said, "I think I can find one. Hold on."

She then vanished into a large office near the vault.

Kate took one step toward box number eighty-six. She had just started lifting her key when a sweet-sour scent wafted to her on the soft electric breeze. Ralph K. Thornton, apparently even more upset than he appeared, had fouled himself.

Thornton stepped up then and put his key into place. Or tried to. He was shaking so badly it took him three tries.

Kate tried hard not to feel disgust toward the man. She wasn't any braver than he was. But there was something about his arrogance collapsing this way that sickened her.

He turned his key. "Now you turn yours."

"Pull it out," Doyle said.

Kate angled her head to see him. Doyle and Riki stood tight together, in front of the door. Something in the way they stood suggested that they were . . . partners. But God . . . that couldn't possibly be true.

Could it?

Ralph K. Thornton slid the long, narrow box out.

"Bring it over to the table."

Ralph K. Thornton brought it over to the table.

"Set it down."

Ralph K. Thornton set it down.

Doyle took two steps forward and brought the butt of his

weapon down hard across the back of Ralph K. Thornton's skull.

Ralph K. Thornton struck the floor so hard Kate felt her stomach knot. Doyle hadn't simply knocked the man out; he'd done him great damage.

Doyle took another step forward, bringing him close enough that he could reach out and touch the box.

As he extended his hand, a smile broke across his face and Kate thought that she'd never seen Brad Doyle look boyish before. But just then, that's exactly how he looked. Young . . . and almost innocent.

He opened the top of the box and stuffed his hand down inside. He picked up two pages of what appeared to be photocopied material, folded them and put them in his pocket.

He grabbed Kate, put a hand on her shoulder, guiding her toward the door. "This gun is about two inches from your head, Kate. You know I'll kill you if you try anything. Riki, open the door."

McGivern saw the Fidelity woman returning from the office in the rear. He hurried to meet her, eager to get the key.

Then the door from the safe-deposit vault began to open—

Doyle eased Kate out the door. As the people gathered in the center of the aisle saw the gun Doyle held on Kate, they began to move back, away from the path the three were taking.

"Let's go inside and talk to McGivern, Mr. Sayler," Grogan said, and opened the entrance door.

Grogan was two steps across the threshold when he saw Doyle leading Kate down the center aisle toward the front door, Riki trailing behind.

• • •

McGivern crouched behind a desk near the vault. He had his weapon drawn, ready to fire, but he had to be certain that Doyle wouldn't have time to fire first.

And with somebody like Doyle, there was always the possibility that he would get angry and start shooting without much provocation at all—

Doyle recognized the guy with Sayler right away. Not by name, of course, but by occupation. The guy was a cop.

"She's dead if you try anything at all," Doyle said, steadily moving Kate toward the front door.

The big cop froze.

Sayler looked at his life disintegrating right in front of him.

Doyle might get out the door, but how far would he get from there, even with Kate as a hostage?

And then the papers that had been in the safe-deposit box would be found.

McGivern eased his way around the desk. He was about ready to fire. But he had to be absolutely sure—

Frank Sayler snapped. He pushed Grogan aside.

"Give me the papers, Brad! Give me the papers!" he shouted, running directly at Doyle.

Without hesitating, Doyle shot Sayler in the chest—

When Doyle opened fire, so did McGivern.

He squeezed off three shots.

Brad Doyle screamed and started to sink to the floor.

Kate dove forward—

Riki screamed—

And Frank Sayler, though he'd been shot, though he was

bleeding from both chest and mouth, threw himself over the fallen figure of Brad Doyle—

The hospital was discreet voices on the public address system; the squeak of rubber soles on the high-gloss tile floors; the furtive scent of medicine; laughter from one room, tense and sad whispers from another—mortality, something we all face eventually, Kate knew.

McGivern said, "I hate to be a cop."

"You're going to ask me about the safe-deposit box again, aren't you?"

"It's my job."

"It was empty."

He stared at her. "Kate."

"It's the truth."

"Doyle killed all those people and came all this way for an empty box?"

"He didn't know it was going to be empty."

"He didn't say anything before he died?"

"No."

"And Riki didn't say anything? After Sayler was shot and threw himself on top of Doyle, Riki went over to him and leaned over and started talking to Doyle, before he died there on the floor. One of the customers later on told us that she thought she saw Riki take something from Doyle's pocket, but there was so much confusion and yelling and—did *you* see her take anything from Doyle's pocket? You were right next to her."

"No."

"They changed."

"What changed?"

"Your eyes. They shifted. Which means, if I remember my Psych 101 courses, that you probably just told a lie."

"Did I?"

"You sure aren't making this easy for me."

She looked at him and said, "Some things aren't our business."

McGivern had just started to protest again when Ann Sayler suddenly appeared. She came directly to Kate and they embraced and she said, half laughing, half crying, "He's going to be fine, Kate. Three bullets and he's going to be fine." She paused. "He'd like to see you." She smiled at McGivern. "He wants to see her alone. Sorry."

McGivern nodded and indicated that she should take Kate's chair.

Kate walked down the hall.

The room was big and white. Frank was connected to so many pieces of medical equipment he resembled a robot from an ancient science fiction movie.

He was asleep when she reached the side of his bed.

She watched him for a long time. She'd always liked Frank despite his best efforts to present himself as a bad guy, a role he sometimes seemed to delight in.

"Hi, Kate," he said, coming awake and looking up at her.

The strength of his voice startled her.

"Hi, Frank."

"It's over, huh?"

"Yes."

"Doyle—" He didn't finish his sentence.

She nodded. Doyle was dead.

He lay there for a time and then said, "How's Riki doing?"

"Fine."

He stared at her. "You were in there when the safe-deposit box was opened, right? Did the cops or anybody ever get their hands on it?"

"No." She paused. "Riki took it from Doyle when he was dying."

"Do the police know?"

Kate smiled. "They suspect but they don't know. And I'm sure Riki has destroyed it by now." Kate laughed. "Riki still has her career and so do you. I just hope she buys this new song I'm working on for her."

"You're a nice kid, Kate, anybody ever told you that?"

"Not often enough." She leaned over and kissed him on the forehead. "Now you'd better get some rest."

"Thanks again, Kate. I mean it."

A minute later, Kate left the room and walked down the hall to meet Robert McGivern.

So it was over, Frank Sayler thought as he fell into his deep sleep.

It was over and nobody was ever going to know that Riki was actually a man who had been Brad Doyle's cellmate in prison—a man who'd gone to Europe and surgically become a female star named simply Riki.

Poor David Greene had been at Riki's one night and had come across some medical papers and . . . Brad Doyle had had no choice but to pay the blackmail . . . and for two reasons. One, if it were ever known that Riki had once been a man, her career would be over. But besides that, whatever else he was guilty of, Brad Doyle was guilty of love. He had first loved Riki as a man and then as a woman. A sick, possessive love, true, but the only love he'd ever been able to feel for anybody or anything. And up till David Greene, Brad had been good about keeping Riki's secret . . . especially with the misleading lies about Riki's early "pregnancy" and abortion, a story designed to make everybody think Riki was a perfectly normal woman. Riki had had everybody fooled.

Frank closed his eyes, still unable to believe his luck.

It was over, all of it. Finally. The secret safe with him . . .

and with Kate, who, though curious, had chosen not to learn the truth . . . even though she clearly had her suspicions.

"This is going to be cold."

Frank opened his right eye.

The nurse again, the nurse who smelled of hair spray, perfume, medicine, and who sounded of squeaky rubber-soled shoes, starchy white uniform and tiny beeping digital wristwatch.

She had a big silver needle in her fingers.

"It's that time again, Mr. Sayler."

He smiled. "Yes, I guess it is, isn't it?"

And for being such a good boy, not crying or even making an especially ugly face as the needle went into his right buttock, Frank Sayler was rewarded.

When he rolled over onto his back again, there stood his two daughters at his bedside.

And then they were leaning over him and kissing him and giggling and crying—and he wondered why the hell they were both giggling and crying . . . and then he started giggling and crying, too, and holding his two precious girls tighter than he ever had.

66

TWO nights later, Kate sat at her apartment window watching the streaked red dusk paint the sky above Lake Michigan. She saw a plumed jet trail. A few birds soared majestic and lonely across the bright silver half-moon, and then disappeared in the starry gray that was beginning to consume all daylight.

On the tape deck was a ballad she'd written recently for Riki. The melancholy tune was exactly right for Kate's mood as she sipped wine and watched the dying day.

She'd been sitting for nearly two hours, thinking of so many things, from her parents to life on the farm to her failed first marriage—and of dear Sally, dead so young.

And, of course, the last few days—the crazed trip with Brad Doyle.

Sometime during her ruminations, McGivern had called and said he'd like to stop over. But she'd asked him not to. There was a peculiar pleasure in the pain she was feeling— some kind of purgation—as if the trip with Doyle had forced her to evolve into a different, stronger kind of person. And she wanted to feel the full effects of this transformation, a quiet truth in the wine she sipped, a majesty in the loneliness she felt, especially now with the raw power of an alto sax doing a solo in the tape on the deck.

She sat like this for a full hour more, unmoving except to

sip more wine, happy-sad and sad-happy, knowing herself better, and liking herself better, than she ever had.

At some point when there was only moonlight in the sky, when the distant tugboats hooted like lonely dinosaurs in the gloom, she went to the phone and dialed a certain number and said, "Is it all right if I change my mind? About having company, I mean."

Half an hour later, laden down with Chinese food and a new bottle of wine, McGivern stood in the doorway, smiling.

And Kate smiled right back at him.